the Revealed

ALSO BY SARAH KLECK

The Concealed

the Revealed

The Lakewood Series

Sarah Kleck

Translated by
MICHAEL OSMANN and AUDREY DEYMAN

amazoncrossing

This is a work of fiction. Names, characters, organizations, places, events, and incidents are either products of the author's imagination or are used fictitiously.

Previously published as *Die Macht der Verborgenen* by dotbooks Verlag in 2016 in Germany. Translated from German by Michael Osmann and Audrey Deyman. First published in English by AmazonCrossing in 2016.

Published by AmazonCrossing, Seattle

www.apub.com

ISBN-13: 9781503954847
ISBN-10: 1503954846

Cover design by Laura Klynstra

Printed in the United States of America

For Sarah, Anna, and the Little Dot

Doubt thou the stars are fire,

Doubt that the sun doth move,

Doubt truth to be a liar,

But never doubt I love.

—*Hamlet,* William Shakespeare

PROLOGUE

"Evelyn," Enid said, gently shaking my shoulder from where she sat next to me in the backseat. "Evelyn, wake up."

I blinked and barely held on as the Jeep turned off the paved road onto bumpy gravel.

"We're almost there," Enid explained.

"How far is it?" I asked numbly, rubbing my tired eyes.

"About five miles," Colin said, glancing at me in the rearview mirror.

"We have to walk the last three miles," Irvin added from the front passenger seat, while looking at the yellowish map. The lights of our group's second car briefly flashed behind us.

Still half asleep, I tried to sort through my thoughts and, for a fleeting, drowsy moment, felt a glimmer of hope. Was I dreaming it all? Maybe the black witch was just a nightmare, the product of my overactive imagination. When I opened my eyes, surely Jared would be lying beside me sleeping peacefully, his arms crossed behind his head, his mouth open a tiny gap. I could almost see that satisfied, relaxed expression he would have on his face when he felt me lying close to him in our room at the headquarters of Legatum Merlini. I would be sheltered and protected in the place that had become my home.

I breathed in deeply as reality started to sink in. It was true. All those horrible things had actually happened. I gulped and nearly broke out in tears. There those feelings were again: despair and helplessness, the familiar companions of my youth. They bound me mercilessly and threatened to crush me. I gasped for air. I remembered the day I'd seen Jared for the first time. Those incredible blue eyes. Everything around me had ceased to exist when I looked into his eyes for the first time. Gravity had shifted, and from that moment nothing else mattered to me . . . only he did. I had lost my bearings after my sister Zara's death and drifted through life without direction. But suddenly there he was, captivating me. Only he existed . . . from that moment to this.

No! I thought, clenching my fists and breathing deeply. No! I would not drown in this despair. Not so long as a ghost of a chance remained that Jared was still alive. That I could save him. Determined, I opened my eyes and dug my fingernails into my palms. We'd be there any minute, and I'd go into the fog alone. Then I'd get Jared out of Avalon—no matter what.

CHAPTER 1

"Ruth *Hayman*?" Irvin repeated in disbelief. He sat up in his chair, bracing his hands against the huge table in the headquarters' council chamber, where we'd all gathered.

"Yes," I confirmed. "I don't know anyone who knows more about Merlin, Nimue, and probably even Morgana."

"*Mary* Hayman's daughter?" Irvin sounded astonished—to put it mildly.

"I don't know her first name, but Ruth told me her mother devoted her entire life to searching for the truth about Merlin and Nimue."

Thinking of the loving way Ruth had spoken of her deceased mother made me a little sentimental.

Irvin looked across the room to where Enid stood by the window. She seemed torn for a moment but finally nodded, giving Irvin permission to speak. He took a deep breath, stood, and turned toward me.

"Twelve years ago, we became aware of a certain elderly lady by the name of Mary Hayman who was conducting some . . . research." Irvin paced up and down the spacious council chamber. He paused for a long while, frowning in thought, before continuing. "As we later found out, she had collected everything related to the legend of Arthur, especially regarding Merlin and Nimue, since she was a child. She read every tale, visited every site, and followed even the slightest lead. Somehow, she pieced the puzzle together bit by bit."

"Ruth told me her mother was pretty obsessed with it," I said.

Irvin nodded. He stopped in front of one of the tall windows, clasped his arms behind his back, and stared out, lost in thought. "Mary spent almost her entire life on it . . . and finally uncovered the Order's secret."

His words carried hints of appreciation and accusation.

"We didn't know if we should trust her and run the risk of having the secret of Legatum Merlini exposed." Irvin paused. When he spoke again, he seemed strangely affected. "Karen classified Mary Hayman as a danger to the Order and the Calmburry family. She constituted a risk the high priestess was not willing to accept. That's why she had Mary . . . disappear."

Embarrassed silence filled the room. I didn't miss Enid giving Gareth a meaningful glance. He looked at the floor.

My hair stood on end. How many people had the Order made *disappear* over the years at Karen's behest?

Irvin continued. "It's a puzzle to this day. We knew Morgana had become aware of Mary, just as we had, because she constantly appeared at significant places—Glastonbury, Stonehenge, Dozmary Pool, Caerleon . . . Morgana could under no circumstances be allowed to get her hands on Mary. That's why it had to happen so fast." Irvin clenched his fists. "Morgana must have found Mary's notes. She knew everything Mary knew. The Calmburrys were no longer safe in Oxford. That's why the Order decided to take the entire family to a secret place, a safe house in Boston."

Irvin took a moment to calm down. Anger and grief were written on his face. He shut his eyes and continued. "The plane was supposed to take them to America . . ." His voice cracked.

I recalled the horrible images of the wreck.

"Morgana killed all the members of the Calmburry family," Enid continued in Irvin's place, her voice breaking. "All—except for one," she added with a whisper of pride.

"Jared," I said.

She nodded. "He's the last Calmburry, the last of Merlin's bloodline."

Irvin stepped beside me and put his hand on my shoulder. "After Morgana killed the family—except Jared—Karen became very paranoid. Anyone who constituted a threat to Jared, or who might reveal his existence and draw Morgana's attention to him, was killed. Karen knew Jared would be drawn to Nimue's descendants. There's a centuries-old magical connection between your families—you are two parts of a whole. She knew you would find each other sooner or later." Irvin looked at the ceiling. "Karen set everything in motion to find Nimue's heiresses," he said, his voice trembling.

"She killed my parents. And my sister!"

Enid gave me an empathetic look. "First Karen found your mother and arranged for the car accident that killed your parents. But she couldn't find you or your sister. The amulet was powerful enough to hide the two of you because you were so close."

She lowered her eyes. "Three months before you arrived in Oxford, Karen succeeded in finding Zara, and"—she swallowed—"she assigned a member of the Order to murder your sister."

There was silence in the room.

"The past can't be changed," Enid continued, almost whispering. "I don't want to shirk my responsibility, but you must know that Karen ordered these actions on her own, despite the resolutions of the High Council."

Burning hatred spread inside me. Struggling against it was difficult. Karen Mayflower was nothing less than a ruthless murderess. For a second I wished Morgana had killed her, but in the next instant I regretted that thought. Morgana would have killed me, too, without giving it another thought, had she not needed me. She had used me. I clenched my teeth, enraged.

"We can't sit around here doing nothing. We must do something. Now!"

"Evelyn," Enid admonished me gently, "we will. But first, you must tell us everything you know. Anything you saw or heard could help us. Perhaps Morgana overlooked something. Some trivial detail . . . perhaps . . ."

While Enid struggled for words, I closed my eyes for a moment, breathed in, and tried to focus. The sooner we got this out of the way, the sooner we could start searching for Jared.

Then it bubbled out of me. I told them everything—about Frank Tempton, whose name I had discovered in the book in the relic room that listed all the members of Legatum Merlini since the Order's foundation in the fifth century; about the argument between Jared and Karen when he confronted her with his discovery that she was guilty of killing my family; my flight, followed by my encounter with Morgana in the forest clearing. How she had stood there in the midst of her army of damnati. I wanted to drive that memory from my thoughts.

"Had you ever seen Morgana before?" Irvin asked after I reached the end of my tale.

"No." I shook my head but suddenly stopped, frozen, as the image of an amazingly beautiful, dark-haired woman in a flowing white dress appeared in my mind.

"No, wait—that's not right. I *did* see her once before. In my dreams, the night I came across the Calmburry family chronicle in the library." I hesitated. "But the woman I saw in my dream was not Morgana but . . . *Eowyn*. Myrddin's mother—Merlin's mother." Uncertain, I looked at Irvin, who to my surprise was nodding in agreement.

"It's astounding how deeply Nimue's magic remains rooted in you after so many generations," he said. "How your subconscious intuitively grasps and correctly interprets." He laughed, then noticed the irritated expression on my face. "Morgana is Eowyn's *twin sister*, making her Merlin's aunt and, if you wish—twenty-nine generations later—Jared's great-great aunt."

My jaw dropped. "What?"

"Yes, they're all descended from the same magical bloodline. Their magic works the same way." His voice suddenly took on a dark tone. "Only matters are a bit different with Morgana. She violated the most fundamental of all laws of nature when she killed her sister in cold blood to bind her power and magic to herself." He shook his head.

"She killed her twin sister?"

He nodded.

"But . . . I read in the Calmburry book that Eowyn died while giving birth to her youngest daughter."

"That's the official, censored version of the story. The truth is, she suffered a cruel ritual death at the hand of her own sister when Morgana attempted to yoke her magic to herself."

"Tried?"

"She didn't succeed; in the end, she simply killed her." Irvin smiled darkly. "The fair lady overlooked a detail! Magic can only be transferred with the consent of the donor—and that requires a certain . . . voluntarism."

"Jared . . ." I was barely able to say it. "She will . . ."

Irvin nodded. "He consented. To save you. He entered a magical pact with that witch. Breaking it means he'll die."

"What? What do you mean?"

"If Jared doesn't keep his word and tries to double-cross Morgana, his own magic will turn against him. That's how the pact works. Breaking the oath would kill Jared."

No! No! No! That couldn't be! Jared was not yet lost. I wasn't willing to give up. There must be a way. Any way. I would do anything, no matter what, to save him. But first I needed Irvin and everyone here to tell me everything they knew. There *had* to be a way!

"What's this about the laws of nature?" I asked. "You said Morgana violated them?"

Irvin cast me a harsh look. "All magical beings originate from the harmonious order of nature and draw their strength from the all-embracing energy that is the source of the four elements: earth, water, fire, and air."

He paused to see if I had followed so far. When I nodded, he continued. "Some, like Nimue, and also you, are bound to the energy of a particular element. Water, in your case. Others, including Eowyn, Merlin, and Jared, master the energy of all elements. The magic of each creature is one with nature and its energy. It acts in harmony with nature. This means energy in its natural context and natural flow can be directed and affected by magic." He looked at me skeptically. "Do you understand?" His manner of explaining things reminded me of his lectures. He was an excellent teacher.

"Yes . . . I think so. I saw Jared make crocuses bloom over an entire glade."

"Exactly!" he confirmed, clearly relieved that I had understood what he was driving at. "He just *accelerated* the natural course of things with his magic."

"And how does Morgana's magic work?" I asked, eager with anticipation.

Irvin opened his mouth, but it was Enid who answered my question.

"By ending a life violently or casting a creature into darkness by binding its soul to herself." She halted and looked at me with pity as I shuddered. "Such a cruel, unnatural deed will not be without consequences." She shook her head.

"What consequences are we talking about?" I tried to push aside the terrible memories of my encounter with Morgana.

"She crossed a line with the murder of her sister and the countless others she committed over time. The moment Morgana raised her hand against Eowyn, she set her magic against the natural order and unbalanced her own bond with nature. She was no longer part of the greater whole. With the murder of her sister, Morgana excluded herself for all time from the natural, harmonious order of the world."

"Does this mean Morgana's magic embodies the . . . opposite of everything natural?" I asked, hoping I had understood correctly.

"Exactly," Irvin answered. "She brings death to all living beings. Where love reigns, she fans hatred. She lays waste to anything pure, and everything beautiful she turns ugly."

"The damnati . . . ," I mumbled as I thought of those creatures covered in repulsive scars and sores.

"Yes." He turned up his nose in disgust.

"There were *so many of them* in the clearing." I found it difficult to picture how much suffering had to be in the world to create those legions of scarfaced monsters. I shook my head to drive away the thought and concentrated on what mattered most now. I had to find a weakness.

"Why did Morgana want to kill Jared's entire family? If it's true she wants to bind his magic to her, why didn't she try it with any of the other family members?" I asked anxiously.

Irvin took a step in my direction. "The failed attempt to bind Eowyn's magic to herself not only cost her sister's life but almost killed Morgana as well. She realized magic was not simply for the *taking*."

He paused to find the right words.

"The plane crash twelve years ago was supposed to wipe out the entire Calmburry family. I presume Morgana felt that if she was not able to have this magic, then at least no one would be able to challenge her. Until very recently, she believed they had all died, because the protective magic grew stronger when it no longer had to protect an entire family but instead only a single person." Irvin again stepped toward me. "Even newspaper articles and newscasts about the accident, which always mentioned there was a single survivor, were obscured by the spell. The Order set everything else in motion: falsified reports, doctored photos, disappeared evidence, bribed witnesses . . . Karen did everything humanly possible to protect Jared. This lulled Morgana into believing she had gotten rid of all the Calmburrys." Irvin smiled for a moment, but then his face hardened. "Morgana didn't have the slightest notion until . . ." He swallowed.

"Until Madison went to her and asked her to kill me so she could have Jared for herself," I completed the sentence.

"Exactly," Irvin rasped.

"Madison not only betrayed Jared to Morgana," Enid continued, "but she also provided her with suitable leverage." A weary smile spread across her face. "Never forget that magic must be given freely!" She looked into my eyes. "Morgana used you from the start."

The torment I felt at the thought must have shown on my face. I stood up, clenching my fists. "No, that's not how it will end. It *must* not end that way!" I burst out, looking at them one after the other. "I must speak with Ruth. I'm sure she knows what needs to be done."

Irvin looked at me skeptically. "All right," he finally answered. "Colin, please tell Ian to bring Ruth Hayman here. And take Gareth with you."

CHAPTER 2

"Nimue's heiress," Ruth repeated, shaking her head. I'd told her everything I knew, much to the displeasure of some members of the Order. Well, almost everything. I'd kept silent about the circumstances of her mother's death. It just wasn't the right moment for that. But there were no other secrets—we needed to move forward.

Ruth did not appear too surprised—and this seemed to make some other members of the Order particularly nervous. I'd snorted. What did they expect? I had said no one knew more about Merlin and Nimue than Ruth. And I figured the Order should be grateful for any help, any straw to grasp, to free Jared from Morgana's clutches. But now that Ruth was here, the High Council was split into two camps: for one faction, initiating an *outsider* into the secrets Legatum Merlini had closely guarded for centuries bordered on high treason. Judith McHallern and Montgomery Grey had even left the room just before Ruth arrived.

The others, the faction to which Irvin and Enid fortunately belonged—and which now held sway, since Karen had been sidelined—were giving their everything to rescue Jared. Even if that meant spilling a few secrets. Still, I was sure they would never have brought Ruth here had they seen another possibility. They had clearly tried everything.

Gareth, Ian, Colin, and a few others had followed Morgana and Jared while I was unconscious.

"We never had a chance," Gareth told me, pulling his shirt up to show me a deep wound a damnatus had inflicted below his collarbone. Jared couldn't bear the thought of his friends suffering injuries for his sake, Gareth told me. So he wiped out his and Morgana's tracks with a spell to prevent the posse from pursuing them. As much as they tried—and I knew at least Colin well enough to be certain he wasn't the kind to give up easily—they couldn't help him. Jared had entered into a magical pact with the dark witch from which there was no escape. Jared knew. We all knew.

It was silent far too long. A mixture of nervousness and embarrassment pervaded the room. When the tension became almost unbearable, Ruth finally said: "Morgana wants to bind Jared's magic to herself."

Enid and Irvin nodded.

"Yes, but how? Where is he? Where did she take him?" I burst out. I was on the verge of fury—every moment we sat idle diminished our chances of finding Jared, alive!

Ruth stared into open space. Then her gaze cleared. "Do you still have the book I gave you? About Nimue?"

I hesitated. "The book? Um . . . it was—"

"It's in Karen's office," Irvin interrupted me and nodded to Ian, who immediately left the room.

I looked at Irvin with raised eyebrows. Saying anything would have been superfluous. How stupid was I back then, to believe these fanatics when they told me that, of all my things, the fire in my residence room had destroyed *only this one book*? Serious doubt overcame me. Was I trusting the right people? But was there a choice?

Ian returned and pressed the thick green book into Ruth's hand. She licked her index finger and hastily leafed through it.

"Aha. Here it is." Ruth inhaled deeply, pressed down the page, and began to read:

> "The blind heart tormented by longing
>
> Readily walks into darkness so far.
>
> Deprived of its light, deprived of its might,
>
> Only Death watches over the wight."

"Yes." My voice sounded far more impatient than I intended. "The Prophecy of the Nymphs of Avalon."

"There, you've got it," Ruth said calmly, looking at me.

"What? I don't understand."

Colin, Enid, Irvin, Gareth, and Ian gave Ruth irritated stares.

"The nymphs know no world outside Avalon," she explained, as if it were an obvious thing. "For them, it's the only place that exists."

"What are you trying to say?" Colin asked. I was relieved I wasn't the only one who didn't grasp it.

"Everything the nymphs, well, perceive is linked to Avalon, and that means everything this prophecy speaks of—"

"Happens in Avalon." I completed the sentence as if in a trance.

"Do you mean to say that Morgana took Jared to Avalon?" Colin burst out in disbelief. He pulled at his hair with both hands. So far he'd held back, but now he seemed close to despair. He seemed beside himself with worry for his friend.

"But of course," I mumbled. Though my voice was little more than a whisper, all eyes were on me. I stared into space as if under a spell, far away in thought.

Feeling, intuition, magic, or a long-forgotten truth resurfaced—I had no idea where it came from or what it was, but suddenly it all made sense. Suddenly I *knew* what I had to do.

It wasn't just a premonition, an idea, or a feeling. No. I *knew* deep inside me, with unassailable certainty, what I needed to do. Where I had to go. Images coalesced inside my head. Things I'd never sensed before in real life but were still so . . . familiar.

Glades crossed by streams, overgrown clearings, majestic trees, singing birds.

"Where's the entrance?" I wanted to know.

"Glastonbury Tor," Irvin and Ruth simultaneously said, staring at me with confused expressions.

"A hill in the midst of the Summerland Meadows, with the ruin of St. Michael's Tower on its summit," Irvin continued. "If you wish to believe the old legends, it's the entrance to Avalon."

"And how do you get into it?" My voice sounded harsh.

Ruth pressed her lips together. "It's hard to say with certainty—after all, no one ever made it in. Not even Nimue was able to return to Avalon, if you remember the story I told you." I remembered only too well. She had lived on as a normal human, taken a husband, and given birth to a daughter named Viviane. My great-great-great—oh, I had no idea how many times great—grandmother!

"But there must be a way," I shot back. Worry and desperation arose in my chest. My nerves were fraying.

"Well, according to my mother's notes, if there's any possibility at all, one can only get there in a mist. During the magical hour between night and day."

"So at dawn?" Colin deduced from Ruth's words.

Ruth nodded.

"Then we should leave right away." I rose.

"I'm going with you," said Colin, holding his hand out to me.

"That's very courageous of you, Colin," Ruth countered, "but I don't think you'll make it through the portal."

"What's that supposed to mean?" He sounded deeply offended.

"That's the catch in this business. I'm certain that *if* the portal opens, it will *only* open for Evelyn. No one else."

"Then I'll go alone," I said.

Colin dropped his hand. "And how are you going to do that?" he asked in a huff. "Do you want to take on Morgana and her accursed damnati army all by yourself?"

"Do I have a choice?" Of course I would have loved to have him by my side.

"All alone?" Colin was vacillating between anger and desperation. "That's crazy!"

"If it works," Ruth interrupted in a calm tone, "Evelyn will not be alone."

"What are you trying to say?" Enid asked.

Ruth smiled. "Avalon is *Evelyn's* island," she said, extending her chin in my direction. "Every being at home there will serve her."

"You mean the nymphs?"

"Yes, the nymphs and all the other creatures who live in Avalon."

I swallowed. What was waiting for me there? Provided I even made it through the portal . . . "You mean the nymphs will fight for me?" It came out sounding like a stupid question.

"Fight?" Ruth reflected for a moment. "No, I wouldn't think so. The literature describes nymphs as thoroughly peaceful creatures. Fighting isn't in their nature. But that doesn't mean they can't be helpful in other ways."

Ruth herself didn't quite seem to know what she meant by that. There was silence for a moment while everyone stared at me as if they were weighing whether I was up to the task. To be honest, I wasn't sure myself.

"Good," Enid said and got up. Though she didn't appear totally convinced, the urge to do something had taken hold of her. We had to do *something*, after all.

"Colin, Ian, look after Evelyn's baggage," Enid commanded, now all high priestess of Legatum Merlini. They nodded. "Gareth, you're responsible for the Jeep. Get it filled up and ready for the road. Irvin, you're coming to the library with me. Maybe we'll find something that'll help us."

Enid looked at me with a tense expression. "Rest, Evelyn. You'll need your strength. Ruth, thank you for your help." It was clear that Enid believed Ruth knew too much.

"We'll get going tonight," Enid continued, addressing everyone. "It's a hundred and twenty miles from here to Glastonbury, and we don't want to miss the dawn."

***

At my pleading, Ruth stayed and accompanied me to the headquarters' garden. Just sitting around would have driven me crazy. I reviewed what I'd experienced one more time. I needed perspective—and maybe, just maybe, I'd find something I hadn't considered yet. Something that might help. So far, I didn't have the slightest inkling of a plan. I'd go—if I made it—to Avalon. Alone. That much was clear. I didn't have a clue what would happen next. What if I dropped in on a damnatus party? Or ran straight into Morgana's arms? What if Avalon itself attacked me? What if the beings who lived there weren't on my side after all? Or—the worst of all scenarios—what if I arrived too late? What if Jared . . . I didn't dare finish the thought. I closed my eyes and shook my head. Too many questions; too few answers.

While Ruth and I walked together in silence, one of our first conversations popped into my mind.

"If Nimue was such a magical and mighty creature, why did she want to live as a normal human with Merlin? What happened to her magic?" I had asked one evening at Ruth's place.

Nimue's magic was inseparably linked to Avalon, she'd explained. *"If she hadn't left her magic there, Avalon would have died."*

Hmm. At first I struggled with admitting my absurd thought, but it kept pressing itself further into my consciousness.

A mixture of courage and shame overcame me, but I simply had to ask. I swallowed. "You once said Nimue left her magic in Avalon," I carefully began, slowing my pace.

Ruth nodded.

How should I say it? "Do you think it . . . it's still there?"

She nodded again.

"You mean . . . I might . . ." I didn't know how to finish this sentence. Was it hubris, or was it really possible?

Ruth stopped and looked into my eyes. She seemed to understand.

"If it has the choice, magic always returns to its source, its rightful owner," she said, and her intensity gave me goose bumps.

I stared at Ruth, letting her words sink in. Then I shook my head.

"Rightful owner," I repeated, full of self-doubt. I looked at the ground. Now that Ruth had spelled it out so clearly, this business sounded much less credible. At that moment, I didn't feel like the rightful owner of anything.

Ruth's firm grip on my arm surprised me. She looked at me with urgency in her eyes. "Evelyn, you're the last of Nimue's bloodline, the last descendant of the Lady of the Lake. You're the heiress to Avalon. It's nothing less than your *birthright* to return there. Just as it's your birthright to claim Nimue's magic for yourself."

Oh, well, if that's all there is to it, I sarcastically thought.

"And how am I supposed to accomplish that?" Discouraged, I sat down on a garden bench.

Ruth sat beside me, took the green book from her purse, and flipped through it.

"It says here," she began, taking that respectful tone in which she read from old books, "that one should consider one's right with light and love, then ask for entry."

I frowned. "Aha."

"Oh, don't be so skeptical," she said, arriving at the end of her patience.

"I'm just wondering how that's supposed to work. *In light and love . . .*" It sounded ridiculous.

"You'll just have to try."

"Excellent advice. Jared only has days, maybe only a few hours, and I'm supposed to calmly *ask for entry in light and love*?" Desperate tears welled up in my eyes. "Damned shit!" I shouted, burying my face in my hands. To my surprise, it gave me a little relief.

Ruth gently stroked my back. "I'm so sorry, love. But that's all we've got. You'll just have to try it."

Angry and frustrated, I wiped the tears from my face.

"Listen." Ruth forced me to look at her. "You must never doubt yourself, do you hear me? Never! Go through the portal. Just go through the portal."

I snorted. But Ruth was right—there was nothing left for me to do but go and try.

I got up and continued walking. She followed.

"Ruth?" I asked after a while.

"Yes?"

"You once said Morgana killed Merlin with his love for Nimue . . ."

"Hmm."

"You said she used Nimue to blackmail Merlin. And he gave his life to rescue her."

"Yes." She was clearly curious to hear what I was driving at.

"But . . . how did Merlin stop Morgana from binding his magic to herself?"

After a long pause, she said, "I'm not sure. Maybe it was just . . . *too much* for her."

"Too much?"

Ruth thought for a moment. "Despite her magic, Morgana's body is a living organism made of flesh and blood."

The image of the gaping wound on her lower arm, the warm blood—*her* warm blood, which she had smeared on my naked body—flashed through my mind.

"She can definitely bleed," I said tersely.

"What do you think? How much magic can such a bleeding human body hold?"

"No idea. But both Merlin's and Morgana's magic in only one human body . . . that seems a bit crowded to me." I stopped for a moment as I began to understand. "So you think she was a bit too greedy and in the end was not able to, well, how shall I say, keep any of it?"

"Yes, I think you could say it like that." Ruth almost grinned. "As if she had to throw up—in a magical way."

I had to smile at that thought. "Like a kid who quickly gobbles up all her Halloween candy at once." I caught myself latching on to this idea. Even Morgana's slightest weakness gave me new courage. Was Jared perhaps simply too powerful? Could it be that Morgana would be . . . overburdened by his magic? I really wanted to believe it.

"Well, something like that." Ruth smiled, but then her expression turned serious again. "The problem simply is that magic is inseparably linked to the human body of its owner. Even if Merlin's magic was too much for Morgana to handle, it cost him his life. The body itself cannot survive without magic. It seems to have been a little different with Nimue."

"Yes, I was just thinking that. How could she leave her magic in Avalon and simply continue to live as a normal, non-magical human?"

"Hmm. My mother believed that it was different for Nimue than for other magical creatures. Most *consist*, in a manner of speaking, of two components: the human body and magic. One cannot function without the other—they're a unit." She stopped, appearing strangely affected. Then she took a deep breath. "But Nimue's existence didn't seem to rest on these two pillars alone but on three: her human body, magic, and Avalon. All three would survive as long as two of the three remained firmly linked."

"Nimue's human body could survive as long as her magic was firmly linked to Avalon?" I thought about that for a moment. "But then why did she have to leave her magic there at all when she wanted to be together with Merlin? I mean, Nimue's body and her magic would have been firmly linked, and Avalon, as the third pillar, could have continued to exist. Right? Or . . . ?"

"Yes, Avalon would have continued to exist. But all the other beings who live there . . . none of them can survive without the magic. Avalon would have continued existing as a physical place, but magical life there would have been extinguished."

I felt sad. Would I be capable of making such a decision? Between the place and the beings one loves and one's own life?

"Now she's dead," I mumbled.

Ruth lifted my chin and looked at me lovingly. "But you, Evelyn, are alive." Her voice was imploring and determined. "You're alive, and you will reclaim what belongs to you."

CHAPTER 3

My mobile rang while I was on my way to our room to pick out clothes for the upcoming trip.

"Sally!" I called out in surprise when I answered. I had totally forgotten my best friend during the events of the last few days.

"Would you like to tell me why you weren't in class today?" she asked, point-blank.

"I . . . um." Classes were the last thing on my mind right now. It was almost as if I was leading a completely different life in which everyday things such as studies and old friends didn't exist.

"We've hardly seen each other for weeks now. You only hang out with Jared, and I'm lucky if we see each other for lunch once in a while! Look, it's been weeks, and I want an explanation." Sally took a quick breath, and then her voice switched from angry to sad. "Now you don't even come to classes anymore and can't be bothered to at least tell me why."

"Sally, I'm really sorry about how I've treated you lately."

I could hear her begin to cry. "Colin isn't calling." She was struggling to keep composed.

"He's been . . . we are . . ." What could I tell her?

"Yeah, yeah," she answered, her voice heavy. "That's what I keep hearing from him, too. This bloody stammering all the time." Then she really got mad. "You know what? If you see him, tell him he can kiss my butt!"

"Sally, no, you're taking this the wrong way. Colin really cares for you. It's just—"

"What?" she screeched. "Just *what's* going on?"

"I . . . I can't talk about it." *Bloody hell.* How dumb did that sound?

"Duh. That's really original," Sally said crossly. "I can't believe you're trying to babble nonsense, too, Evelyn."

"Listen, Sally," I interrupted with a firm voice. This discussion was leading nowhere fast. "Jared's in bad shape. Colin and I have to help him. Colin's not contacting you because he doesn't want to get you involved. He's totally mad about you. So am I. So calm down and trust me. It'll all turn out fine!"

Silence. Apparently, we were both surprised by my firm and self-assured tone. Where did I get this sudden certainty, this confidence? Would everything really be all right? I wanted to believe it.

"Sally?"

"Yeah?"

"Please trust me."

She was silent for a long time.

"Okay," she finally said.

"I'm sorry about the way things have been lately. You're my best friend, and I don't want to lose you."

Silence.

"Are you there?" I asked.

"Yes," she answered with a tear-choked voice.

"Oh, Sally." I would have loved to hug her.

"It's okay. It's fine," she said, acting strong. "Have you heard about the thing with Felix?"

I frowned. "No, what?"

"He raped a first-term student."

I was speechless.

"Two days ago. Then he disappeared. The police are looking for him."

I was so shocked, I couldn't say a word. We were silent for a while. I clasped my hand over my mouth as tears streamed down my face.

"It's my fault," I said.

"Don't go there, Evelyn." Sally breathed deeply. "We should have gone straight to the police." The reproach hung over me like a dark cloud.

"There's a rumor going about," she eventually continued, "that the girl's friend and a few of his buddies went after Felix and he won't be found any time soon. At least not in one piece . . ."

I swallowed. "So . . . he's . . . dead, then?"

"No idea. But how bad would that be?"

How bad, indeed. I didn't know how to feel about it. To be honest, I felt a certain relief that Felix would never be able to hurt anyone again.

"Take care, Evelyn," Sally finally said.

"You, too—I love you."

***

"Is the Jeep ready to go?" Enid asked when we returned to the council chamber a few hours later.

I'd had a lot of time to think about what Sally had told me. Maybe it was better that way. Right now only one thing counted: Jared.

My lot was cast. I wore a tank top, green cargo pants, and a breathable softshell jacket with innumerable small pockets and zippers. I looked down at my black army boots, which still had a hard and stiff feel. I had my hair in a tight ponytail and looked as if I was going to war. It was really starting to feel that way.

"Filled and warmed up," Gareth answered, giving the key to Enid before Colin took it away from her.

"At least let me drive, if I can't do anything else," he said.

"The equipment?" Enid inquired.

Colin held up a high-end black backpack. "Check."

"Hang on," Ruth interrupted, pulling the green book from her purse. "I'd like you to take this. It could be very helpful once you're in Avalon." She held out the book with a gentle smile.

"Thank you, Ruth," I said, stashing the volume in the backpack.

"Good," Enid continued. "We found a map in the library that marks the energy currents leading from here to Glastonbury."

"The Jeep has a GPS," Colin said mockingly, earning a severe look from Enid. "Just saying."

"It's not just about finding Glastonbury. It's having the energy current guide us to a magical place," Irvin explained, but Colin couldn't help rolling his eyes.

"Are you ready?" Enid gave me a probing look.

"Yes." I didn't sound very convincing.

Ruth gently squeezed my arm. "Just go through the portal. You mustn't doubt, even for a smidgeon of a second—or you'll fail."

I nodded and tried to memorize her words. Enid would have preferred not having Ruth along. I'd snorted, shaking my head. Old habits die so hard—once a bunch of paranoid secret hoarders, always a bunch of paranoid secret hoarders.

But I'd insisted Ruth should come along and, in the end, won.

I was just putting on the backpack when I noticed that the room had become strangely silent. I looked around and instantly realized why everyone looked embarrassed and nervous.

Karen Mayflower stood in the doorway of the council chamber, right behind Aiden, staring at me.

The moment I saw her, it was as if a switch flipped inside me. My anger boiled over. My temples throbbed as I charged at her, roughly pushing Aiden aside as he tried to protect his mother. Where did this strength suddenly come from? Not even Colin, who grabbed my arm, could manage to hold me back.

Karen's eyes widened with shock when I grabbed her shoulders and shoved her against the wall. I was delighted to hear the back of her head thump against the hard surface.

"It's all your fault!" I yelled in her face.

"As high priestess, it was my duty to do everything in my power—"

"Do you still not get it?" I interrupted her. "You made the Prophecy come true!"

"It was my duty—" she started again, but I wasn't about to listen to her feeble excuses and rationalizations.

"Your duty?" I was beside myself. "You killed my parents and my sister! It's because of you that Jared . . ." My voice broke with rage and sadness.

"I had to . . . ," she started again, but I was completely losing control. I heard no apology, no regret, no expression of remorse from her lips. This woman had my family on her conscience, and all she could offer were lame excuses? I took a step back and punched Karen, with full force, in the face. She collapsed to her knees.

Then I felt Colin's firm grip.

"Come on," he said softly. "We have to get going."

CHAPTER 4

"It must be here," Colin said as he shut off the Jeep and the motor fell silent. The car behind us, holding Gareth, Ian, and Ruth, also came to a stop. I looked around. I couldn't recognize anything in the headlights' beams other than thick, white fog.

We had left at about three in the morning to arrive at Glastonbury well before sunrise—in time, before the mist could dissipate.

I shut my eyes and took a moment to focus on what was about to happen. What if I didn't manage to get through the portal? If it simply wouldn't open for me? But what if . . . it did? What was waiting for me on the other side? Would the creatures living there really be on my side, as Ruth claimed? Or would they attack me? Would Morgana be the least of my problems? And Jared? Was he still alive? Would I arrive in time? Was I already too late?

I checked my equipment again after the others had gotten out. I'd brought a plain black trekking pack, light as a feather but with enough space for everything I needed for survival—at least for a few days. Some water, some army-ration protein bars, apples, a high-tech pop-up tent folded down to the size of a pineapple, a toothbrush, a change of socks and underwear, a compass that may or may not work in Avalon, a Swiss army knife, the blue-sheen dagger Karen had thrust into Morgana's arm—the only weapon we knew for sure could injure Morgana—and, of course, Ruth's green Nimue book.

"Are you ready?" Colin asked, leaning into the car.

"Yes."

I zipped up the backpack and was about to slip the straps over my shoulders when Colin lifted it out of my hands.

"I'll take it. You'll be on your own soon enough," he said in a subdued voice. I knew he'd like nothing more than to accompany me, but Ruth clearly thought the portal would only open if I went through it alone. I smiled hesitantly. Colin wasn't good at sitting around and waiting. He would have preferred to march into Avalon with his mighty sword to chop the head off anyone daring to oppose him. And I would have loved to have him with me.

***

The walk up the hill seemed to take forever, probably because of the fog—a murky, impenetrable brew. Trying to peer through it made me feel like I was treading on the same spot for hours. No one spoke.

Finally, we arrived at the top. I only noticed when I bumped into Enid.

"Sorry," I mumbled, running my eyes along the massive wall before us. I raised my head, perplexed. "That's supposed to be the gate to Avalon?" Not that it wasn't impressive. On the contrary: a medieval tower reaching skyward, with a gate many feet high, situated on a commanding hill in the middle of nowhere—if that wasn't awesome, what was? I would not have hesitated for a moment to call this mysterious place "magical," except . . .

"What did you expect?" Irvin asked.

"I didn't expect anything in particular, but to me it looks as if this gate, well, leads *nowhere*."

Enid, Colin, and Ruth followed me as I walked around the imposing building, and my fears were confirmed when I arrived on the other side. It was just a passage. If you entered on one side, you'd exit on the other. Where was the damned entrance?

"No one said it would be easy—" Enid began.

"Yes," Irvin confirmed, "but you're the last of Nimue's bloodline. If the portal doesn't open for you . . ." He sounded a little discouraged.

Ruth put her hand on my shoulder. "You mustn't doubt, or you'll fail." Her words sounded both encouraging and urgent.

I breathed in deeply as I tried to internalize what she had said.

"Okay," Enid decided, "time to say good-bye."

One after another, they hugged me and whispered into my ear that I would succeed and they'd be waiting for me here when I returned with Jared. Colin held me against his firm chest, and I hung onto him.

"Okay, let go," I finally said, detaching myself from his embrace. I was afraid I'd lose my composure if he held me any longer.

"Take care of yourself," he said, making an effort to keep a firm voice.

I nodded, turned around, straightened my shoulders, and walked into the fog.

"I request entry," I whispered. "In light and love. I request entry." I felt silly repeating this phrase I had learned by heart. But if it worked . . . "I request entry. In light and love. I request entry."

Step by step, I walked into the fog.

"I request entry," I whispered, robot-like. "In light and love."

When I turned a last time, my companions were only recognizable as silhouettes, while the fog ahead of me became denser and brighter—as if it was illuminated from within. *I request entry . . . in light and love.*

Then—I had no idea how much time had passed; neither space nor time seemed to exist in this uniform, grayish gruel—the fog gradually lightened. My heart raced. What was waiting for me on the other side? Damnati? Morgana? Or other frightful creatures whose existence I had not yet dared to dream of?

Suddenly I noticed a shadow in the distance. It became clearer with every step I took. Fear gripped my pounding heart. A man. It was a man—there on the other side. He just stood there. Although I was nearly paralyzed by fear, my legs carried me onward, ever onward. The fog almost became transparent, and then I recognized . . .

"Irvin?"

"What was that?" Colin asked, irritated.

"It looks as if she . . . simply . . . walked through it," Enid said, her voice sounding astonished and incredibly desperate.

I looked around, stunned. "This just can't be true!" I had really gone in at one end and come out the other. I'd simply walked through the damned gate. I angrily kicked at the dirt.

"Try again," Irvin encouraged me, but the tremble in his normally controlled voice betrayed his fear that I would not make it.

Ruth nodded.

I furiously clenched my teeth and trudged around the stone monument.

"Focus," Irvin said in a mantra-like tone, but it was anything but simple to shake off the anger and frustration and to focus on my *birthright,* as Ruth had called it. Blast, I *knew* it was my birthright to return to Avalon and, of course, I would once more think of it *in light and love* and request entry. But that went *super* well the first time, right? Apart from it not working fifteen centuries ago for Nimue. And if this was the right way, she *would* have done it, wouldn't she? I mean, if not her, who? So maybe it was something else that would open this goddamned gate for me. Maybe I shouldn't even try to fight this anger, hatred, frustration, and burning rage? Maybe I should just admit these feelings? Maybe I should try to *force* entry with this rage boiling over and this anger burning inside me.

And, by God, I *was* angry!

Everything, just everything, in my life that meant something to me had been taken from me. Everyone I loved had been torn away while I could only helplessly stand by and watch. No! Not this time! I would not let Jared be taken from me. I would not stand by without doing something, would not let it all just unfold. I would not collapse and wallow in self-pity. No! Those times were gone. For good.

Determined, I set one foot in front of the other. Fists clenched. Teeth clenched. Never again would someone take something I loved from me! Never again! I would get Jared out, and anyone in my way would get to know another side of me. I was Nimue's heiress. I alone. It was my *right* to return to this island that Nimue had left long ago. Moreover, it was *my* island. Avalon belonged to *me*!

Once more, I immersed myself in the fog. But it was different this time. There was something strange about the mist. The way it curled around my legs and crept up on me almost made it seem alive. Again and again, its plumes wound themselves along my body, ice-cold and unstoppable. I withstood the urge to shake them off and marched on. Wildly determined to save the person who meant the most to me in this world. Who was ready to give his life for mine. And that is what I would do for him now. *Jared, I'm coming! I'm coming!*

"Colin, don't! Come back!" I heard someone call from far behind me.

Then I dove into the white fog. Everything was silent.

CHAPTER 5

Um . . . what is that? A woman's voice humming a song? Yes. Very faintly.

It was both familiar and intimidating. Could Colin hear it? He must have followed me into the fog. I couldn't risk having the portal close again, so I continued on. Would we meet after the passage? How far was it still? It seemed like I'd been wandering about in this pea soup for hours. I probably had.

There. There it was again. That humming. I thought I recognized the melody, but it was still too faint to place. Was it a . . . lullaby? Yes, a melody I knew but hadn't heard for ages. Just like the voice humming the melody. An intangible longing arose inside me. But for what?

As I pressed on, the humming grew louder, clearer. It was a woman's voice, I was sure of that now. One I had known. One that I loved.

I squinted, but nothing was recognizable in the shifting whiteness surrounding me. What if I was going in the wrong direction?

"Eve."

I froze.

"Eve," the tender voice whispered again, before resuming its lullaby.

Trembling, I called out, "Who are you?" and then held my breath.

"Don't be afraid, my darling," the voice said softly, then continued humming.

Suddenly I recognized the familiar, melodic sound. The sound of the voice that had comforted me, lulled me to sleep, laughed and cried with me, and sung to me.

"Zara?" I barely whispered.

"Don't be afraid, my darling. I'm with you," my sister's voice said. *"Nothing can happen to you. I'm watching over you."*

"Where are you?"

"You only had a bad dream."

"What?" I desperately turned in all directions. I still couldn't see anything beyond the fog. I peered as hard as I could.

"It was just a dream," Zara said, gently brushing back my hair.

My eyes widened with fright as I looked into my sister's beautiful face. I shrank back, realizing after I bumped against the headboard that I was lying in a bed. In *my* bed. At home. In our flat in Fleetwood. Zara sat, as she so often did when I had a nightmare, by the side of the bed and looked at me tenderly. She gently brushed my face with her fingers.

"Only a dream," she said again.

"Zara," I repeated, unable to form a complete sentence.

"Try to sleep a little more," she said. She was wearing her uniform. "I have to go to work, but I'll be back when you wake up. We'll have breakfast together."

"But you're . . . Frank Tempton . . . he . . . you're . . . *dead*."

"That dream again?" Her expression was soft and compassionate when she took my face in her hands and looked at me. "That was nothing but a dream, Eve. I won't leave you alone. You and I—forever. Have you forgotten?"

She smiled.

"You and I—forever," I repeated. That had been our motto since our parents had died. A promise that we'd always have each other, would always rely on each other.

"Now sleep a little more. I'll bring some fresh bagels when I come back, okay?" She pressed a smooching kiss on my forehead and got up.

"Zara, wait!" I called after her. She turned back to me. I threw the covers aside, got up, and slowly walked toward her. She looked just as I remembered. That amazing oval, slightly heart-shaped, face with the sincere green eyes. The pointed chin with a hint of cleavage. The dense light-blond hair that fell over her shoulders in gentle waves and reached to her collarbones. I took another step toward her. Could this be? Could all those terrible things have been a dream?

"I missed you so much," I finally said. Tears streamed from my eyes.

"Missed?" Zara asked, astonished, but I had already thrown myself into her arms and wrapped mine around her slender body.

"Eve, what on earth is going on with you?" She seemed concerned.

I buried my face in her shoulder.

"It was just a nightmare. Calm down. Sleep a little more, and we'll have breakfast when I get back, okay?"

Zara rocked me back and forth, then led me back to my bed and passed me a tissue. I blew my nose and looked into her deep-green eyes. She sat back down at my bedside. I put my arms around her neck and pulled her close, feeling her warm, comforting skin. I could even feel her heart beating in unison with mine.

Oh God, I'd missed her so much! I'd endured so much time without her warmth. I'd thought of her for so long, dreamed of her . . . but my thoughts were uneasy. Had I just been dreaming? Was any of it real?

She sat next to me. It must have been an intense dream, if I had to struggle with it so long after waking up. It was probably best to sleep a little more. I was wiped out and could barely keep my eyes open. I started to yawn.

Zara smiled. "See," she said. "Everything's fine. Now, think of something pretty before you fall asleep."

"I will," I said, smiling back, and she once more took me into her arms. What would I do without her?

"Good night, Eve."

"Good night, Zara," I answered, letting myself sink into the pillow. The familiar surroundings of home gave me a deep feeling of shelter I could immerse myself in. I closed my eyes and had almost slipped into a dream when I suddenly saw something. An image of dark-blue eyes flashed through my thoughts. Wonderful, glowing, dark-blue eyes.

Odd. I'd never seen those eyes, yet they seemed so real. What's more, they exercised an inexplicable, even magical attraction. Strange . . .

I tried to remember the face surrounding those wonderful blue eyes. I nearly had it, but then it slipped away again. I tried to concentrate but was only able to put the picture together in fragments. Why was it so hard? A small, straight nose . . . auburn hair . . . The image blurred as gently arched lips spread into a slanted smile.

How did I know how those lips felt?

"Zara?" I called into the hallway.

"Yes?" Zara came back into the room, putting on her dark-blue uniform jacket. She moved to my bed and sat down, casting a hurried glance at her watch.

I didn't want her to be late because of me. "It can wait," I said. I wouldn't have known how to tell her that I couldn't get the image of this blue-eyed man out of my head, whoever he was. And yet, I felt I knew who he was. Moreover . . . *loved him*. Did Zara know him?

Instead of asking her, I hugged her. It was amazing to feel her again. The nightmare had been so real. I'd felt with my heart and soul that I'd forever lost her, the sister I loved more than anything. Again the image of the stranger with the indigo eyes crept into my thoughts. Had he been in my dream? I shook my head to cast out these confused images and focused instead on the sensation of Zara's cheek against mine as I snuggled against her.

I once again inhaled the familiar scent of Zara's skin. That scent . . . I inhaled again. Something was . . . different . . . about her. I slowly pulled away and looked at her. Something wasn't right.

"Lie down, Eve." She brushed my hair out of my face, as she had done thousands of times before. I shrank back from her touch. I couldn't explain *why*, but it suddenly felt strange to be touched by her. *Wrong*, somehow. Again the picture of the young man shot into my head. This time it was clearer, more defined. And suddenly there he was: *Jared.*

I could see Jared in my mind! *My* Jared. The man I loved. The one who had been taken from me. For whose sake I'd gone into the fog. For whose sake I was *here*. Here with . . . *her.*

I looked at Zara, frightened. When she recognized what was happening inside me, her attitude suddenly changed. Her hand stopped in mid-motion, and her body became rigid.

"Sleep so you're rested," she said. But the tone of her voice had changed. Become harder. Firmer.

I shrank back but did not let my eyes leave her. For a second everything was perfectly still as we sized each other up.

"You're not Zara." Had I said that? My voice sounded different than usual. Harsh. My tone surprised me, but not as much as my words. It was as if I were speaking with an internal voice. I slowly stood.

"Don't be silly, Eve," Zara countered, waving her hand. She rose and came toward me.

"Stay where you are." I took a step back.

"Just stop it," she said, not nearly as friendly. "You're just tired. You need rest." She came closer, lifting her hands in an almost threatening gesture. "Go back to bed." Her words sounded like a command.

At that moment I was absolutely sure. This was *not* my sister. "My sister's dead. I don't know who or what you are, but you're not Zara."

A dark grin distorted the familiar face. She had recognized that it was pointless to pretend anymore.

Then the room around us dissolved. The creature that looked like my sister slowly approached, while a cold and clammy mist crawled over my skin. Every hair on the back of my neck stood.

One thought burned in my mind and took total possession of me: *Jared!* I was here for his sake—I was here to save him. How could I have forgotten him?

"You're not real." My voice sounded ice-cold and determined. "Get out of my way!"

Suddenly something changed in her face. Her shining green eyes dimmed, and her pupils narrowed into tiny snake-like slits. Her rosy skin turned ash-gray, scaly, and dead as her cheeks sank in. Even her wavy blond hair fell out, leaving a small, bald head with a pointed tongue flicking toward me through tiny, tight lips.

The creature made an awful hiss as it rushed me.

She's not real . . . she's not real . . . she's not real . . .

I ran as fast as I could. Far away from this monster I had just held in my arms. I almost threw up thinking about it. *Just get away from here!* I looked around in desperation. Something was moving about me. My nerves were fraying. Something in the shadows . . . or . . . no—it *was* the shadows! Wavering, grayish-white shadows. They danced about me, awkward and sluggish, whispering my name, enticing me closer.

Hazy apparitions of groaning, half-naked women in ragged clothing pleaded for help. I forced myself not to look. I noticed another movement behind me. I reached for the blue dagger in my backpack and pulled it out.

Children with empty black eyes stared at me from all sides. "Where's my mama?" a sad child whimpered. My stomach clenched. They closed in on me. I felt their shadow fingers in my hair. At my throat. A cold shudder ran down my spine. What was this wretched place? I ran as fast as my legs would carry me, trying to escape the shadow fingers.

Then I held my breath as a damnatus floated toward me, its rotting body wrapped in a filthy dark cloak. A hood concealed much of its sore-covered face. I thrust the dagger in its direction, but the creature simply floated through it. Plumes of fog whirled about the spot where I had struck.

I shut my eyes and kept running, past shadows grasping at me with sharp claws. A damp cold crept over my skin. I opened my eyes and regretted it. The sight before me left me stunned. I cried out, then clasped my hand over my mouth. Was I losing my mind?

The path was paved with human corpses. Some looked peaceful, but others had terror written on their faces—mouths and eyes wide open, faces distorted into pale masks of horror. I wagered that the latter were those who had gone deeper into the fog. Had I stayed with the fake Zara, I would also be lying there, my face forever frozen into a silly grin. Pure terror possessed me. These poor souls . . . men, women, and children. Dozens had lost their lives in the fog. Would I share their fate?

Panic and you'll be stuck, my internal voice said. Quiet and composed, it seemed to come from deep within. *Stay calm. Stay calm.*

I obeyed my thoughts and slowed my pace, difficult though that was. *Keep the goal in mind. Always forward.* The ground was strewn with corpses. There were so many I had to watch where I stepped.

To take in this horrible scene as a whole would have driven me insane.

Only one thought helped me stay focused: *Jared! Jared, I'm coming!*

Thinking of him drove me relentlessly forward into the fog, marching mechanically across the blanket of corpses.

Suddenly, ahead of me: a silver, floating veil. Was that the end of the fog? Had I made it? What would happen if I walked through? Should I take the risk? Turning around wasn't an option. I couldn't do this twice. I gathered all my courage and stepped into the silver mist. A clear, high voice rang out.

"Magical Avalon lets some enter but turns others away."

"I . . . request entry," I answered formally. It was all I could think of on the spot.

"Pass the final test here to leave the mists behind."

"What kind of test?" Would I fail now, so close to the goal?

"Solving this riddle will allow you to enter. But consider: Only the correct answer leaves you unharmed."

I swallowed. "And what if my answer is wrong?"

"A wrong word and you remain here. The fog will take possession of you."

A cold shudder ran down my spine. I cast a glance over my shoulder. Would I end as *they* had?

"Okay," I timidly consented.

The voice rose.

"The powerful being, worshipped by all,

to its home, for love, its back has turned.

Deceived and betrayed by malevolence and greed,

the Mistress finds her return home denied.

The water's might violently displaced,

the heavens with black clouds are hung.

The nymphs' laughter fallen silent,

dark creatures proclaim their evil deeds.

The forest, once flowering in perfect splendor,

without her its might is extinguished."

I swallowed. *Okay, let's think. Don't jump the gun with an answer.* I really didn't feel like becoming the next patch in the corpse quilt.

Focus!

I knew this story. Ruth had told it to me. The verse was about Nimue's love for Merlin, his death, her desperate attempt to return home, and Morgana's invasion of Avalon.

But what was the correct answer? Or rather, what was the correct question? The name of the mighty being at the start of the verse? Or did the voice in the silver mist want to know what had happened there? I reviewed the verse one more time in my thoughts.

Mighty being leaves Avalon. For love. That meant Nimue—that much was certain.

Malevolence and greed—certainly characteristics I would ascribe to Morgana—*betrayed her and she can no longer return home.* I was sure up to that point.

The water's strength—Nimue's magic.

Black clouds—perhaps a symbol for Morgana's dark magic?

The nymphs' laughter fallen silent—I bet.

But who were the dark creatures mentioned? The damnati? That would make sense.

The forest's splendor was synonymous for Avalon; of that I was sure because of the drawings in Ruth's green book.

Without her its might is extinguished. That last sentence cleared up all my doubts. The question was: Who is *she*? *Who* was the riddle speaking about? That had to be the solution! I breathed deeply.

"Nimue," I answered, betting the farm on the Lady of the Lake horse.

The voice was silent for a moment. I held my breath.

"You may pass, but be forewarned: cunning and deceit are well disguised."

I breathed out, relieved. I had done it!

"Um . . . thanks, I'll keep that in mind," I replied awkwardly and stepped through the silver veil. I forced myself not to look back and went forward. On and on. I had to get through this fog and find Jared—nothing else mattered. And so I went, on and on. Until the fog dissipated and the shadows fell behind me.

CHAPTER 6

Where at first I couldn't see my hand before my eyes, now only fine plumes surrounded me, gradually dissolving with each careful step I took forward. And then . . . *unbelievable.*

It was exactly like the pictures in Ruth's book.

An enchanted forest. There was no other way to describe the view. Plate-sized blossoms shining in every color, florescent leaves glowing in the shadows, cupped flowers spraying a dizzying yellow mist when I touched them.

I was nearly overwhelmed by the multitude of colors as I ventured into the forest. The dense, luscious grass muffled my steps. Trees of all kinds surrounded me for as far as I could see. Aspen, linden, birch, spruce, oak, fir, beech, chestnut, larch, pine . . . many I knew, while others seemed to have sprung from a child's fantasies, judging by their forms, colors, leaves, and sizes. Some trees were young and slender; others had mighty trunks and majestic crowns. They must have been centuries, perhaps millennia, old. A gentle breeze set the leaves dancing in the sunlight. A gust carried away the parachute-like tufted seeds of a fifteen-yard-high dandelion clock. The forest floor was covered in luscious ferns, leafy shrubs, delicate grasses, fragrant flowers, and too many different mushrooms and mosses for me to count. My eyes widened in disbelief.

A monkey-like animal the size of a hamster merrily hopped from blossom to blossom, opened its tiny mouth, and extended its tongue—almost three times its own body length—into the flowers. It slurped up the sweet nectar with satisfaction. Next to the blooms were carnivorous vines twining up to the gills of six-foot-tall mushrooms with umbrella-like caps. I watched another hummingbird-monkey giggle while it hopped from mushroom to mushroom, amusing itself by fooling the snapping vines. Just before a vine was about to catch it, the creature quickly hopped to the next fungus. A passing dragonfly-butterfly was not so lucky. It was grabbed by one of the vines, which retracted like an octopus's tentacle and swung the winged insect into the wide-open mouth of a water lily, which devoured its meal with loud smacking noises.

I heard water splashing nearby, accompanied by melodic birdsong coming from all around. I glimpsed a bird's plumage sporting all the colors of the rainbow. Near me, a sparrow-sized brilliant white bird sitting on the branch of a mighty aspen spread its glittering wings in the sunlight. It plunged downward, chirping, while a raptor the size of a goshawk but with deep-green feathers circled above the treetops, presumably looking for a meal. Without warning, the bird of prey swooped down on a fluffy, mouse-like animal. The critter produced a piercing cry, causing such pain in the hunter's small walnut-shaped ears that it immediately flew away.

I was amazed. A giggling squeak drew my attention to a small birch tree with purple leaves where a pointy-eared hedgehog-squirrel was uttering it before hopping down, grabbing a chestnut off the ground, and running back up the slender tree. There it settled in comfortably, cracked open the chestnut by beating it against the spikes on its back, and noisily chomped away on it.

What a marvelous place. I felt like Alice after she fell down the rabbit hole. A green Wonderland was inviting me to stay. It was strange, yet strangely familiar. I somehow felt I'd been here before. And I had—at least in a dream. In the magical sleep Jared had sent me.

I inhaled deeply, taking in the scent of the luscious meadows, ancient trees, splashing brooks, loamy forest soil, and beguiling flowers. My heart knew Ruth was right—this was my home. Avalon was *my* island. And Jared was here. Somewhere.

Suddenly I heard a noise. I slipped behind the nearest tree and pulled the blue dagger from my backpack. I'd startled a small fluffy animal—a cross between a rabbit and cat—hopping from shrub to shrub. I breathed in and relaxed. Still, it seemed best to fasten the dagger to my belt. That way I'd have it handy. Just in case. As beautiful as this place was, I couldn't let it lull me into feeling safe.

The flat ground began to slope downward, leading me into a kind of gulley. I wasn't quite comfortable with that. I would rather have stayed farther up, with a better view over the terrain. Down here, I felt like easy prey despite the cover of the trees. But since I had no idea where to start looking for Jared, I simply went straight ahead. There was no path, which made the task considerably more difficult. I progressed slowly, clambering over roots, ducking under low-hanging branches, climbing over moss-covered rocks, and walking around dense shrubs. Did it only feel this way, or was the forest gradually becoming thicker and less penetrable the farther I went into the heart of Avalon?

***

Except for a few cute forest dwellers, I encountered no one on my hike. Yet I gradually felt less and less alone. I looked about. Nobody was to be seen. I continued onward but couldn't shake the constant feeling of several pairs of eyes following my every move. What's more, the deeper I went into the forest, the quieter it became. Where at first

I'd heard merry bird twitter, excited squeaking, and busy rustling all around me, it was now completely silent. Only the gentle bubbling of the occasional stream and the sound of the wind rustling the leaves accompanied me.

On I went, forcing my way through the thick undergrowth. Time stood still. Hours seemed to pass like seconds, but then a minute would feel like an eternity. The forest looked the same in all directions. I began to fear I was walking in circles.

Finally, I rested at a narrow brook. I filled my water bottle, ate one of the disgustingly sweet protein bars Colin had packed for me, and changed my socks. I took this opportunity to go through my backpack. The tent would be my shelter and was very pragmatic, though I sincerely hoped I wouldn't need it. Should I find Jared before sundown, we might be off the island faster than I thought. To my surprise, I became a little melancholic at the thought of leaving Avalon so soon.

I suddenly thought of something. *The compass!* If there was no other way to orient myself, it might help me find Jared. Hastily, I rummaged through the backpack and pulled it out. But it was useless. The needle spun in circles instead of pointing north. *Great!* Frustrated, I tossed the broken compass into the forest. Then I got up, recovered it, and stashed it in the backpack again. It would be stupid to leave tracks. In the worst case, I'd hurl it against a damnatus's head.

I'd have to use the sun's movement as my guide. How did that work, again? *The sun rises in the east* . . . I cursed myself for not paying more attention in geography class. *It then moves southward*—that's right, isn't it?—*and sets in the west . . . it's never seen to the north.* Exactly! The sun is never in the north sky, right? If only Colin were here. I was sure he'd know what to do. Was he still in the fog? I just had to continue. One way or another.

***

The forest was completely silent now, as if every living being held its breath as I passed. Progress was painstakingly slow now that the sun was mercilessly beating down on me. I crossed shallow, almost soundless streams; avoided overgrown ponds; and trudged around mud holes. Pristine, unspoiled nature as far as the eye could see. Beautiful, yet full of traps.

I took care with every step not to trip over protruding roots, stones, or dense shrubs. A machete would probably have been more helpful in this jungle than that dumb spinning compass.

Suddenly, I heard something like clanging, then a rasping sound that set my stomach churning. I held my breath. *Damnati!*

I hastily ducked behind a knotty fallen tree trunk. My heart beat so loudly, I was afraid they'd hear it. I spied through the root tangle into the shadows. Fear sharpened my senses.

There were four of them: two scarfaces walking ahead, a third right behind them, another straggling behind. On patrol—at least, that's what it looked like.

"Watch where you're going, asshole," the third said to the straggler. "Damn well pick that up."

"Yes, yes, all right."

I clasped my hands over my mouth to stifle any noise. My eyes widened with horror. The voice of the last one didn't sound nearly as raspy as that of other damnati I'd had the pleasure of meeting. It almost sounded human. What frightened me most was not its sound but that I knew it.

It was *Felix's* voice. I swallowed my fright and stared through the thicket. Felix, or whatever had become of him, bent down to pick up some shiny metal objects that were causing the clanging sound. Were they traps? I focused on him. His black cloak didn't show much of him, but as soon as he was upright again, I was able to see his face. I bit my tongue to keep from screaming. He still looked like Felix, but a transformation had begun. His once dark-brown eyes were so turbid that one might have thought he was blind. His skin appeared scaly and pale, and above his right eye a ghastly sore spread, stinking of rotting flesh so badly I could smell it. His hands were covered in scars, warts, and burst boils. I barely kept from puking. How long had Felix been here? Three, maybe four days? And the transformation was already irreversible after such a short time. My mood darkened. Felix was no longer human—he had become one of them.

"Get a move on!" the third one shouted over his shoulder.

I watched in disbelief as the Felix damnatus followed the others. Once more, I held my breath as they passed near my hiding place. I remained in my crouched position for several minutes, then slumped and buried my face in my hands.

I heard Irvin in my head: *Damnati are evil, soulless creatures who have lost their place in the world.* What did I expect? That Felix could redeem himself? That he'd change? That it all was just a *misunderstanding*, as he'd tried to convince me? Surely not after what Sally had told me. *Misunderstanding* . . . that word alone! My God! Just how stupid had I been? Felix had wanted to rape me—I only owed it to Jared that he hadn't succeeded. And what about Sally? He'd poisoned her and would have been fine with her death. Just so she wouldn't get between him and his plan to attack me. And what about the other girl? I shuddered. Though I'd been spared the worst, thanks to Jared, it had not done that girl any good. She'd fallen prey to Felix, who'd been willing to murder and was a rapist. Who knew what else he'd done or what else he was capable of?

What the devil was wrong with me that I'd let him get away with it? Had I really just suppressed it all because I'd been spared the worst? Had I really been dumb enough to give someone like Felix a second chance because the worst hadn't happened? What happened to that girl was my fault. I could have prevented it by going to the police. What had driven me to worry about *his* future? I knew what he was!

So it was true. The girl's friend had taken care of Felix before the police got to him. I felt satisfaction. I didn't approve of murder, but Felix had gotten his just desserts. Though did he have to run into Morgana—however that might have happened? Or had she already been looking for him? She'd obviously offered him a deal: to be spared damnation in exchange for his deformed soul. Now he was a damnatus—and a damned one. Good people don't become damnati. Good people wouldn't ever enter into a pact with that witch. But Felix had. Now he was trapped in Morgana's bondage for eternity because he was too cowardly to face what awaits murderers and rapists.

Once the damnati were out of sight and earshot, I slowly got up, wiped the dirt from my legs, stretched a little, and followed them.

CHAPTER 7

Where were they now? All those fabled creatures that Ruth had promised me, that were supposed to stand by my side? The way it looked, I was all alone on this island—apart from the damnati, of course. They'd tear me limb from limb if they managed to lay hand on me. Provided they didn't think of worse things to do. And I was stupid enough to follow them! But whatever happened, there was one damnatus I would *not* let get away. That one had already gotten away with far too much. Anyway, these stinking monsters would lead me straight to Morgana—and, I hoped, to Jared.

The four trampled an obvious path through the forest. Even a complete idiot would have been able to track them. I didn't have to get close to follow.

Since I'd lost all sense of time, only the sun's position provided me with an idea of how long I'd already been here. I guessed it'd been about two and a half hours—in the scorching heat. I felt it in my bones. The damnati must have felt the same, because they decided to take a break. I snuck in a wide arc around their resting place, taking great care not to make a sound. I fought my way through thorny vines, climbed over a huge tree stump, and pressed myself along a ragged cliff. Then I was there. I had circled their improvised camp, climbed on a jutting rock ledge, and was lurking right above them.

"You stink!" one accused the other as I came within hearing range.

"Shut up!" the stinker hurled back.

I advanced a little to peep over the edge. They were all lying in the shadow of a huge tree, drinking from a hide-covered flask.

"Don't drink it all, you swine," one yelled, ripping the flask from the hand of the Felix damnatus, spilling some of its contents. Felix was apparently not winning any popularity contests among his new friends. That delighted me, and an image entered my thoughts: how he had hovered over me, pinned my hands to the mattress, and looked at me with an awful, greedy expression. Then I thought of the other girl. The one who'd not been so lucky. I didn't know her and had probably never met her, at least not knowingly. And yet I still felt strongly connected to her.

I hadn't had a plan when I started to follow those four idiots below—and, to be honest, I still didn't have one. But I didn't care. Four on one? Whatever. I just didn't care. All that counted at this very moment was revenge and saving Jared. Each of these damnati groaning in the shade had done something horrible in his human life. They would pay for it.

Without thinking, I got up, lifted a football-sized boulder over my head, and flung it down hard against the skull of the damnatus who saw me first and was trying to get up. I heard a bone crack as it struck his temple. He fell, twitching, to the ground. The Felix damnatus quickly sprang to his feet and caught sight of me. He briefly struggled to regain his composure, until the one next to him pushed him in the back with an ax handle and growled, "What are you waiting for? Grab her! Or I'll tell Morgana you let the dirty slut get away!"

The Felix damnatus froze for a moment—as if he were imagining what Morgana would do to him if he failed—then made up his mind. He pulled his scab-encrusted eyebrows together and came at me, bounding up to the rock ledge and charging me. It all happened so fast. I let him approach close enough that I could feel his foul breath in my face, then pulled out the blue dagger, thrust it straight into his heart, twisted the blade, and pulled it out again. I looked at him coldly, free of emotion. I stood there straight as a stick and watched him stagger backward, eyes and mouth wide open, unable to understand, clasping the gaping wound in his chest with both hands. Thick, dark blood flowed in streams through his fingers. He took another step back before tumbling down over the ledge. The dull sound of his impact was the last thing I heard before I ran.

I could hear the other two already coming after me.

I ran as fast as I could and disappeared into the dense forest as if it would render me invisible.

Why didn't Enid give me a gun to bring along?

The two scarfaces quickly caught up, but then the first stumbled and pulled the other to the ground, which bought me a small lead.

"You idiot!" I heard one of them yell, enraged. There was a short scuffle. Soon they were after me again. And gaining. All of a sudden, something struck my head. I tripped, and my vision blurred as pain shot through my skull. My legs gave way, but before I fell, a damnatus caught up with me and rammed his fist into my head. The warm, metallic taste of blood filled my mouth. I coughed and spat. Through a veil of blood and tears, I noticed another blurred black cloak moving toward me. I shrank back, kicking and trying to get on my feet. I was so dizzy that it seemed as if the trees were spinning around me. The first damnatus kicked me forcefully in the ribs. The air escaped my lungs with a hiss. I gasped. My dagger went flying from my hand with another kick. By now my vision was too blurred to see much. Panic took hold of me. I had lost my only weapon. Hold it—no! There was also that Swiss army knife in my backpack! I pulled the backpack off my shoulder and ripped open the front zipper.

"What's that supposed to be?" the damnatus said in a smug tone.

I frantically dug around inside the backpack until I felt the smooth finish of the knife handle. Then I quickly snapped the blade out—or at least that's what I thought was going to happen. Instead, a shiny corkscrew appeared.

The damnatus gave out a ringing, raspy laugh, infuriating me so much my panic was instantly dispelled. I reached back as far as I could and rammed the corkscrew with full force into the stinking scarface's thigh. He stopped in his tracks.

"Ow—you cunt!" he screamed, turning in circles on one leg as he attempted to pull the corkscrew from his flesh. He finally got hold of the shiny red handle and pulled the coil out. A hideous foul liquid bubbled forth from the wound.

He briefly looked at the corkscrew, to which bits of his flesh still clung, and then turned to me.

"I'm gonna shove this up your arse," he croaked, then slowly walked toward me, obviously relishing the prospect.

The second damnatus had also almost reached me. A rotten grin spread across his face as he approached.

I retreated, flailing all the while, and had almost managed to get to my feet when the damnatus struck me in the chest and sent me sprawling into the dirt again. Would they kill me now? Or torture me and take me to Morgana for her to finish me off? And make Jared watch. My eyes filled with tears. The pain in my head was unbearable.

I'm so sorry, Jared! I've failed you.

Suddenly I noticed a lean, black shape approaching from the side, crouching like a silent shadow. Another damnatus? No, this creature moved far too gracefully. Without warning, it leaped on the damnatus farthest away from me. In one smooth motion, the massive black creature tore him to the ground. I heard a wild growl, followed immediately by the death rattle of a ripped-out throat.

The damnatus who'd been about to finish me off glanced, terrified, over his shoulder. His legs shook with fear as this creature, lean as a panther and yet massive as a bear, moved toward him with grace and confidence. The damnatus could do nothing more than tremble and watch as the predator approached for the kill.

"A barghest? In broad daylight?" he stammered in disbelief.

The animal leaped again. In a lightning-fast, smooth motion, the bear-like cat buried its powerful claws in the flank of the damnatus and ripped his head off with razor-sharp teeth. It happened so fast the scarface didn't have a chance for a last cry. The creature—the barghest?—spat out the remains of the stinking skull in disgust. Then it came toward me, uttering a rumbling growl from deep within. I stood frozen. It stopped before me and gave me a penetrating stare with its golden-red eyes for a second, two at most, before turning and disappearing with a graceful bound into the depths of the forest. I fainted.

***

I woke with a pounding headache. How much time had passed? I was so exhausted that I just lay there until I could no longer bear the stench of the damnatus corpses. I tried to get up, but my legs gave way, and I collapsed again. My head felt like it was going to burst. I massaged my temples, then crawled across the ground and collected the dagger and Swiss army knife. I nearly fainted with every movement, but I somehow stayed conscious. *Water! I need water!*

I heard quiet splashing nearby.

If I can only get there . . .

It took all my remaining strength to crawl on my hands and knees to a small stream in the soothing shade. First, I put my hands into the cool water. Then I greedily drank. Finally, I dunked my head and remained under water until my temples stopped throbbing and the warm, metallic taste of my own blood had washed from my mouth. The pain relented. *Thank goodness*, it relented. Glancing in all directions, I stripped down to my underwear and slid into the water. It felt so good and immediately helped, as though it was washing away my pain. My muscles began to relax, the dull pounding in my head and ribs disappeared, and my swollen hands and feet shrank to their normal size. I moaned, relieved. The effect water had on me here was nothing new, but I was sure *this* water was healing my injuries faster and better than ever before.

For a long time, I simply lay in the stream, closed my eyes, let the water flow over my body, and healed.

It was dusk when I opened my eyes again. Had I fallen asleep? I hastily climbed out of the water, dressed, and nervously looked about. I'd already had a taste of what might be lurking behind the trees, and, to be honest, I wasn't eager to find out what else was concealed in the darkness of the forest. But . . . was I really in danger? The black panther-like creature—what had the damnatus called it? Barghest?—had spared me. No, not just spared me. It had killed the damnati, and so . . . saved my life. Was Ruth right? Were the creatures here in Avalon really on my side? I wasn't sure if this was the moment to put the theory to the test. Better to find a resting place for the night and wait for the next day. Could Jared wait? Would he last through the night?

***

Darkness was closing in, making me feel less and less comfortable. I was also incredibly hungry. I had eaten nothing all day except for the ultra-sweet protein bar, which had almost made me sick, and an apple. I walked upstream along the bank for about half an hour. Straining, I stopped and listened to the forest. Nothing. Not a peep. Still, I didn't want to see what creatures were hidden in the growth, and wandering around in the dark was certainly not a good idea. Reluctantly, I found a hidden place under a willow with low-hanging branches and went about making camp for the night. The pop-up tent Colin had packed did honor to its name. Setting it up, with one motion of the hand, was child's play. After looking around once more, I crawled in, pulled the zipper shut, ate an apple, curled up, and placed my head on the backpack. It was uncomfortable. I was lying on top of something hard and flat. The book! I awkwardly pulled the volume out of my backpack, turned on the flashlight, and flipped through the pages until I found a picture of a black creature that was part panther, part dog.

> *The barghest (also bargtjest or bargest) is a mythical golden-eyed creature with monstrous claws and razor-sharp fangs. Swift as a panther, enduring as a wolf, and strong as a bear, it is a malicious example of the "black dogs." Its name is of uncertain origin. According to some sources, the name is derived from the German Berggeist, or mountain spirit. But "bear ghost" has also been suggested. The barghest is a native of the high plains of Avalon and only appears at dusk. It is an omen of death.*

I swallowed and turned the page.

The behemoth, I read next, and brushed my fingers over a picture of a gigantic, armored primeval creature that looked like a cross between a hippopotamus and an armadillo. The description made the behemoth seem like a rather peaceful soul, although it could level entire villages when it felt itself or its young threatened. The thought of meeting such a colossus was frightening.

I turned the page to encounter another inhabitant of Avalon:

> *The kelpie (or kelpy) is a supernatural water spirit that inhabits both the innumerable lakes and rivers of Avalon and the flowing waters of the Scottish Highlands. It has the appearance of a large horse with a fish tail. It can be found near deep rivers and promises travelers that it will carry them across the river. If the traveler consents, the kelpie drags him to the depths to be devoured.*

Wow. Those were lovely prospects. Malicious barghests, trampling behemoths, devious kelpies . . . I continued to read on and glanced over the next few pages. Goblins—ill-tempered, trap-setting imps living underground . . . Pixies—small, winged, and blue-skinned, prone to mischievous pranks . . . something for every taste. Were there any *nice* creatures here?

Tired and somewhat disconcerted by what I'd read, I shut the book. Jared's face was the last thing I thought of before falling asleep. *Hang in there! I love you!*

***

Shortly before sunrise, I pulled open the zipper and crawled out of the tent. I stretched my stiff limbs in all directions, like a cat. Then I gathered my things. It was a challenge, pushing that damned tent back into its original shape, but I managed. It was dawn when I set on my way along the stream. I followed it until I arrived at a spot wide enough to wash myself. As I brushed my teeth, I wondered where the water came from. The damnati I had wanted to follow wouldn't be going anywhere now, so maybe I should try my luck with this stream. I followed the gurgling water toward the source. Was I mistaken? Hadn't I seen this place before? A stream, a mountain, a cave . . . a tree underground . . . the . . . *the source*? I couldn't remember. Yet from deep inside came the calming feeling that I was on the right path.

The sun rose slowly over the treetops to dapple the forest in a golden green light. I walked for some time before I noticed the terrain becoming increasingly steeper. I was going uphill. Soon, I could see over the tops of the smaller trees. The good thing was that the higher I climbed, the better the view I had. But it also meant that my route became more difficult with every step.

As on the previous day, the forest around me turned strangely silent. I could hear neither birdsong nor the rustling noises of forest dwellers moving about the undergrowth. Nothing. The forest, except for the sound of the wind in the leaves, stayed silent. Still, it felt as if I wasn't alone. As if I was being watched.

My route became so steep I almost had to support myself on my hands. Sweat covered my face. I'd tied my jacket around my waist and rolled up my pant legs. The brook I'd been following for hours became shallower and narrower until it finally disappeared as a trickle inside the mountain. I decided to continue. Straight ahead, to the peak.

The forest was still unusually silent. By now, I was certain that I was being observed. My feelings about things like this had never let me down. I wasn't afraid. It didn't feel threatening, like I was being hunted. No. It felt like curious eyes were eagerly watching to see what I might do next.

Finally, I stopped and asked in a gentle, friendly voice, "Why are you hiding?"

Have I gone mad?

What if I'd been wrong and would be torn apart by wild beasts? But this flight of panic was only in my head. I felt in my heart—I don't know why, I just felt it—that no real danger loomed. The barghest could have easily killed me but had spared me and even helped me. Whatever creatures had been watching me for several hours probably were more scared of me than I was of them.

I dared again. "Show yourselves. I won't harm you."

I waited to see what would happen. Suddenly, I spotted some pointed ears peeping out from behind a nearby tree trunk. I swallowed, excited. A cheek followed the ears, then a nose, until finally I was looking at a gorgeous, alabaster elven face, attentively watching me with intelligent moss-green eyes.

"Who are you?" I asked, surprised by the assured, friendly tone of my voice.

Shouldn't I be running away screaming now?

The nymph just looked at me. She whispered something I couldn't understand, and then repeated it.

"Mistress," the creature whispered, barely audible.

Um, pardon? Did she just call me Mistress*?*

As if on command, numerous pointed ears and green eyes appeared from behind the trees. I gasped at the brilliance of these creatures. Had I ever seen anything more beautiful? They looked just like the drawings in the green book. So delicate and pure, so . . . innocent.

"Mistress," they whispered, one after another. *"Mistress."*

Silently, they circled around me, out of reach. Moving like spirits. Again and again, I glimpsed a bit of a dress or flowing white hair briefly disappearing behind a tree.

I took a step toward the nymph who had first shown herself to me, but she immediately shrank back and was gone in a flash.

"Don't be afraid. I won't hurt you," I implored her, and looked around for the others. But there was no trace of them, either. I stood still to see if they'd show themselves again. I waited and waited. When nothing happened, I went on. I couldn't waste time. I had to find Jared.

I wouldn't have thought it possible, but the route became steeper. To top it off, the sun beat down mercilessly. Sweat ran down my body and collected in my boots. I was terribly thirsty but knew I had to carefully ration the remaining water in my bottle. Why hadn't I filled it one last time? No water was in sight anywhere. I should have returned to the stream, which had disappeared several miles back. But I didn't turn around. An inner voice commanded me to carry on.

My mouth dried out more with each step forward under the full sun. I'd have a problem if I didn't find water soon. When my throat hurt from the dryness and my temples beat to the rhythm of my heart, I climbed up a tree with wobbly legs to get a better look around. No water. Only forest around me. Then I spied something else. The peak!

It wasn't far now. I was almost there. I hurried down and climbed the rest of the way with a final burst of strength. Completely exhausted, I retreated under the shade of a tree, pulled my boots off, and sipped the last drop of water from my bottle. I wiped the sweat from my forehead and looked around.

Strange. Although there was no water, the vegetation up here seemed more abundant than below in the valley.

"You wouldn't happen to know where I could find a few drops of water?" I asked the trees. Although I hadn't seen them for a while, I sensed the nymphs had followed me every step of the way.

I didn't expect an answer. I dropped down, exhausted, against the tree trunk—the afternoon heat was almost unbearable. To my surprise, I saw a set of pointed ears.

I almost forgot to breathe as I watched how the nymph—I wasn't sure if it was the same one who had first shown herself in the valley—stepped with slow dignity from her hiding place. She approached me, then stopped at a safe distance and nodded toward a huge tree, with extended branches, that seemed to be growing from a moss-covered cliff. Its mighty roots were wrapped like long, gnarled tentacles around the cliff, its lower half hidden by dense shrubbery.

"Is there water anywhere here?" I asked, and slowly raised myself—very slowly, to avoid scaring her off again.

She nodded her pretty pale head, sending a strand of her long, almost white hair forward over her shoulder. I took a few cautious steps toward her and was surprised that she didn't move. Then I walked a little faster, with resolute steps, until I stood directly in front of the moss-covered cliff to which the delicate creature had repeatedly pointed. I reached into the dense growth and pushed aside the small sharp branches. It took a while before I uncovered the spot and found myself at the entrance of a cave. A pleasant coolness flowed over my skin as I stepped inside. The cool cave air was a blessing for my burning, throbbing body. It felt moist—so there probably was water in here. Was this where the spring in my vision was?

I entered the darkness. I saw little before my eyes but was entranced by the inside of the cave. Then, as if from nowhere, something I thought was a firefly appeared before my nose. A tiny light speck danced up and down before me. Then a second, a third, a fourth . . . and suddenly I was surrounded by small light specks. They merrily bounced about, seeming to move purposefully in one direction, as if they wanted to show me the way. I instinctively followed them ever deeper into the cave as they guided me along dripping stone walls through a labyrinth of branching corridors. I had to suck in my tummy to squeeze through the narrowest passages. Then on to a dangerous-looking gap, which I leaped across after taking a run at it. I only slowly penetrated the mountain on this untrodden path. The whole time, I had to watch where I stepped. Along the way, I began to doubt that I would be able to find my way out on my own. Briefly, I considered marking my trail like Hansel and Gretel, but I had nothing I could easily leave behind. Besides, I felt an unfamiliar inner peace. A profound sensation of trust, as if only my mind was worried I would get lost in these dark corridors while my heart knew the way. As if I had been here before. Following my inner voice, I set one foot before the other.

Finally, my glowing companions stopped at a stone bridge. At the other end stood a marvelous stalagmite, as tall as a man, in the middle of a crossroads. The light specks guided me around it. I followed them without hesitating. This dark, damp cave and all that was hidden inside—visible or invisible—felt like my home in some marvelous way.

After I passed the statuesque stalagmite, my eyes took a second to adapt to new lighting, and then—my breath stopped—I was in an enormous underground cavern. The light specks spread out to illuminate the entire cave. Incredible. At the foot of a magnificent, flowering apple tree, with roots trailing across the bare rock, a subterranean lake spread out with the clearest deep-green water I'd ever seen. Sighing with relief, I stepped close and filled my water bottle, then cupped my hands to drink.

That's when it happened. *My God!* The second my skin touched the water, movement began under the surface. Something sparkling pushed upward from the depths. I bent forward.

Tiny light specks floated gently, like snowflakes, to the surface, filling the grotto with a wonderful bright golden light. I watched my little guides join the others, weightless and wonderful. More and more continued to rise, surfacing like a thousand sparkling diamonds, their light reflecting off the cave walls. I watched the spectacle wide-eyed, as if a spell had been cast on me. I moved closer, attracted as if by magic. The closer I looked, the more little diamonds of light rose from the green depths—until the entire water surface shone and glittered like a million stars in the firmament.

By then I was standing knee-deep in the water and wading in deeper, watching the gentle waves with fascination, enraptured by the sight. Suddenly I heard something. I spread my arms, as if in a trance, and an all-penetrating woman's voice struck me to the core. No one but me was here, and yet I heard the voice clearly and unmistakably in my mind. I'd never heard it before, yet I knew it was *her* voice.

Nimue.

She only said one word. *"Welcome."*

I closed my eyes, submerging myself.

Ready to give myself.

With all that I was.

Everything became bright, and brightness flowed through every fiber of my body.

My soul.

My spirit.

My being.

CHAPTER 8

Everything was so clear.

So light and fluid.

As if everything were happening by itself.

I almost laughed out loud. It had been ridiculous to believe I needed Colin by my side to protect me. Power flooded every cell in my body with pure, unadulterated magic. How had I existed before? Even now, the memory felt strangely murky—as if I were looking through opaque glass. Only my head was completely clear, my thoughts ordered. Structured. Entirely together. My body also felt different. My muscles were strong, my skin sensitive, my senses sharp. I heard, smelled, tasted, saw, and felt everything. I missed nothing of what was happening around me. Only now, when I felt Nimue's magic, *my* magic, in every fiber of my being, did I feel whole. As if I had formerly walked through this world as an empty shell. As if an essential part had been missing. I was only complete now that I had absorbed what was mine by birthright. It was next to impossible to find the right words for what I felt. No fear, doubt, or weakness, only . . . power. I was mighty and strong—freed of the weaknesses limiting me as a human. And I would stop anyone who dared to come between me and Jared.

I couldn't remember how I wound up outside again. Had I walked? Floated on air? Been carried?

The first thing I remembered was the nymphs, *my* nymphs, waiting outside the cave for me. Twenty-two of them.

At first nothing happened. They watched me attentively. Then one stepped out, lifted her arms, faced the sky, and raised her melodic voice. She pierced the silence the way a beam of light pierces darkness. It started as a hum; then I recognized a word in the angelic sound.

"Mistress," sang the nymph.

"Mistress," the others joined in and began to move. Without touching, they circled each other with extended arms. Then they took me into the middle of their dance.

"Mistress," they sang, one after the other, with magical voices. *"Mistress, Mistress."* First quietly, then louder, clearer.

"Mistress," they repeated, again and again. Their song sent goose bumps over my entire body.

"Our Mistress has returned."

They surrounded me, fleet-footed, touching my hands, arms, and face.

A welcome ritual.

All my senses aroused, I gave myself to the nymphs' ecstatic dance. I closed my eyes, spread my arms, let them lead me, and moved to the sound of their song. Filled with the power, filled with the . . . *magic*.

***

When I awoke, I was alone, gazing at the starry night sky. I carefully propped myself up on my elbows and looked around, then shut my eyes and rubbed my temples. It was almost like I had a hangover after a wild night of partying. But my vision and head cleared after a few seconds.

I felt my body needed a little more time to adjust to the power. That's probably why I'd fallen asleep. It had overcome me. This feeling of unanticipated strength, the living, pulsing magic in my arteries. Pure, unspoiled power.

Power . . . a word that didn't normally fit me. But there wasn't a better word to describe what had happened to me inside the cave. I was powerful. I was magical.

I slowly sat up and closed my eyes to explore the sensations inside me. I felt myself more clearly and more consciously than ever before. But it was not only that. First I thought I was imagining it and once more went inside myself to check my sensory experience. I was not mistaken. Indeed, I was able to sense every nymph around me, even if I could not see them. It was like they were part of me. I reached deeper inside. There was more—*my God*, there was so *much* more. Trees, grass, birds, butterflies, even stones . . . the impressions threatened to overwhelm me. I felt the *whole* island. Every creature, tree, drop of water, blade of grass—I felt it all. Avalon was firmly bound to me. And I to it.

Then I froze. There was something else. Something dark. Something evil. Something that did not belong here.

And then I felt *him*.

He was alive! Jared lived!

He *still* lived.

I quickly packed my refilled water reserves and other belongings into the backpack and started my descent. It was true child's play. Unbelievable, how much I had exerted myself a few hours ago. I felt every stone under my feet long before I touched it. I pressed toward my goal.

A few moments later, I reached the stream I'd followed toward the peak. It would lead me straight to Morgana—of that I was sure.

The day gradually dawned to cover the forest with its intoxicating green light. Life had returned with twittering, chirping, rustling, and giggling from all directions. Occasionally, I saw a small, furry forest dweller scurrying through the underbrush. Once I even spied a grim-faced goblin. He poked his green head out of an earth mound like a mole. A swarm of four pixies flapped excitedly about me before pouncing with squeals on a rabbit-cat, pulling it by the tail and ears, then rushing off, chortling as it snapped at them and hissed.

I didn't feel the slightest touch of exhaustion, even though I had been wandering for hours. It appeared as if the laws of physiology had been abolished, so I could walk forever. Since I did not have to focus on movement as such, I had time to think of other things.

How does my magic work?

I knew it had to do with water. Nimue as the Lady of the Lake, my innate ability to heal my body with the help of water, Irvin's explanation of the energy of the elements—those were clear signs. I happened to be walking along a stream ten feet wide. I closed my eyes. I could really feel the flowing water next to me. I plugged my ears to be sure. Yes. It wasn't my vision or hearing. I knew the consistency, direction, strength of flow, and even the presence of water simply by *feeling* it.

I stopped walking and looked into the stream. I reflected. If I could feel every drop of water so clearly . . . would I also be—it was slowly dawning on me—would I be able to *influence* it? Did Nimue's magic—*my* magic—work the same way as Jared's? Was I able to affect the natural course of water, even control it?

It was worth a try. I just wasn't sure how to go about it. I strained to remember how Jared had made the glade of crocuses bloom. Back in the clearing, when he revealed to me who he was. And who *I* was.

I could almost see him before me with that focused yet relaxed expression on his face. He had kept his eyes closed while spreading his arms and turning the palms of his hands upward and . . . that was it! There had been a sudden glow around his hands.

Okay, let's do it. I excitedly stepped from one foot to the other, rubbing my hands together. I considered rolling up my sleeves, but decided that might be overdoing it. I had resolved to tackle this issue and was incredibly eager to see if it would work. I stood up straight, spread my hands, and tried to stem the water upstream against its natural flow. I held my breath and looked with strained eyes. And saw . . . nothing. I dropped my arms, disappointed. Except for a few bubbles on the surface, the water seemed completely unimpressed by my wizardry.

One more time! I probably hadn't waited long enough.

Legs shoulder-width apart, back straight, arms spread.

I closed my eyes and concentrated on forcing the water in the opposite direction. I held this stance for a while, then quickly opened my eyes, as if to surprise the water. A few more bubbles had appeared on the surface. That was all. Maybe I had done something wrong with my hands? Or did I have to shut my eyes first and then spread my hands? Suddenly I heard a voice in my head.

Relax, it said in a stoic, almost hypnotic tone. It was the same voice that had guided me through the fog. *My* voice, coming from deep inside. I calmed down instantly. My arms and legs were at ease, and I closed my eyes.

Reach inside yourself, my inner voice said, and my arms spread out. And then I understood the obvious. These gestures were not the essence of the matter but merely expressions of my inner state. Only when I became one with myself and let the magic flow from inside could I also feel the water. Its coolness, wetness, motion . . . I felt all aspects of the water. As if it were part of me. I held gently against the current, without force or violence. And if I were to move one of my body parts in a particular direction, the water would obey. I knew it without opening my eyes.

Excellent, my inner voice praised me. *Now let the magic flow.*

I slowly opened my eyes, with my chest arced forward. I had spread my arms outward with an inviting gesture, and a golden-green light shone around my hands, very delicately. My glance shifted from myself to the stream. Indeed, the water flowed smoothly uphill.

What a sight! I closed my eyes in a trance-like state. I felt the water again as if I were touching it. Could I make it flow faster? I could. The water flowed wildly and irresistibly against its proper direction. Fast. Even faster. The magic pulsed within my cells, and I directed it at the water and . . . *splash!*

A six-foot tower of ice-cold spring water poured over me in one grand wave. I forgot to breathe for a moment, then gasped for air, exclaiming, "What the . . . ?"

Was that giggling behind the trees?

Okay, so I could affect water by steering it in another direction. What else could I do with my newfound abilities?

I tried to remember what I had felt when I gave my magic free course. I had felt the water's direction, that much was certain. Feeling the direction of the flow was necessary to change its movement. What else had I felt? Its wetness. But was that good for anything? Water happens to be wet. So?

I thought for a moment. Then I had an idea, remembering my physics lessons from grade six. I'd never been close with Mr. Spennen, my teacher in those days. Physics had been an annoyance—too many numbers for my taste—but the topic of water had fascinated me for reasons I only now understood. On that test I got my one and only perfect mark in physics, which I proudly presented to Zara at home. As far as I could remember, water existed in the world in three material states: solid, liquid, and gaseous. Wet, liquid water could be transformed from its original state into other states by changing its temperature. Didn't I also feel the water's temperature? Water freezes at temperatures below 32 degrees and becomes ice. When raised above 212 degrees, it evaporates. I closed my eyes to focus. Oh yes! Then there also was sublimation, when ice turns straight into steam, and resublimation, when steam freezes into ice without becoming a liquid in between. That's how hoarfrost forms.

Okay, let's do it.

I closed my eyes again and let the magic flow through me. I felt the water, flowing, wet, cool. Cool—that's what I had to focus on.

Cool . . . cooler . . . cold.

I breathed in deeply and concentrated my magic on the water's coldness.

Cold . . . icy . . .

The splashing became quieter and finally fell silent.

Ice . . .

When I opened my eyes again, I was looking at a frozen stream. The water had turned to ice in the middle of its flow.

CHAPTER 9

Ice, steam, water, steam, boiling water, steam, ice, cold water—I couldn't get enough of it. I practiced tirelessly as I walked along the stream. *Practicing* doesn't quite hit the mark—it was a riot testing my new skills, and even in this short time I had found a few ways to maximize my magic. For example, the angle of my palms really did make a difference. They gave direction to the magic's action. The more precisely I aimed my fingertips at the object I wished to affect, the more accurately the effect found its mark. I discovered that closing my eyes was unnecessary. Watching how I could make an entire stream freeze was the icing on the cake. However, I didn't want to just affect a small area with my magic; I wanted to hit large areas as well, and closing my eyes helped me feel a larger area as a whole because otherwise I'd rely too much on my vision. In short, it was much easier to rely on feeling if one could not see. Antoine de Saint-Exupéry already knew that.

After a while, I decided to broaden my experiments, so I turned my attention to a green blade of grass. I made it freeze without much effort, but the hidden nymphs, who had accompanied me behind the trees, were horrified.

"Now, now," I calmed down the peaceful creatures when they reacted with an outraged cry to my experiment with the blade of grass. I understood them well because I had sensed their sacred relationship with nature from the time I'd left the cave.

I immediately awoke the blade of grass back to life by liquefying its frozen moisture.

***

With every step I took—down into the valley, up a gentle slope, and then across the island—I came closer to Jared. I would reach him soon. I'd be with him and would . . . well, would what? I suddenly realized I still had no plan for freeing Jared from Morgana's clutches. Sure, I had more abilities than I'd have ever dreamed of before, but I was still not certain I could take on Morgana. At least not alone. I'd experienced what that witch was capable of, what she was *willing* to do. Not to mention her army of damnati, who'd love to see me bleed and beg. The thought brought a defiant smile to my face. I may not be equal to Morgana, but her rabble of stinking, scarfaced monsters . . . I couldn't wait to deal with them. I just couldn't wait.

***

At some point, I realized the island was changing with every step I came closer to Morgana. The sky alerted me first. A moment before, the sun had shone from a clear blue sky, but now dark clouds drew up, covering the forest in a strange murky veil. I continued and noticed that the trees, bushes, and plants looked increasingly stressed. The grass shriveled, the leaves wilted, and the umbrella-sized flowers and mushrooms spread a rotten, syrupy odor. Soon I was surrounded by bare branches and gnarled tree stumps. The nymphs no longer followed me. Pointed, thorny branches lent Avalon, only a moment ago full of life and color, an atmosphere of dreary doom. All life had escaped. The colors had faded. A fog drew up. It was like walking through a nocturnal cemetery. Blue smoke surrounded me. The forest was dead. Nature was decaying.

The animals and small magical creatures also acted in stranger and stranger ways. I watched two of the usually so-cute hedgehog-squirrels. They seemed sick and had bloodshot eyes and straggly, scruffy fur. They quarreled over an acorn. First, there was a malicious screaming match, and then they began fighting, trying to scratch each other's eyes out in a blind fury, constantly snapping straight at their opponents' throats.

"Hey!" I angrily shouted and extended my hand at the little animals to end the fight. One of them turned, hissed at me, and bit my finger.

"Ow!"

I pulled back my hand. The creature pounced upon the other and slit open its belly. Entrails burst out of the wound, thick and red. I gagged.

Then two birds clashed midflight and plunged their talons into each other's dull feathers. Their eyes narrowed as they pecked at each other with their sharp beaks.

What was happening? These peaceful animals had turned into greedy, deadly monsters, attempting to kill each other in the most gruesome ways.

She brings death to all living beings. Where love reigns, she fans hatred. She lays waste everything pure, and everything beautiful she turns ugly. Irvin's words rang in my head. I angrily scrunched my eyes. Morgana was poisoning the entire island with her presence.

Suddenly, I heard cruel, rasping laughter from behind a mighty, black, knotted oak tree. I whirled around. This could only mean one thing: damnati. Hatred welled up inside me—it was time to put my abilities to the test. I snuck closer. What I saw made me freeze.

There were three of them. Two had grabbed a nymph by the arms, while the third tore her dress from her body. She was trembling with fear. One of them licked her cheek. Panic and disgust were written into the poor creature's face. She stared at me with pleading eyes while I watched one of the three scarfaces try to press between her legs. He laughed and licked his sore-covered lips. The nymph struggled with all her strength, but the delicate creature was powerless against the three monsters. I had to step in. Now! I walked up to them without saying a word, causing them to whirl about, momentarily startled. But once they saw me, they broke out laughing, as if I couldn't do a thing to stop them.

I said nothing and just stared at the hideous creatures. Didn't these three boneheads wonder what I—in their eyes an ordinary human—was doing in Avalon? Did they know who I was?

"Just wait your turn, slut," the smallest said and pulled on the nymph's arm. "You'll get your fun, too, as soon as we're done with her."

I remained where I was and said nothing.

Again, rasping laughter.

Then another said, "You really want it bad, huh? Well, maybe we can take care of you right away."

Two of the three scarfaces approached while the third held the nymph by her hair. I looked at my fingernails and tried to appear as bored as possible—even though I was boiling inside with rage and hatred at the sight of the nymph in her tattered dress.

"You're already dead, bitch. You're just too stupid to get that," the first one said in a smug tone.

I'd soon wipe that dumb grin off his face.

I breathed in heavily.

"Water makes up sixty percent of the human body," I finally said, feeling very satisfied with the relaxed, scholarly tone of my voice. Then I looked straight at the damnati. They seemed surprised.

"Let's see what it's like with your rotting bodies." I raised my hands, sensed the stinking, wobbly stew pervading these creatures, let my magic flow, and brought them to a boil with a single wink. The largest of them managed a short scream, but the other two burst immediately, covering the ground in their stinking, rotting entrails. Except for a beastly smelling mash, nothing remained. I took a moment to enjoy the view and, especially, the sensation of power and magic.

Then I blinked, straightened my shoulders, and went to the nymph lying on the ground, who looked at me with shy awe. I extended my hand and helped her up.

"Don't be afraid," I said, while gently brushing over her white hair.

"Mistress," was all she uttered before a tear ran down her cheek.

"Go to your sisters," I said.

I continued on my way without resting. I was in top physical shape and only felt mentally drained after I exerted myself experimenting with my new powers. I needed time to get used to them. Still, I grew confident after my encounter with the damnati. It had been child's play. How many would I be able to kill in one go? How many were there? Had Morgana brought them all to Avalon? Was I strong enough to take on Morgana and the damnati by myself? Jared was still alive; I clearly felt it. But . . . how long would he be able to last?

The forest turned gloomier. It couldn't be far now.

CHAPTER 10

A cry of pain and helplessness pierced the silence. I knew that voice; it was the man I loved. Sick with horror, I crawled silently on my belly through mud and shrubs to a clearing—toward Jared's piercing shriek.

It was already dusk, the sky darkened by blue-gray smoke, and turning into night when I sought cover in a thorny thicket, a good hiding spot. The thicket was at the edge of the clearing, and the densely ingrown sharp twigs allowed me to effortlessly spy on the damnatus camp.

I carefully peered through the decaying foliage and immediately froze. This wasn't a simple clearing, as I had first thought. No, I was at the edge of a giant slashed and burned area. A lump formed in my throat. They'd burned everything down, trees, shrubs, grasses, flowers—leveled them entirely. Not satisfied with everything near Morgana rotting, no, they had to annihilate what had remained. The sight scorched my soul and was heavy to bear. Nothing but black, charred earth as far as the eye could see. Avalon was such a wonderful place—it was a crime to destroy it.

They had set up a tent city, similar to one in a Roman siege. I tried to count the tents, but there were too many. How many damnati? Hundreds? Thousands, even?

I leaned farther forward. Black clouds rose over the clearing, blocking my sight. I clasped my hand over my mouth. I knew I couldn't deeply inhale this smoke—a cough would betray my presence. The area stank of charred wood, singed fur, and carbonized fat. I held my breath while I crawled closer. I made out coarse, raspy shouts through the dense smoke. I dared inch slightly farther. Four damnati sat drinking and swearing around a fire. They were roasting a skewered animal. Judging from its size, it was probably one of the fluffy rabbit-cats. They pulled the charred animal from the fire to quarrel over the best parts. *Revolting.*

I looked around and discovered three more fires near the edge of the clearing, with four damnati sitting around each—one for every direction of the compass. They must have been the camp guards, as they were heavily armed with knives and spears, though they were inattentive and totally drunk. It wouldn't be a problem to wipe them out. I just had to be fast enough for the other guards not to sound the alarm.

Somewhat farther back I saw something like a birdcage suspended in the air. It had been fastened to a low-hanging branch of a half-charred tree. Three pixies cowered inside, pressed closely together, their faces distorted with mortal fear. A damnatus standing below the cage amused himself, tormenting the little creatures by poking a pointed stick, which he occasionally heated in the fire, through the bars. He screeched with joy over the pixies' panicked escape attempts, which attracted another damnatus who didn't want to miss out on the fun. This one had the glorious idea of lowering the metal cage to hold it directly over the fire.

"Look at 'em hop," he croaked excitedly, as he watched the hapless attempts the pixies made to stay off the metal floor as it became hotter, while the other damnatus poked at them with the sharp stick he jammed between the metal rods.

"Got 'im!" the scarface finally called, pointing to the end of the stick from which a limp pixie dangled.

Further into the tent city, a shouting mass gathered around two scarfaces trying to beat each other's skulls in. Their sore- and puss-covered naked torsos were smeared with blood. One went down after a kick but tossed a handful of dirt into the other's face. Blinded for a moment, the second one stumbled into the crowd of onlookers but was thrust back into the ring, where his opponent waited with a club. The cheering and shouting bystanders egged them on. Such disgusting, shifty, and cruel creatures. When they couldn't find anyone else to torment, they turned on each other. This same scene was playing out in several places throughout the camp. Their ordinary pastime. *All the better,* I thought. *Less work for me if they do each other in.*

As I edged forward a little more, I heard a roar. I looked around and caught sight of the massive body of a behemoth captured under a coarse net of thick rope. Three spears were jammed into its armored body. Again, the hippopotamus-like creature roared when a fourth spear hit its mark and remained stuck in the animal's neck.

"Bull's-eye," a cloaked figure congratulated himself after inflicting the fatal wound. The massive creature collapsed, panting. A fountain of blood shot from its neck and spilled onto the ground. After a final deep breath, it closed its eyes. The damnati removed the net and went to work with curved butcher's knives. I couldn't bear the sight and turned away.

Focus, I admonished myself. It made no sense to charge ahead now and kill the damnati. The longer I stayed unnoticed, the better. If you want to kill a snake, chop its head off. Morgana was my target—she was the source of all this evil. But I had to get deeper inside the camp.

It was difficult to estimate how many damnati there were. Probably at least a thousand. Morgana had gathered an army around her.

I gave up my cover and silently crept by the guards. The four drunks were so busy brawling over their supper that they probably wouldn't have noticed if I'd passed them with a marching band. Still, I tried to be as silent as possible, slipping from shadow to shadow.

I hopped over a puddle and pressed against the nearest tent when two damnati came toward me. They'd have discovered me if they'd been a little more attentive, but these two hideous monsters felt so safe and untouchable they didn't look left or right while walking. They passed so close that their stench nearly seared my nostrils. Their skin was gray and shriveled, almost like leather; their lips were practically nonexistent; and their noses were snake-like slots in their faces. Their pitch-black eyes were sunk deep into their skulls. There was nothing human about them. These two must have been part of Morgana's following for some time. I held my breath, afraid of throwing up. Damnati stench pervaded the entire camp—sometimes more, sometimes less, but always present. Having nothing else, I pulled my shirt over my nose and snuck on.

The scene was pretty much the same throughout the tent city. Here, a few completely wasted damnati were lying about, there, a few others. They were often trying to slit each other's throats in front of a howling crowd. Spread all through the camp were nets and cages where the magical inhabitants of Avalon wasted away, serving only as food or amusement for these sore-covered miscreants. In this, the damnati's inventiveness knew no bounds. Snares, sticks, knives, spears, or fire—anything these monsters got into their hands suited them to torture and torment these poor creatures.

Pixies, goblins, behemoths, and nymphs were victimized. I spotted a kelpie in a basin filled with murky water. A dozen arrows were stuck in its massive horse head. To perfect the humiliation of this imposing creature, three damnati stood at the edge of the basin and urinated on its face.

A few feet away, another cloaked figure dumped four rat-sized, green-skinned goblins out of a cage into a bulging cauldron. Thick clouds of white steam rose from it. The impish creatures' screams died in a gurgle.

I crept on until I heard whimpering. I turned. Golden eyes flashed behind cage bars. I quietly tiptoed over to the unguarded cage. A barghest was lying, mewing, in a huge puddle of blood. He was only half the size of the one who had saved me—almost a cub. I felt intense pain at the sight. When I reached through the bars and stroked his soft fur, I felt something wet and warm. My hand was covered in blood.

"What have they done to you?" I quietly asked.

The little barghest pressed his muzzle against my palm and exhaled with a rattle. Then he closed his eyes—dead. My eyes overflowed with tears. I continued to stroke the lifeless head and was hardly able to walk away. I became enraged. I clenched my teeth and squeezed my fists.

This cruelty would end once I'd saved Jared. I swore on my life!

I'd already penetrated several hundred yards into the tent city when I had to evade another group of damnati. I was pressing myself against a linen tent when a sudden, intense tumult erupted inside.

"I'll stab you," a raspy voice said. Then a lean damnatus tumbled out of the tent.

Another followed with a raised knife. "You pig! You stole from me!" he roared.

The first one scrambled back, became entangled in his cloak, and went down. The hood slipped from his head. I was shocked that he had most of his hair left. His face still appeared human, the color of his cheeks almost rosy. Merely a blistering, boil-like wound from his left ear to the corner of his mouth betrayed his fate. As with Felix, the transformation had not progressed far. Looking for help, he turned around while his knife-wielding adversary calmly approached. At that moment, he saw me in the shadows of the tent. He stopped, astonished to find me there, raised his arm, and pointed silently with his finger.

Fuck! Couldn't the other have just stuck him?

"Well, well, what do we have here?" said the knife-wielder, happily excited while scanning me from tip to toe. The one lying on the ground scrambled to his feet and fled, tripping over his cloak again.

"What hole did you crawl out from, my beauty?" the pursuer asked, slowly coming toward me. "Hey, guys! Look what I found!" he yelled, and a moment later, I was surrounded by damnati. Splendid—so much for staying unnoticed. But here I was.

"Take me to Morgana," I demanded.

The knife-wielder burst out laughing, baring a row of rotten tooth stumps. "Who do you think you are, to make demands?" he taunted.

Well, I thought, *a little demonstration couldn't hurt.* I felt the stinking broth of this scarface's body but only focused on his skull. Within fractions of a second, his head boiled and burst into a mess, like a melon hitting the pavement. Then his headless body sank to its knees before tipping over. A nervous murmur went through the crowd. They weren't laughing now.

"Take me to Morgana," I ordered more forcefully.

Keeping a safe distance, several damnati eventually complied. A small crowd led me through the torch- and fire-lit tent city. Hundreds stared at me. After a while, they stopped and opened a narrow passage leading to the entrance of the largest tent in the camp. A cloaked figure tried to raise the flap to announce my arrival, but I pushed him aside and entered unbidden.

***

There she was. Morgana stood in the middle of the tent, before a wooden cross about ten feet high to which the body of a young man was lashed. It took my brain a moment to absorb this horrific sight.

I had heard him scream. I had imagined what she would do to him—dozens of times and in a hundred different ways. I was braced for her hurting him. But . . . what was happening in reality made me falter.

Jared's hands and feet were bound, Christ-like, with leather straps to the cross. His torso was naked. His head lay limp on his chest. His disheveled hair was sweaty. Stubble covered his jaw. Sweat ran down his body. He groaned with unimaginable pain while Morgana, hands spread as if in meditation, absorbed a white-shining light ray—delicate as a freshly spun thread of molten silver—through her fingertips. The shimmering white thread came directly from the highest point between the rib arcs in Jared's chest. Morgana was gradually taking it in. Her face showed how much pleasure and satisfaction it gave her.

Jared cried out again. But it was more than a scream; it penetrated to the bone and ended with a drained breath as his eyes rolled back.

I choked back a cry of horror. *Jared!*

I took this in so fast that neither he nor Morgana had time to become aware of my presence.

I acted reflexively. Instinctively. I charged Morgana, let my magic flow, and thrust my hands forward as if I wished to drive her away. A bright green energy field burst, shield-like, as fast as sound from my palms—*oh, that one's new*—pulled the black witch off her feet, and hurled her into the farthest corner of the huge tent.

Now everybody was aware of me, and I had their attention. I ran toward Jared. He barely raised his head to look at me, but his eyes widened when he recognized me. Thousands of emotions were written on his face. Surprise, joy, love, worry, despair . . . hatred. I looked into his eyes. "Jared!" My voice sounded desperate. I wanted to tell him it would be all right, that I was here to save him, that I loved him above all else.

"Evelyn," Jared faintly whispered, surprised and anguished.

Then he closed his eyes. "You shouldn't have come." His voice was distorted by the pain.

Morgana, still lying in the corner, looked around, stunned. Seeing me, the expression on her face suddenly changed. Her enraged cry almost burst my eardrums. She stood at once and swept away the tent with a single motion of her hand so that we stood under the open sky. It wasn't for a better view, but for the damnati, who by now were surrounding us by the hundreds. Her army stood ready. She nodded to them, and they rushed me. At least, they tried to. I killed any who attempted to come near me or Jared. I raged like a fury, evaporating some damnati and leaving others in piles of burst, frozen, and shriveled corpses. Jared watched in amazement.

Morgana, too, seemed to find my abilities difficult to believe. Angry and aghast, she pressed her lips together. But then she composed herself. A mist crept over the ground and curled around my legs.

"Well, whom do we have here?" Morgana said exuberantly, as if she were greeting a long overdue guest. She put a lot of effort into coming across as superior, even though I had just forced her into a corner and paved a hundred-foot radius with damnatus corpses.

For a moment, it looked as if she were going to say something. Then she nodded to her remaining subjects. A murmur of discomfort went through the crowd as they looked at their fallen comrades. They seemed less aggressive at the sight of their burst, frozen, and shriveled fellows. Even though they had a thousand-to-one advantage.

I looked around with raised eyebrows, spoiling for a fight. None dared oppose me.

Morgana was infuriated. "So, you made it through the fog," she began, clapping her hands as if congratulating me. She chose not to comment on her subjects' disobedience for the time being.

"And I see you've found . . . Nimue's magic."

Now it was my turn to grin mockingly. Apparently, *I* made Morgana feel insecure, no matter how much she tried to sound superior and unaffected. My magic stirred inside me, as if it were yearning for a duel with Morgana.

"Found?" I repeated. That sounded as if I had accidently tripped over it by dumb luck. Really? *Oops, what's that? Nimue's magic? Shoot, I might as well take it with me.*

A hint of a smile crossed Jared's tense face. My new abilities seemed to have flabbergasted him. Perhaps he, too, was burning to know how I'd done it. Morgana pressed her lips together for a fraction of a second, and then she put on her haughty smile again.

"Now, show us what you can do," she challenged me and puffed her chest. As she had during our last encounter, she raised her right arm and slowly formed a fist. Her gaze was highly focused. I felt her fingers around my throat as if she stood right in front of me and not a dozen yards away. She squeezed. Like a natural reflex, my magic stemmed hers. The pressure on my throat gradually lessened and eventually disappeared. It was as if a mechanism had been set in motion. I barely needed to make an effort.

Morgana opened her eyes in surprise and let her arm sink. She could be forgiven for being a bit rusty. For centuries she had only used her magic on ordinary people and mostly harmless magical beings. Opposing the new Lady of the Lake required more effort than she had just mustered. Jared attentively watched what was happening. He seemed impressed and worried at the same time.

Morgana needed a moment to control herself, but then she put on her artificial smile and turned to Jared. I knew immediately what she intended. She was going to make *him* pay. A silver thread broke through his chest and found its way to Morgana. He was immediately overcome by another wave of pain. Tormented, he threw his head back, closed his eyes, and clenched his teeth until his jaw muscles stood out. He was making every effort not to scream. It was unbearable to watch.

I raised my hands without hesitation and released energy in such a burst that I cried out when the powerful force field left my body. Morgana had anticipated this reaction and raised her hand in a defensive gesture. But she had seriously underestimated me. My power was somewhat broken by her protective shield, but the force of the impact was strong enough to make her fly through the air like a rag doll until she landed on the muddy ground. Dirt splattered in all directions. Two damnati rushed to help her up.

"Let go of me, you cretins!" she barked, shaking off their scar-covered hands.

As if pulled by invisible strings, she righted herself without placing her hands against the ground. Burning rage showed in her flawless face. The damnati looked, discomfited, back and forth between Morgana and me. She quickly came at me, paying no attention to her disheveled hair and muddy gown.

"How dare you!" she screamed, exasperated. Her sharp teeth clenched, she raised a hand against me as if to simply sweep me away. I had no time to react. Before I knew it, her mighty dark energy had seized me and hurled me against a tree. The impact knocked the wind out of me. Morgana smiled and brushed her tangled black hair back. Then she went toward Jared and raised her hand, and another wave of pain overcame him. This time the silver thread was more like a rope—she seemed to be in a hurry. A moment later I was on my feet again and hurled my magic at her with all the force I could muster.

Morgana looked up. Suddenly, she was gone. Where she had stood, only a thin black fog remained. I hastily looked around. There she was! She had materialized again only a few yards from where she had disappeared. How the devil did she do that? She quickly went to work on Jared again, and I focused my magic and hurled it at her as fast and hard as I could. The hatred I felt at seeing Jared in pain multiplied the effect, and it hit her with full force. Pivoting on the spot, Morgana was again hurled into the air and came crashing down. A few damnati fled into the forest.

"Come back!" Morgana commanded, gasping. Two damnati stopped, then rejoined the others. Three of them were determined to desert. Morgana sat up and made a sweeping motion with her hand toward the escapees. I heard a short croaking before the three scarfaces went down in unnatural contortions and lay motionless on the ground.

I used the commotion to rush unnoticed across the space, quickly undid the ropes from Jared's wrists, and gently lowered him from the cross. I almost collapsed under his weight. Then I laid his limp body on the ground and unbound his feet.

"Water," he moaned but failed to keep his eyes open. Only now did I notice his cracked lips. His skin felt like brittle paper. He was completely dehydrated. He must not have had anything to drink for days. I quickly pulled out my bottle, put it to his lips, and gave him a big gulp to drink. His mouth was so dry that half of it spilled. He got some down his throat on the second try and coughed. On the third try Jared swallowed a small amount, then more, and finally emptied half the bottle.

"Evelyn," he said with a faint voice, then blinked strenuously. "How did you . . . you can't . . . the pact. You shouldn't have come." A tear ran over his cheek.

"Don't say that." I made an effort to sound confident. "We'll make it."

But . . . would we?

Jared opened his mouth a little to contradict me, then closed it again. "I love you," he said. "More than I would have thought possible." Then he closed his eyes.

Morgana rallied her troops and brushed herself off before coming after me again.

"How dare you, you bitch!" she yelled. She squinted maliciously, then hurled a powerful curse at me. Then, as before, she disappeared into a black mist, only to reemerge in front of me in the blink of an eye. With lightning speed, I took a defensive posture against the powerful curse she immediately hurled.

The thought of Jared lying helplessly on the ground triggered a primal instinct inside me. I raised my hands. There was a deafening bang when Morgana's dark magic hit mine. I managed to deflect most of the curse, but the force I had to apply knocked me off my feet. Exhausted, I fell on my hands and knees, desperately trying to breathe and ignore the aftereffects of the pain. Jared moved beside me protectively but was so weak he could barely sit up. Encouraged by my clearly weakened state, Morgana seemed wildly determined to finish this. Again she sent a powerful wave of dark magic in our direction. Again I defensively lifted my hands. Morgana's curse hit me with maybe a tenth of its original force. It was enough to numb me. Then, unbearable pain exploded in every fiber of my body, as if poison was corroding my cells.

The dark witch raised her chin in triumph. A satisfied, smug expression spread across her face. The surrounding cloak-wearers burst out in ringing laughter. She pointed her finger at Jared and me. "That's what you get, slut!"

Morgana extended her hand at Jared. She lifted the other defensively at me.

Determined to give it my all, I bundled my magic, focused, and hurled it toward her. A golden-green light flashed from my fingertips at the very same moment a dark fog, black as ink, emerged from Morgana's hands. They met in midair. Suddenly my hands began to vibrate as if electrified. How long could I hold firm?

I felt my feet leave the ground. Something was lifting me. An invisible force. I was floating in the air—as was Morgana.

The vibration crept across my hands into my arms.

"No matter what you do," Morgana said firmly across the energy beams buzzing in the air, "the boy and I have a pact. He consented to leave me his magic in exchange for your soul. You cannot save him. Whoever breaks a magic oath dies."

Her words struck my heart. She was right. I was powerless against the magic pact. My arms trembled. We stared at each other for what felt like an eternity.

What was I to do?

What could I do?

I knew I would not be able to resist for long. Morgana shot a second, at least equally strong, fog beam in my direction, and I was swept away. I didn't stand a chance. Her own magic and that part of Jared's she'd already made her own were just too much. She was too powerful. Morgana's poison ran in my arteries and spread through my body, unstoppable.

Roaring, malicious laughter sounded from the crowd of scarfaced onlookers.

I panted with exhaustion.

"Let's bring this to an end, my boy," Morgana said, as if she were about to do Jared a favor. Her black eyes were empty and pitiless. Numbness and the feeling that it was just a bad dream took hold of me. Morgana extended an open hand to Jared as if she were asking him for a dance. Although she did not touch him, Jared's face immediately distorted into a grimace of pain. A white light beam, thick and firm, burst out from his naked chest and shot directly into the fingertips of Morgana's extended hand. She passionately moaned while Jared twisted with pain. I was still lying completely exhausted on the ground while Morgana's dark magic continued to corrode my veins like an insatiable cancer.

Was this it? Would we die now? Had it all been for nothing?

No! I wouldn't allow it! Not as long as there was the tiniest spark of life in me.

I breathed in as if having a seizure, breathed against the pain, and raised myself. Morgana looked at me, astounded.

"Leave. Him. Alone!" I screamed. Then I bundled the magic inside me into a pulsing sphere, pushed it at her with all my might, and . . . forced the witch to her knees. The link broke, and I immediately felt relief. My magic reclaimed my body and pushed Morgana's poison from my cells. I rushed over to Jared. He was lying on the ground with his eyes almost closed.

"Jared." My voice sounded remote. I took his face into my hands. "Jared."

I cast a quick glance at Morgana and saw that she was losing control. She charged at me, floating in the air, her black eyes narrowed. I immediately got up. Determined, I stepped into the dark witch's path, unyielding. I would never again allow a loved one to be taken from me. Never again! Let her come. I was ready.

The energy fields collided in a gigantic explosion. First there was a deafening burst. Then there was a penetrating rumbling, like metal bending underwater. The pressure wave pushed me off my feet, boomed across the clearing, blew tents away, swept damnati across the ground, and snapped trees. The impact's intensity hurled Morgana into the air. She was flung several yards over the camp and crashed into a tent. The colors dispersed in a mighty aftershock, like pulsing shields.

Black, green-blue, and . . . white.

White?

There weren't just two fields of energy—there were three!

I turned around.

"Jared! What have you done?" I shouted, horrified.

Half lying, half kneeling, both palms held up toward Morgana, his face distorted by the exertion . . .

I froze when I understood. He had hurled the last remainder of his magic at Morgana.

Then he collapsed.

CHAPTER 11

Jared didn't move.

I hunched over him, shook his shoulders. Panicking. Helpless. I lifted his head into my lap. I was trembling with fear and desperation as I felt his neck for a pulse.

Come on! Come on!

Nothing.

The damnati were approaching. I threw myself over Jared's body and snarled. Whoever wanted to harm him had to get past me first. I was wildly determined to let none of them live.

My fingers tirelessly wandered over his neck.

No . . . no . . . this cannot be . . .

My hands pressed on his chest.

One . . . two . . . three . . .

I wrestled with panic and tried to keep an even rhythm.

One . . . two . . . three . . .

I stopped, put my mouth against his, and forced air into his lungs. Then I started over.

One . . . two . . . three . . .

Everything blurred. My eyes overflowed with tears. I forced even more air into his lungs.

"Jared." It sounded as if something was stuck in my throat, as if I was suffocating. I heard my blood pulse in my ears. My surroundings turned surreal. It felt as if I was falling.

Suddenly, a strange noise. It ripped me out of my trance. A strange, powerful moaning. Morgana's moaning.

I shuddered.

My hands trembled like aspen leaves.

No . . . no . . . that can't be . . . that mustn't be . . .

I again frantically felt Jared's neck in a panic. "No . . . no . . . no . . ." I put my ear against his chest until I thought I heard a heartbeat, but realized it was only my own heart's panicked thumps. "No . . . no . . . no . . . Jared . . . no . . . please . . . don't leave me alone, Jared . . . don't leave me . . ."

I forced even more air into his lungs, but . . . nothing. His lifeless chest was only rising and sinking with my breath.

I massaged his chest.

One . . . two . . . three . . .

I raised my eyes and looked at Morgana in disbelief.

She spread her arms triumphantly and let Jared's power flood her while she breathed in deeply and moaned.

Horror seized me.

This mustn't be!

Again I felt along Jared's neck. I desperately attempted to get him back. It was as if my nightmares had come true.

No!

Tears clouded my sight again. Numbness and a feeling that it was just a bad dream took hold of me again.

Morgana's moaning continued, turned to sighing and, finally, sounded like a kind of . . . *whimpering*.

I listened intently. The whimpering had nothing lustful to it. I managed with difficulty to turn my eyes away from Jared and forced myself to look at Morgana.

Her whole body began to writhe. She breathed in short, panting bursts, as if she were trying to suppress a building panic attack. Then she bent forward, doubled over, and contorted herself as she worked to find the right place for Jared's magic inside her body. I tirelessly felt Jared's neck, listened to his chest, looked for a sign of life. Pulse, heartbeat, breathing . . . any sign of life.

Morgana's body bent unnaturally backward as she floated above the ground.

Breathe! Damn it, Jared, breathe!

White light shone outward from Morgana's eyes, mouth, nose, fingers, and toes. Then it irresistibly broke out of her, blazing and so bright I had to lift my arms to shield my eyes. When I looked again, I saw both the most beautiful and most frightening thing I had ever seen. A vibrating ball of light floated between Jared and Morgana. A small pulsating sun. She was simply floating. A second, maybe two, and it was still almost impossible for me to look.

Breathe, Jared, breathe!

There! A weak pulse under his skin! But it was quickly gone again.

The expression on Morgana's face changed abruptly.

"No!" she commanded, tensing every muscle of her body. I couldn't believe my eyes. As if it was following Morgana's orders, the blazing light ball slowly moved toward her. Away from Jared. "Not this time!" Her voice acquired a strangely ringing, doubled sound, as if she were speaking with male and female voices simultaneously. The light ball moved irresistibly toward her. With a quiet moan escaping her lips—whether from pain or arousal, I could not say—she righted herself as the ball of blinding light rushed into her with full force. The sudden impact hurled me back.

Morgana doubled over in pain, her body bent unnaturally in all directions. Her eyelids fluttered. The arteries in her face and hands alternated between light and dark, as if something were crawling underneath her skin. She squeezed her black eyes shut and screamed. Then, suddenly, as if she had received an electric shock, her body straightened like a candlestick. She was still floating. Complete silence surrounded us.

It happened.

The change was immediately visible. Morgana's skin became clean, smooth, and alabaster-colored. Her hip-long black hair straightened and became silky and shining. Her body relaxed, and her flawless face radiated youthful splendor. Her talon-like curved fingers unclenched. Her lids opened, and she looked at me with glowing crimson eyes. Then she smiled.

What my mind had already grasped and correctly interpreted, my heart refused to believe. My hands shook as never before. The realization slowly spread through my arms, belly, face, and legs, and down to my toes until my body became one trembling mass. The pain tore me apart. My knees gave way. I fell to the ground . . . next to Jared's dead body.

***

The black night enveloped me. My skull wanted to explode. I opened my sore eyes, stared into Jared's angelic face. His blue eyes no longer shone. They gazed at me like the windows of an abandoned house, empty and expressionless. I sat there and watched my tears drop on his face. I could not turn my gaze from him.

I remained in this position of numb rigidity for what felt like an eternity. There was tugging on my legs. I felt my shocked body being dragged over the ground, but I did not defend myself. Something like a belt was first strapped around my wrists, then my ankles. The angle changed. I was no longer lying on the ground. Something lifted me upright. Stinking, strained breathing brushed over my face. I perceived my surroundings through blurred vision. They had tied me to the cross.

Jared's body lay close. It was so unbearable to see him lying there. Then a searing pain flashed through my chest. I gasped. Morgana stood before me, with an expression of satisfaction in her glowing red eyes. I stared through her. She stared back. Then she lifted her beautiful face into the air.

"Do you see now that you never had a whisper of a chance?" she asked, as if demanding a confession of guilt from a child. "There was no point in coming here, love. Though I admit . . . I was surprised to see you here. Perhaps even impressed. Not to mention that you somehow possessed Nimue's magic." She tenderly laughed and brushed her fingers over my cheek. "Say, child, how did you do that?"

My tired gaze turned toward Jared, who lay unchanged on the ground. Or . . . hadn't his arm been angled differently before? Now it was extended. Was I holding his hand when they pulled me away?

Morgana roughly grabbed my chin, yanking my head so I would have to look at her. Her sharp fingernails dug into my jaw. I made no sound.

"Well, do tell, how did you come by Nimue's magic?" Her nagging undertone betrayed that she was burning to find out. How many times had she combed the island looking for it?

I looked at her numbly. She let go of my chin, stepped back, and sized me up with an iron look.

"What should I do first?" she asked the damnati and put on a pretend smile. "You know, now that I'm more powerful than any other magical being—dead or alive." She happily clapped her hands.

Nervous laughter went through the ranks. A mistress this mighty was probably dreaded by her subjects. The damnati seemed about to shit themselves with fear of becoming her guinea pigs.

I felt nothing but emptiness. It was like waking from anesthesia. She had taken everything from me.

A sudden and brutal pain penetrated, and I cried out into the night. It took me a moment to register that I had given off that sound.

"Have I got your attention now?" Morgana asked, giving me a threatening look. The flicker in her glowing red eyes irritated me. "Where did you find Nimue's magic?"

I looked at her for a drawn-out moment, then breathed deeply. "If magic has the opportunity, it will always return to its rightful owner." My voice was flat, as if I was in a trance. Those were Ruth's words. I was surprised by my answer. Why did I say that?

Morgana frowned.

"That doesn't answer my question, love." Her tone showed that she was at the limit of her patience.

My thoughts were adrift. Was I about to lose my mind? I kept looking at Jared. Words coalesced in my head. Words I'd heard before. A verse. In the fog. When I opened my mouth, my voice sounded odd, strange. Almost as if I were speaking with the voice in the silver fog.

"The powerful being, worshipped by all,

to its home, for love, its back has turned.

Deceived and betrayed by malevolence and greed,

the Mistress finds her return home denied.

The water's might violently displaced,

the heavens with black clouds are hung.

The nymphs' laughter fallen silent,

dark creatures proclaim their evil deeds.

The forest once flowering in perfect splendor,

without her its might is extinguished."

Morgana seemed stumped, then gave me a look as if I had lost my marbles. Maybe that was it . . .

To be honest, that's what it felt like. Why had I repeated that verse? I couldn't latch on to a single clear thought. Text fragments, statements, and scraps of conversations shot through my head without any apparent connection—the voices of Ruth, Irvin, and Enid.

Magic must be given—freely!

Despite her magic, Morgana's body is a living organism—made of flesh and blood.

What do you think? How much magic can such a bleeding human body hold?

Maybe it was just . . . too much for her.

As if she had to throw up—in a magical way.

Like a kid who quickly gobbles up all her Halloween candy at once.

Magic must be given—freely!

Suddenly it all made sense, hitting me like a slap in the face. Reason, magic, intuition—or whatever may have been working behind the scenes—had sent me a message. Shown me a way out.

Overkill.

Wasn't that how Merlin had done it?

He had overexerted Morgana with his magic.

Had Jared tried that? Was that it?

But why hadn't it worked? How was she managing to handle so much magic? Had she taken up so much in droplets that chasing those with the remainder, which Jared had injected into her, couldn't harm her? Was it simply too late?

Maybe.

But I . . . *I* was still in possession of all *my* magic. I weighed this, looking straight at the dark witch. Would she be able to handle it?

"What shall we do with you?" Morgana asked. "You can't stay here."

She began to pace in front of me, thinking.

"Kill her, Mistress," one of the damnati thoughtlessly said. He immediately pulled back his neck as Morgana fixed her eyes on him.

"Who allowed you to speak?" Morgana snapped at him, then put on a sweet smile and slowly approached the scarface. This total moron had obviously volunteered.

"No one here speaks without being spoken to. Understood?" she warbled in a honey-sweet voice.

"Beg your pardon, Mistress," the addressed whispered. He trembled so badly that his spear blurred before my eyes.

"Now you did it again," Morgana said, coldly but with satisfaction. She spread her arms, raised her palms toward the sky, and slowly lifted them. The damnatus tracked her movement, and soon he was levitating and trembling above the ground. Morgana indicated a circular motion with her long index finger.

"Mistress, please," the damnatus pleaded. Then he whirled about on his axis, with his insides appearing to rotate faster than his outside. A second later, he hit the ground with a strange, slopping noise. The sight was so repulsive that even the damnati, who were no doubt capable of stomaching almost anything, stepped back in disgust. A bag of skin wrapped in a stinking cloak, filled with a gel of innards and bone splinters—that was all that was left of the damnatus who had just wished death upon me.

Morgana smiled, satisfied. A second later she was with me again.

"So, what shall we do with you?"

No one answered this time. Morgana looked at me smugly, as if I were still the same helpless girl I'd been back at the clearing in Oxford when she had made this pact with Jared. Again, I looked at him. He had entered into it to save my life. A tear ran down my cheek. Now he had done it again. He had forced his magic into Morgana. To protect me. I knew my plan amounted to a suicide mission—but I didn't care. Nothing was left for me to live for. If I couldn't save him, perhaps I would at least be able to rid Avalon of this blight. Wasn't there something heroic about sacrificing oneself to rid the world of this evil witch's tyranny?

That had to be worth something. Maybe that had been my destiny all along. Maybe that was what the Prophecy spoke of. Maybe I never stood a chance of saving Jared. Maybe everything I had experienced—all those terrible things happening to me and all the people I'd encountered along the way—had led me to this place, to exactly this moment. Maybe I was the only one who could do it. I had to try.

With grim determination, I lifted my head and stared into Morgana's eyes. For a moment I thought I saw something akin to fear reflected in them.

"What are you doing?" she asked wearily.

At that moment my power returned.

Power, hatred, and fire. Blazing flames shot through my body. I felt myself start to tremble but did nothing to prevent it. The fire spread. It took hold of me from head to foot, from inside to outside. I closed my eyes to arm myself for what stood before me. Maybe it was only a gesture of departure to say farewell to the part of myself I was about to inject with all available force into Morgana.

I looked at Jared one last time.

“I love you!” I whispered.

Then I reared up and, with a piercing cry, pushed out a glistening golden-green cone of light from my chest—straight into Morgana.

***

I felt torn from my body. The pain surpassed anything I’d ever experienced. My bones were burning brightly. I feared my skull would burst open along its crest at any moment. My eyes turned in their sockets. All that linked me to this life was severed. All I’d once been and all that made me was shredded in an instant. My name, my life, myself. The last thing I heard was my own scream. Then I slumped down into darkness.

CHAPTER 12

I felt angry, snorting breath on my neck.

Am I dead?

Something moist and cold was nudging me. Sniffing my hair.

I heard a strong wingbeat.

I blinked and willed my eyes open. A giant eagle-like creature with mighty wings had landed at my feet. Something nudged at my back again, more firmly this time. I turned sideways and looked into the golden-red eyes of a monstrous barghest leaning over me. When he saw that I was awake, he sat on his haunches.

What is happening? Where am I?

I propped myself up on my elbows, looked around . . . and couldn't believe what I saw. There was war. No other word could describe what was happening in the clearing.

Nymphs—those beings Ruth described as utterly peaceful—were riding with flowing hair on the backs of gigantic behemoths. The reverberating roars of these primeval armored animals sounded like a horn blowing the signal for an attack. The earth shook under their massive legs. They trampled everything and left paths of destruction like whirling tornadoes. There was growling and hissing throughout the tent city, always followed by golden-red eyes flashing in the dark, then hoarse cries that immediately died off. Panic spread among the damnati. They ran like frightened chickens, bumping into each other, tumbling to the ground, and scrambling up. Wherever glowing eyes flashed, a cry went through the crowd, and then it was silent. One by one, the barghests fought—or rather, *tore*—through the camp. I counted thirteen of the huge cats around me. They stormed in from all sides and soaked the ground with stinking damnati blood. Shrill screams and thundering roars drove the scarfaces apart, crumbled their protective walls, and mowed them down.

I blinked and caught site of a freshly cast-up earth mound. Goblins appeared by the hundreds from holes in the ground, set traps, and cut the throats of the scarfaces they brought down. Little blue pixies swirled in swarms through the air, biting, pinching, and jabbing the fumbling damnati. One they drove to the basin in which the kelpie was captive. The damnatus stumbled and fell into the water, thrashing wildly. The water foamed up, then turned red. Mighty eagle-like creatures circled high above in the overcast sky, dived on the cloaked figures, plunged huge talons into their shoulders, lifted them in the air as they screamed, then dropped them from high up. Some died immediately, while others lay whimpering and moaning on the ground, limbs twisted in all directions.

Though I was having trouble believing it, Avalon was striking back!

The mewing of the barghest over me drew my attention. Again and again he nudged me with his cold muzzle as if to tell me something. I looked around—then my eye caught it. Less than five yards away, Morgana floated in the air, shaking as if in a fever. Her eyes were rolling in their sockets, flickering wildly. Her long fingers curled into claws as her body curved and twisted as if possessed by the devil. Her mouth foamed. Somehow I managed to get on my feet. I held my breath. At that moment the golden-green light broke out of her, bundled into a pulsing ball, and stood still halfway between her and me as if waiting for my consent.

The battle raged around us, but at that moment I was enshrouded in silence. I straightened my back, arched my chest, and spread my arms. For a fraction of a second, the light ball hesitated, but then it began to move.

Whoom!

It rammed into me with full force. I gasped and went down on my knees. Pure, unadulterated magic flooded every cell. I groaned while the power pulsed inside me. It filled me, took complete control, and flowed wildly inside me. Then it found its spot. The pressure relented. I slowly rose.

I looked back at Morgana. It wasn't over yet. Her teeth chattered. She still foamed and trembled as she fought to control the demon inside her. Her eyes fluttered as a white-golden light erupted from her. It made its way out through the witch's eyes, nose, mouth, fingers, and toes to bundle, just as my magic had, into a ball. I needed a moment to understand what that meant. My eyes widened.

"Jared!" I turned about, searching.

My heart stopped. There he stood. More dead than alive, but he was standing with his own strength. My legs gave way with relief. I sank to my knees, watching Jared spread his arms to welcome his magic. The pulsating light ball rushed at him to charge with full force into his body. The pressure wave blew the hair strands out of my face. Jared sank down, panted, coughed, and breathed in deeply. He lifted his head and looked into my eyes. Tears ran down my face. I wasn't able to stand, but he was on his feet. A moment later he was beside me and embracing me so hard it almost hurt. Then he kissed me. First very tenderly, almost like a whisper, then more intensely, passionately. It was as if we'd never kissed before. As if this was our very first kiss.

He looked into my eyes and kissed me again.

I couldn't say a thing. I just focused on breathing and trying to understand what had just happened.

"You're alive," I whispered.

Jared nodded, clasped my face, and kissed me so intensely that I became dizzy.

"What were you thinking?" It just tumbled out of him. For a moment it looked as if he didn't know whether to slap me or keep kissing me. "You could have died!" He pressed his lips so hard against mine it hurt.

"You're alive!" I repeated, this time louder, and wrapped my arms around his neck. I pressed against him as tightly as I could. "You're alive!"

"Thank you," Jared answered, barely audible, before raising his voice. "But what were you thinking?" He was almost yelling at me. Once again he kissed me as if he needed to feel I was there. I struggled for air. Jared put his hand on the back of my neck, pressed his forehead against mine, and looked in my eyes.

"How could you put yourself in such danger?"

"I had to try." It sounded like an apology.

Jared laughed, nervous but happy. "I was so worried about you." He took my face into his hands.

I took his hands and looked at him. "*You* were worried about *me*? Have you looked in the mirror lately?"

Jared chuckled. Then he held me tightly to him as if he would never let me go.

The barghest growled with raised hackles. My personal guardian had not left my side. I first thought the hostile gesture was directed at Jared but then followed the barghest's watchful look. I was shocked. Morgana's struggle was not over yet. She still shook, her fingers bent back unnaturally. An orange light erupted from her, and another pulsing light ball bundled itself together outside her body. For a moment, the sphere stood still, hovering above the ground. Then it began to move. But where was it going? My eyes followed it as it moved toward a figure waiting calmly by the forest edge. The entire clearing shone like a light in a glowing sunset. It blinded me so much that I had to shield my eyes. Faster than sound and with the force of a wrecking ball, the magic united with the figure. When the body had absorbed the trembling sphere . . . I nearly lost my balance. Could this be true?

"*Ruth?*" I blinked into the dawn. "Is that you?"

For an instant, I'd forgotten to breathe. Jared was already on his feet, drawing me to him in a protective gesture.

The barghest growled and nudged me in the back. I followed its glowing eyes to the east.

No!

Morgana was fleeing! Three of her most trusted servants were carrying her into the woods. With a trembling hand, she pulled Nimue's amulet—*my* amulet—from her pocket and put it on. Then she vanished among the trees.

"She has my amulet!" I shouted, horrified. "We must stop her!"

"In which direction?" Jared hadn't noticed and was trying hard to focus.

"There," I replied, pointing to the spot where I'd last seen Morgana.

Jared ran that way. I looked over my shoulder, but Ruth had disappeared. I started to run, faster than ever before. A group of daredevil damnati tried to stop us, but the barghest took care of them.

Jared was fast even though he must have been terribly weakened after his ordeal. Maybe it was rage that drove him on. We flew past the trees. I tried to keep up with Jared's superhuman speed while looking for Morgana in every direction. The glowing light of the rising sun blinded me. Jared ran on. The forest became denser. We soon left the barren area behind to enter a colorful landscape that was still unspoiled. The witch had no influence here.

Still no sign of her. The wind whipped my face. I tried to discern something in the sounds of the awakening day. Steps, voices, something that would tell me which direction we needed to take.

"Did you see her?" Jared called over his shoulder. He briefly stopped, looked around, then ran on. "I can't feel her energy." Helpless rage echoed in his voice.

"She's wearing my amulet!" I called, panting, looking around frantically. Then I slowed down. "Jared, wait."

He looked back at me, frowning, but didn't slow down. I stopped.

"It's useless," I said, resigned. "The amulet will hide its wearer from anyone wanting to harm them. We won't find her this way."

Jared slowed down, clenched his fists, and turned around, searching with his teeth gritted. Then he ran on.

"We've hidden from her long enough!" he growled. "Do you hear?" he shouted into the echoing forest. "We've hidden long enough!" He took a deep breath and yelled louder. "Run as fast and far as you can—I'll find you!"

It wasn't a threat; it was a promise.

I hurried after him, tried to stop him, put my arms around him. Jared was so tense the air around him began to crackle. His tension only lessened when I gently enveloped him with my magic. Finally, he stopped, stood still for a moment, and attempted to control his rage. He had difficulty giving up the chase and kept looking around, hoping to catch sight of Morgana somewhere between the trees.

"It's useless," I repeated with a soothing voice, "for as long as she's wearing my amulet."

Jared's facial muscles twitched. "Maybe she's even left the island." After all, not much was left of her following. Avalon had struck them down. The thought filled me with pride.

Jared nodded. Then he took a few deep breaths. For a while we were silent as he tried to calm down.

"Who was the woman in the clearing?" he asked. "Do you know her?" His voice was still trembling. I didn't know if this truly interested him or if he just wanted to switch topics.

"That was Ruth Hayman," I replied with excitement. "She helped me uncover your and the Order's secret. She's the friend I told you about. She helped us find you."

"Us?" he followed up as his face finally relaxed.

"Yes, Enid and Irvin and Colin . . . Colin!" My eyes widened. "He must have followed me into the fog!" Deeply worried, I put my hand to my forehead and started to nervously walk in circles. "But he didn't arrive on the other side. I don't know what happened . . . no idea where he . . ."

"Calm down," Jared said, taking me in his arms. I was so upset I felt electrified. I would have preferred to run off to look for Colin in the fog.

"Colin knows what he's doing. He can handle himself. He's probably the last one we need to worry about. Tell me everything. What happened since you woke up at headquarters?"

I was still beside myself. A thousand questions raced through my mind. What about Colin? Was he all right? What had Ruth been doing there? How had she gotten to Avalon? *Why on earth did she not tell me she had magical abilities?*

Jared must have sensed I was ready to burst and gently laid his hand on my forehead.

"May I?" he asked.

I knew what he was up to, so I nodded. I was suddenly overcome by a warm feeling of confidence and optimism. I breathed in deeply.

"Let's start over again," Jared said. "What all has happened since you woke up?"

I considered where to start but was overwhelmed by the memory. Jared had put me into a magical sleep, then made a pact with Morgana. I was steamrolled by my anger at him for simply deciding that—while rendering me incapable of acting so I couldn't prevent it.

Jared's expression betrayed that he saw it coming, and he took the slap in the face without flinching.

"I deserved that," he admitted, subdued, rubbing his cheek.

I stared at him angrily but, to my horror, a grin spread across his face. He wrapped his arms around me and lifted me up.

"I love you," he said, spinning me around so my legs flew in the air. "I love you!" He grinned from ear to ear, then kissed me and lowered me back down. He was completely relaxed.

"Never, ever do that again!" I said, but it didn't sound as serious as I meant it.

"I won't," Jared promised, without making it sound ridiculous, then kissed me again. I felt his hot breath on my cheek and cuddled against him. Then I kissed him. I finally had him back. We were safe again.

***

"So Morgana possessed Ruth's magic. That would mean that Morgana somehow got Ruth to give up her magic in the past," Jared surmised. "Magic can only be *given* . . ."

I'd told him everything, left nothing out. It was so good to finally talk about it with him.

"Yes, and it would appear she has her abilities back." I fell silent.

"What's on your mind?"

I exhaled. "I wonder if this was Ruth's plan all along. I really like her, you know?"

Jared embraced me.

"I can't believe she was pretending all this time. I believed she was my friend." The disappointment and hurt in my voice were obvious.

"I don't know Ruth, but perhaps you shouldn't judge her so quickly. Maybe it's not what you think."

I nodded into his shoulder. "I hope you're right," I began, detaching myself from him, "but there's one thing I don't understand. It was

Ruth who told me the body of a magical being and its magic can only exist together as a unit."

"That's right. If you take the magic from a magical being, it'll die."

"How was Ruth able to continue living without her magic?"

"I don't know how she did it." Jared paused. "But . . . *we* should be dead. Both of us."

With that, he said what I had pushed aside. I had believed I'd lost Jared forever and had embarked on a suicide mission. "Yes, I didn't assume I'd . . . *survive*," I conceded, thinking everything over one more time. I'd really believed Jared was dead. The memory of him lying on the ground tightened my throat. How he had pushed the last bit of his magic into Morgana to protect me. How it had felt when I'd done the same to destroy Morgana with my magic, knowing I would not survive. So how was it that we both still lived?

Then it struck me like lightning.

"What is it?" he asked.

"Jared," I answered, my eyes wide open, "I think I've found the source of eternal life."

CHAPTER 13

"Thus I turn my back on immortality,
preferring your love to eternal life.
For all the time in the world is meaningless,
compared with just one day by your side."

"You've got something?" Jared asked.

"I've found the source of eternal life," I repeated, thinking back to my dinner at Ruth's.

"Was Nimue immortal?" I'd asked her after she'd read from the verse.

"She was the Guardian of Avalon, the legendary, mist-enshrouded island that's said to contain the source of eternal life."

"I drank from it . . . filled my bottle with it . . . and then I gave you some of it to drink!" I spoke so fast I tripped over my words. "Do you understand, Jared? The water kept us alive!" I was beside myself.

He looked perplexed. "Are you sure?"

"You yourself said we should be dead." I hastily rummaged in the backpack and pulled out the book.

"Let's see if there's something about it in here," I mumbled, leafing through the pages like mad. My mouth gaped. There it was! A faithful drawing of the source! Why, for Heaven's sake, hadn't I looked in the book before?

"Here! Just look." I flattened down the page and held the book up to Jared. "I was there. Nimue's magic came to me from this source."

Gothic letters proclaimed *Vita Aeterna* below the drawing. But there was no explanatory text.

Jared took the book from my hand to have a closer look. He glanced at me, then back at the image again. His eyes widened.

"You're a genius," he said, casting an admiring glance at me. "Entire generations have spent their lives searching for it . . ."

I stared at him.

Suddenly, he frowned. "Wait a second. Do you think Ruth also found the source and, therefore, was able to survive without her magic?"

I shook my head. "I doubt it. The nymphs showed me the way. I can't imagine they'd have led anyone else there."

Jared looked at me while thinking aloud: "I knew you didn't age as long as you were on Avalon. But I'd always thought it just exaggeration that the water would make you immortal." He stopped and thought. "Probably only the water right from the source has that effect," he surmised.

"But all the water on the island *originates* from the source," I objected. No idea where I got that from—I simply knew.

"Right. The effect probably weakens the farther the water is away from the source. That must be the reason for Morgana's eternal youth."

"So you think the water from the lakes and streams everywhere here on the island stops the aging process, but one remains mortal?"

Jared frowned. "Yes, you don't age, don't die from illnesses or old age, but—"

"If you get a dagger in your heart—" I completed his thought.

"Yes," Jared interjected. "The damnati must have drunk from the water as well, but there's not much left of them." He smiled darkly.

"That means Morgana—as long as she never drank from the source—is mortal."

"I'm sure she hasn't found it. She was burning to know how I'd come upon Nimue's magic." I paused when I suddenly had a thought. I looked pensively at the book, which Jared still held in his hand. "Do you think," I started hesitantly, "that we're *immortal* now? Forever, I mean?"

Jared scrunched his eyebrows. Then he shook his head. "No, otherwise Nimue would surely be alive today."

"The effect must be limited. You have to drink again and again from the source to maintain its effect."

He returned the book to me, and I put it safely into my backpack.

"So what do we do now?" I asked.

"We'll go back and start looking for Morgana."

I felt a sting in my chest.

"She's surely not stupid enough to stay here now that the whole island is against her—" Jared stopped abruptly. I had tensed involuntarily, and he had noticed at once.

"That is . . . if you'd like." He looked at me.

At the thought of leaving Avalon, an oppressive sadness overcame me. Jared took me into his arms and kissed my forehead.

"Would you rather stay here?" he asked, so cautiously that I knew he was afraid of my answer.

I sighed and fought against the sadness. "What matters most is that we're together." It was true, but I started to cry. This was anything but easy. Since Zara's death, nothing had felt more like home than this place. I loved it and its magical inhabitants—every flower, every tree, every blade of grass, every stone. For the first time, I understood what Nimue had gone through. But she chose Merlin in the end. And I—I chose Jared.

"Let's find Morgana," Jared said, with a gentle but firm voice. "Then you can return here whenever you feel like it."

"Sounds good," I answered in a tearful voice. I could never have said farewell to this place forever. Even departing for a short time was difficult. But he was right. The sooner we'd rendered Morgana harmless, the sooner I'd be able to return. Whenever I wanted. "But there's something I have to do before we can leave."

***

I cried a lot as we traveled to the peak. Jared watched helplessly. He tried to comfort me, but I assured him it was all right. I just needed to cry. My tears were a gesture of farewell to Avalon. Farewell to my magic. I had no choice—I had to leave it here so Avalon and all its magical creatures would live.

"There." I pointed to the shrub-covered cave entrance when we arrived at the peak. This time I'd found the way on my own. Jared followed me through the dark, narrow passages. We were silent all the way. When we arrived, once again, in my presence the subterranean lake began to shine. I swallowed. All I had to do was go into the water and . . . I breathed in deeply. Why did I find it so incredibly hard? As if . . . someone were about to die.

I hesitated. Jared took my hand.

"You don't have to do this," he said gently. His look was sincere, and I knew he'd make this sacrifice for me. He'd stay here with me if I asked. Give up everything.

"No," I answered, trying to pull myself together. "It's okay." Would it be easier if I did it really quickly? Like tearing off a bandage? My voice didn't sound as firm as I would have liked. "Let's go back. Let's go back and find Morgana."

Jared pressed my hand. I looked down. He didn't want to see me cry again. But he pulled me to him, brushed his fingers along my cheek down to my collarbone. Then he placed his finger under my chin and lifted it so I could look at him.

"We'll return," he said earnestly. "I promise."

I hesitantly nodded and swallowed the pain tightening my throat. I put my arms around his neck. He pressed me tightly to himself, giving me the support I needed. It felt so good to just drop, and do so in his presence. Why was I acting this way? I had come for *his* sake. To save him! Now that I had done it against all odds and Jared was safe, why was I so sad to have to leave again? He'd been ready to give his magic and, therefore, his life for me, dammit!

"I love you, Jared," I said. Nothing else counted.

His breath brushed my ear.

"I really thought I'd never see you again," he whispered, holding me as if he'd never let go again.

"I thought that, too," I answered and rubbed my cheek against his.

Jared slowly detached himself and looked into my eyes. His look was honest and filled with love. He put his hand over my heart and placed mine on his heart, both our hearts hammering loudly. Then he kissed me. First on the cheek, then on the lips. I felt his hand run down my spine. His touch was tender and light. Yet I perceived it so intensely that my skin sensually tightened. He hugged me tighter and, suddenly, something changed. The way I felt in his arms was somehow different. From one moment to the next, I knew that this was more than a comforting hug.

Jared's breathing picked up its pace, and mine did, too. I closed my eyes and opened my mouth. Then he kissed me as he'd never done before. As if he'd always held back. My lips melded with his. His fingers brushed over my collarbone, then slowly wandered downward. I felt as if I was going to burst when they slid over my breasts. I tilted my head back. We stroked each other. First cautiously, then firmer, more demanding. My fingertips wandered over his hard abdomen. He bent down, kissed the hollow between my neck and shoulder. My legs felt like Jell-O. I thought I was melting when he pulled me in, even firmer. He raised his head and looked at me with his wild blue eyes. I was swept away. Heat rose inside me, streamed through my body, and pulsated in my belly. Flames burned brightly inside me. He had already touched me, stroked me, caressed me so many times before. But this time was different. There was no longer a need to be cautious. I was almost as powerful as he was now. He no longer held back. No. We'd go through with it this time.

A throaty sound escaped my lips, and Jared seemed to completely lose control. His fingers closed around my waist, dug into my behind. His mouth wandered along my neck and back to my lips. I opened them and met him with my tongue. My hands trembled with desire as they moved down his torso. I didn't want to wait any longer. I heard my blood flowing in my ears and found the buttons of his jeans and yanked them open. He pulled my top over my head in one skillful motion. His hands returned to my hips and moved forward. I dug my fingers into his hair and pulled. He unzipped my pants with his right hand as his left pulled them over my legs. Then he stripped off his own pants. I took his face into my hands and kissed him. Without inhibition, without embarrassment. It couldn't be fast and firm enough. He let my bra snap open. I pulled it over my shoulders, and then he pulled me over to the water. I stripped my panties off and tossed them. Jared's boxers lay on the shore. We slid in. It was warm, almost like a bathtub. The lights danced on the water. Our magic shone, immersing the grotto in a golden-green shine. Then he pulled me into the water and let me feel how much he desired me.

***

We cuddled on the shore. My head rested on Jared's chest. The water gently washed over our legs, tickling our feet. Though we were naked, I didn't feel cold. An unfamiliar heat pulsed through me. We just lay there in each other's arms. Jared finally fell asleep, and I listened for the regular flow of the air with which his chest lifted and lowered at every breath. I could probably have lain there for the rest of my life listening to that sound. And maybe we should have stayed in the cave. Just the two of us. Forever. I closed my eyes. *What a thought* . . . for a second I was lost in it. Then I opened my eyes, took a deep breath, and slowly got to my feet. There was no point in delaying any longer. Better to get it over with. I swallowed hard, casting a glance at Jared's peacefully sleeping face. The memory of his promise gave me the strength to turn around.

I moved to the water. The steady waves splashed around my ankles, and I breathed in deeply. It was harder than I thought possible. I was doing the right thing, there was no doubt about that, but my emotions overcame me. I was glad Jared slept—I didn't want him to see me this way. He surely would have tried to stop me if he saw me suffering like this. I took another step in. The water was up to my knees. Then I took another step and another until the water was at my hips. I was petrified. Then I let the magic rise one more time. I spread my arms. The grotto was immersed in a shimmering green light. It was reflected on the pool's surface. Everything pulsed. Every one of my cells. I felt the power flow out of me and took a last deep breath.

I dove under.

And released the magic.

CHAPTER 14

"Oh, Evelyn. I'm so sorry." Jared took me firmly into his arms. I was still naked when I came out of the water, but I *felt* naked without magic. More than that. Amputated. A special part of me was missing. The extent of my sacrifice exceeded the power of my imagination.

"We'll return. I promise!" Jared said, full of passion. He was so aware of my pain that his voice cracked.

We just stood there for a while beside the source, and I let him hold me. It took a while for me to find my voice again. I didn't dare speak until I was sure it would be steady.

"Let's go" was all I had to say.

***

The walk down the mountain was exhausting. I still felt uniquely connected to this wonderful place, but without magic, I just felt like any idiot walking down a mountain.

Weak. Tired. Slow. Worthless.

Why was it so hard for me? Why did I suffer so much from this loss? I'd lived without magic before, for nineteen years—so why did I feel incomplete now that everything was back to normal?

I looked at Jared and at once felt guilty. He looked the way I felt. Could it be that he was suffering even more than I was because he saw me suffer? I swallowed and tried to pull myself together. I had Jared back—that was all that mattered.

***

"Ready?" Jared asked, taking my hand.

I only realized we'd arrived at the portal when I looked down and noticed the smoke-like fog snaking around my ankles. The time had come to leave Avalon. I looked around one last time to see dozens of pairs of eyes light up among the trees. They had come to say farewell. An iron fist gripped my heart.

"I'll be back," I whispered into the woods, praying that I'd be able to keep this promise.

I straightened my back and nodded to Jared, and then we plunged into the fog. He didn't let me go, firmly held my hand, and led me. Soon it became difficult to see my hand before my eyes. I shuddered at the thought of what awaited us. The carpet of corpses, Zara turning into an awful snake-like creature, groaning women, crying children with soulless eyes . . . those images were etched into my memory.

Soon we had left the silver fog behind. I was on the lookout but couldn't see anything in the fog. No dead, no damnati, no phantoms grasping for me—nothing. Nothing but the uniform, shifting whiteness. At first, I didn't know what it meant, but then I understood that all the horror I had experienced before must have been Morgana's handiwork. Now she'd lost her power over Avalon, and the fog and phantoms had disappeared with her. The fog was no longer terrifying. I looked at

Jared, about to say something about not being afraid, when his expression changed. My eyes widened. I followed his look. *There!* The outline of a shadow. I held my breath and grasped Jared's hand even tighter.

Had I been wrong? Were the apparitions still here? Jared squeezed my hand as we marched on.

There was a figure sitting on the ground. Jared headed straight for it—a dark-blond shock of hair over muscular shoulders.

"Fuck!" Jared shouted. He ran ahead without letting go of my hand, pulling me after him. I suddenly realized who was sitting on the ground.

"Colin!" I shouted, as Jared sprinted the last yards toward him, grabbed his shoulder, and shook him.

"What's wrong with you?" Jared wanted to know as he searched for injuries. Colin was completely out of it. His legs were stretched out, his shoulders slumped. His head was tilted forward, and his arms hung limp. His hands rested in his lap, and every muscle was slack.

"Oh God, what's with him?" My voice sounded far too shrill.

Jared examined his best friend's body one more time. Lifted his eyelids, pressed his fingers on the jaw joints to open Colin's mouth, looked in his ears.

"Nothing." Jared's voice cracked.

I couldn't see anything that might have caused his condition, either. Did he have internal bleeding?

Suddenly, Colin opened his mouth and mumbled.

"What?" Jared and I asked simultaneously.

Colin was totally out of it, as if paralyzed. He might as well have been on another planet, he was that unreachable. It was strange to touch someone physically when they were so remote.

"Can't you do anything?" I asked Jared desperately.

He grasped his hair with both hands. "If he were injured, I could try to heal him, but like this . . ."

Jared and I stood helplessly beside Colin.

Colin mumbled again.

"What?" Jared asked, grabbing Colin again by the shoulders. "I can't understand you. What happened?"

Colin's lips trembled. "Sss . . . all . . . yyy," he mumbled. "Saaa . . . llyyy."

I knew what was wrong with him. "The fog!" I shouted. "The mirages in Morgana's fog!" My memory conjured up those hideous images. Colin must have seen terrible things, just as I had. His fog nightmare must have something to do with Sally. I grabbed him by the collar and forced him to look at me. His eyes rolled.

"That wasn't real, Colin! Whatever you saw in the fog wasn't real! Those were just phantoms, conjured up by Morgana, do you hear?" I shook him. It was as if I were trying to wake a comatose patient. "Nothing but delusions. None of it is real. Do you hear me, Colin?"

"Saaaaally," he mumbled again, this time more clearly. His look steadied.

"There's nothing wrong with Sally," I assured him. "She's at home in Oxford, sitting bored stiff in some lecture."

Suddenly, his eyes cleared up, and he looked at me.

"Go on," Jared encouraged me. "It's working."

"Colin, whatever you saw, none of it's real," I repeated. "Sally's fine. There's nothing wrong with her. Do you understand?"

He hesitantly nodded.

"Come," Jared said. "We're taking you to Sally."

Colin nodded again and tried to get up. He was too weak and had to lean on Jared. He kept tripping over his own feet.

"He's really gone," Jared moaned under Colin's weight. "We've got to get out of here as fast as possible."

I nodded and forcefully walked on. Only a few yards to the human world. Then, we left the fog behind us . . . and landed in the middle of chaos.

CHAPTER 15

"What the hell is this?" I yelled, exasperated.

Hundreds, no, thousands—no, *tens of thousands* of people were partying around us. Young women in shorts and crocheted tops stomped about in rubber boots, dancing ecstatically in the mud. A guy who looked as if he'd just had a lobotomy drummed without rhythm on a set of homemade bongos. He only wore one shoe. Beside him, a couple rolled in the mud, uninhibitedly making out. The two bumped into a young woman who was giving a palm reading prophesizing a long and happy life. Mud splashed my pants. I sidestepped a guy who'd wrapped his T-shirt around his head. He yelled, "Mud surfing!" and slid on his belly into a huge puddle. Four others dove in behind him.

My eyes widened with disbelief. Where the hell had we landed? Behind us, men and women were playing chicken and trying to shove each other into the enormous puddle. Others were sitting farther back where one guy played a guitar, another a tambourine. They were in a circle on the mushy ground, offering up an exotic version of Oasis's "Wonderwall" and heavily drugged—or that's what it seemed like. A redhead in a colorful hippie skirt was walking on her hands around the song circle. She wasn't wearing any panties.

Jared, who had more than enough on his hands keeping Colin upright, looked around, confused. Suddenly it dawned on him. "It's the Glastonbury Festival," he said in a flat voice.

As if on cue, the penetrating sound of an electrical guitar started up.

"The Who—woo-hoo!" a girl with a wreath of wild flowers in her hair shouted as she charged downhill. I looked after her. Only then did I realize the extent of the chaos. The huge terrain of the Summerland Meadows surrounding Tom Tower had been transformed into a giant tent city. At its foot stood a huge, pyramid-shaped stage on which The Who were playing a melancholic tune about a sad man with blue eyes. Thousands of people enthusiastically partied along.

"The Glastonbury Festival?" I asked, taken aback. "But that's not till the end of June . . . Wait a minute—how long have we been in Avalon?"

"Hey you," Jared asked a guy walking by. "What day is it?"

The guy looked back, startled. "Um, Sunday." He looked at us as if we'd missed something really obvious and pointed to the spectacle on the pyramid stage. "The Who are on. The big acts are always on—"

"What date?" Jared interrupted sharply.

"Um . . . the twenty-eighth . . . I think."

"The twenty-eighth?" I repeated skeptically, then used my fingers to count. I looked at Jared in disbelief. "We were gone for two weeks."

He'd come to the same conclusion and nodded. "It was only three days in Avalon. Time must move slower there. This means Morgana has a much greater lead than we thought."

I wanted to say something, but Colin suddenly broke out in heavy sobbing. It took me a moment to realize what had churned him up. But then I heard it. The Oasis song circle had finished "Wonderwall" and now was trying its hand at "Don't Look Back in Anger." At the line "So, Sally can wait," Colin's floodgates had opened, and he clutched Jared.

"She knows it's too late as we're walking on by," the group sang, out of tune, as Colin's legs gave way.

"Pull yourself together, bro," Jared admonished as he tried to pull Colin up.

"Her soul slides away," the improv circle sang.

"Saaaaaaallyyyyy," Colin cried. His nose was running.

I rolled my eyes. "We'll never find Morgana here," I said, resigned, looking around at the turmoil. "She's probably a million miles away by now."

Jared, still supporting Colin, nodded with a sour expression. "I still can't feel her energy."

"And Ruth has probably gone to the ends of the ear—"

Just then I saw a black cloak slip through the crowd.

"Damnatus!" I shouted, and started running.

"Stay here," Jared ordered, placing Colin on the ground with the Oasis singers where he'd be inconspicuous. Then he followed me.

"Where?" Jared asked.

"There, up ahead." I pointed at the flowing black cloak as it cut through The Who's audience. Jared and I charged after it. The wind whipped about my ears, blew hair into my eyes, and robbed me of my sight. I plunged into the crowd and bumped a guy who spilled his beer over the person in front of him. The latter turned around and pushed the guy with the beer, who tried to rescue the last of his slopping drink with a balancing act. There was no passage, no gap between the tightly pressed bodies. I used my elbows to move ahead. Hands pushed back. A few even hit me. Jared showed up next to me, pushed in front, and cleared a path. Were the others noticing the angry flare-up of his magic?

"Jared!" I tried to draw his attention, but he didn't seem to hear. He moved forward, focused as if he knew exactly where the damnatus was. A dark-haired woman bitched at me and pushed me in the back as I wormed past her. The crowd abruptly pushed me in the wrong direction, and I was separated from Jared. He fought his way through, grabbed my hand, and pulled me to him. It cost us valuable seconds, and Jared lost the damnatus's trail. He searched in all directions.

"Ugh, man, you stink!" I heard someone call ahead of us. Then I smelled it myself: the unmistakable rotten damnatus aroma. There he was! Jared leapt. It was impossible to overlook the glow of his magic.

"Cool special effect," a spacey curly-head said appreciatively, raising his hands, presumably to have Jared high-five them.

"Jared!" I yelled again, because everybody could see that something was different about him. But he was furious. He landed in the tight pack, spread his arms, and grasped a black hood. He yanked the figure toward him. But instead of the damnatus, he had grabbed a terrified festivalgoer by his Foo Fighters hoodie.

"Shit!" Jared shouted, frustrated, and let go. He furiously looked around.

"Alien!" a girl shrieked, pointing at Jared with wide eyes.

"Jared!" I cried, trying to draw his attention to the rather obvious magical aura surrounding him. He finally noticed and looked down at himself. Then he closed his eyes, breathed in, and dimmed the light. The girl frowned, startled, as if she was wondering if she was imagining things.

"I can't sense the damnatus's energy anymore," Jared said, still busy gaining control over his magic. "There are way too many people and way too many energy fields."

We stood in the midst of the press of the festival crowd. The Who played the last chords of "Behind Blue Eyes" and the crowd broke out in tumultuous applause. The damnatus was gone without a trace.

"Fuck!" Jared roared. He usually didn't swear, but he was obsessed with finding Morgana. That stinking cloak-wearer might have provided a clue.

"Let's look after Colin," I suggested, taking Jared's hand. It took an eternity to struggle back through the crowd and up the hill again. When we got there, Colin sat crying in the mud, just as we had left him.

"Come on," Jared said affectionately and pulled him up.

Suddenly, I spotted a familiar face in the crowd. "Enid!" I ran toward her and threw myself into her arms. Irvin rushed to Jared to help with Colin.

"Evelyn! Jared!" Enid exclaimed. Unbridled joy spread across her face. "You made it!" she whispered into my ear, hugging me as tightly as she could. She looked up. "You were gone for so long, we thought . . ." She stopped, noticing Colin. "Colin. Oh God. What happened? Is he . . . how did you . . ." She hurried to them and examined Colin with expert hands. For a moment I felt irritated but then remembered that Enid was a doctor and knew what to look for.

"We found him like this in the fog," Jared explained.

"There's nothing physically wrong with him," Enid muttered, placing her hand on Jared's cheek before focusing on Colin again. It was a tiny, tender gesture, but everyone could see how much Jared meant to Enid and how incredibly happy she was to see him alive.

"Looks very much like shock," Enid diagnosed.

"Yes, he must have seen something horrible in the fog," I said.

Enid nodded, giving me a look that seemed to ask what *I* had seen there.

"Ruth followed you into the fog," Irvin explained, his voice strained from helping Jared support Colin. "Colin ran after her."

"Did you see Morgana emerge from the fog?" Jared asked, as he finally managed to keep Colin on his legs.

"Saalllyyy."

"No," Irvin replied, breathing heavily. He had to raise his voice so we could understand him over Colin's whimpering and the festival brouhaha.

"What about Ruth?" I asked. "She was there—she was . . ." The expression on Irvin's face caused me to fall silent.

"What's the matter?" I asked.

"She's in the car," he said curtly. "Gareth is with her."

My jaw dropped. "You . . . *nabbed* her?" That wasn't quite the word I was looking for, but it came pretty close to what I meant.

Irvin nodded. "She ran into our arms when she came out of the fog."

"But her magic . . . didn't she try to . . . *defend* herself?"

He thought for a moment before conceding: "She tried. But I think she doesn't know how to use it."

"She doesn't know how her own magic works?" I looked at Jared in the hope he'd know what that meant. But he just looked surprised and uncertain.

"But how can that be?" I wanted to know.

"Why don't we just ask her that?" Jared said.

***

We sat in the backseat. Jared put his arm around me, and I rested my head on his chest, listening to his heartbeat. Although I was tired as a dog, I stayed awake almost the whole drive. My thoughts would not stop spinning. Colin, who was finally becoming himself again, took his phone from his pocket as soon as he'd sat down on the passenger side and attempted to call Sally with trembling hands. He misdialed twice. So I took the phone from his hand, searched the directory for Sally's name, pressed Call, and returned it to him.

"Sally," he said, relieved when she picked up. He sank deep into his seat.

***

"We're here," Jared said, stroking my hair. I must have fallen asleep.

I lifted my head to find that we'd already turned into the headquarters' underground garage. The other car was already there. I watched closely as Gareth led Ruth in handcuffs into the building. Gareth was no longer young, but few could take him on. As a former detective constable in the City of London Police, he exuded the requisite self-confidence and authority to intimidate anyone with a single look. But seeing Ruth in handcuffs was more than strange. She was my friend. At least, that's what I thought.

We got out. Jared walked around the car and took my hand. He had hardly let go of me since we were reunited. My heartbeat accelerated as we walked up the stairs from the underground garage. Our steps echoed through the corridors. No one spoke.

Finally, we stopped in front of the ornamented, mighty double door. Colin pushed against it, then held it open for the rest of us. The others were already there. Gareth and Ian stood at the front of the room; Montgomery Grey and Judith McHallern, the two oldest members of the High Council, sat at the long sides of the huge table. Ruth had been placed at the head of it. I sat down beside Jared as the others also took their seats. Gareth and Ian remained standing behind Ruth. Enid, at the far end, placed both hands on the table and leaned forward in Ruth's direction.

"Why did you follow Evelyn into the fog, Ruth?" she asked with a firm voice that demanded respect. The interrogation had begun.

Ruth avoided my look.

"Is this really necessary?" she quietly asked, rattling her handcuffs behind her back.

Enid's face remained frozen for a moment, and then she nodded at Gareth. He reached into his pocket, pulled out a key, and undid the handcuffs with a metallic click. Ruth rubbed her wrists.

"Why. Did. You. Follow. Evelyn. Into. The. Fog?" Enid repeated.

I tried to read Ruth's thoughts from her expression, but she turned away.

"Because of Morgana."

"And that means?" Enid followed up, glaring at Ruth. Little progress was being made.

Ruth stared at her wrists, which she continued to rub. It didn't look as if she'd answer any time soon.

Jared pounded his fist on the table. Everyone jerked with fright. Especially Ruth. She swallowed.

"Morgana had something that belonged to me," Ruth finally answered. "I wanted it back."

"Your magic," Enid said.

Ruth nodded.

"How did you make it through the fog?" Colin asked. He seemed to consider it a personal humiliation that she'd made it and he hadn't.

"I was . . . prepared for what was waiting for me in the fog."

Colin leaned back angrily, crossing his arms over his chest. Clearly that answer was less than satisfactory for him.

"How did Morgana end up possessing your magic?" Jared asked, pressing on. The sooner we found out Ruth's story, the sooner we could search for Morgana.

Ruth exhaled. "It's not exactly *my* magic," she started.

We all looked, astonished, at each other.

"It's . . . well, it was my mother's."

"Mary Hayman was a magical being?" Irvin asked, trying to play down his amazement with a soft tone.

Ruth nodded and lowered her head.

That explained why Ruth didn't know how to handle her abilities, just the way it had been for me. I had to *learn* how Nimue's magic worked. Ruth obviously hadn't had time to figure hers out, and I could imagine it was difficult to practice while handcuffed. She didn't really know what she was capable of.

"My mother was a light guardian," she quietly explained. Suddenly, she raised her gaze and looked at me for the first time. "Light guardians are peaceful creatures. They shine light into dark places and can brighten even the darkest night." She seemed to be choking back tears. "If the light magic falls to a creature like Morgana, the light turns to darkness. It gives her the power to turn even the brightest day into the darkest night." Ruth paused, staring into space. "Light magic passes from generation to generation. After my mother's death it was to pass to me, and after my death, to my daughter." Ruth sounded incredibly sad.

"What happened?" Irvin asked.

"Morgana lured my mother into a trap and threatened to kill me if she didn't turn over her magic."

There was dismay throughout the room. We all knew what that meant. Mary had given her magic and, with it, her life to protect her daughter. From the corner of my eye, I saw Enid turn her head and look at Gareth in shock.

Jared also saw it. "What does that mean?" he prompted Enid.

Ruth was silent for a moment but then fixed on Jared, who raised his eyebrow, which I interpreted as a warning. The air around him began to crackle. It was probably best if she put all her cards on the table. It was not particularly advisable to continue to irritate Jared.

"When Mary Hayman discovered the secret of Legatum Merlini," Enid began, "Karen ordered Gareth to kill her." She looked at Ruth, who had frozen. I searched in vain for a sign of surprise on her face.

Gareth, who remained in his guard stance behind Ruth, cleared his throat. "I decided against it," he said. "Instead, I told Mary to disappear because the Order would never give up looking for her. I led Karen to believe I'd killed Mary." He cleared his throat again. "To be honest, I believed that Mary had run."

Enid gave Gareth a long look. I could read her face like a book. As unreasonable as it may have seemed, at that moment, it was clear that she blamed him for the death of the Calmburry family. Had he killed Mary as Karen had demanded, she would not have run into Morgana's arms and put the witch on the trail of the Calmburrys. Enid left all that unspoken, but I knew what was going through her mind.

But if Gareth hadn't been who he was and hadn't resisted Karen's orders, I, too, would be dead. My fate would have been sealed the moment he found me in Fleetwood. I was the last one who should think poorly of what he had done. Or, rather, had not done. Should a man be faulted for refusing to kill an old woman? Hardly.

"If I've understood it correctly," Jared said to Ruth, as if he had listened in on a conversation inaudible to all others, "it was in your interest for a struggle to arise between Evelyn and Morgana." He gave her a penetrating look before continuing. "Should Evelyn win, your mother's magic would return to you. Should she lose, everything would remain the same." Jared stood up and slowly approached Ruth, stopping in front of her. "At the very least, it was in your interest to get Evelyn to Avalon." He was silent for a long time, staring at Ruth. Then, without turning away from her, he raised his voice. "Claire, come in."

To all our surprise, Claire McAdams, Madison's mother, entered the room. Had she been listening at the door?

I prepared to receive her typically hate-filled look, but instead her gaze was neutral. As if I only played an incidental role in what was to follow.

Claire stepped to Jared's side, raised her hand, and slapped Ruth.

I flinched. "Are you nuts?" I shouted, leaning over the table.

I couldn't believe Jared had allowed this. Didn't he realize Claire's intentions? I could see no sign of surprise on his face. He had actually approved of Claire striking Ruth!

Jared raised his hands. "Listen to what Claire has to say first, Evelyn."

I was baffled. It wasn't long ago that Jared had sent Claire away, but now he was allowing her to barge in here and slap Ruth in the face?

Foaming with rage, Claire turned away from Ruth. She looked at me with glistening eyes.

"This woman used you from the start," she said, lowering her pained eyes. "You and . . . Madison." Her voice broke as she uttered the name of her dead daughter.

Searching for answers, I looked at Claire, then at Ruth, who stared at the floor.

So, Ruth had used me after all! She had followed me into the fog to recover her mother's magic should I vanquish Morgana. She had used the situation to her advantage. But . . . could I reproach her? She had become Morgana's victim as much as I had. Maybe I would have done the same thing in her place. So she followed me; so what? Should I feel used for that? Maybe a little. Though I could also understand why she had done it. But something in Jared's look told me that this was only part of the truth. Why did Claire think Ruth had used Madison? As far as I knew, they hadn't even known each other.

"What does she mean by that?" I asked Ruth.

She was silent.

"Speak!" I demanded, walking over to stand in front of her. "What does Madison have to do with this?"

She looked into my eyes but remained silent. It was Claire who answered. She looked at me, then shifted her ice-cold stare to Ruth.

"You took my daughter to Glastonbury, didn't you?" she said. "You sent her into the fog to lure Morgana." Claire stepped closer, clenched her teeth, and hissed: "You gave her Nimue's amulet."

"What?" I shouted. "No, it cannot be. Madison ripped it from my neck. At the swimming pool." I went around the table.

"Oh, really?" Claire retorted. "Did you see that it was Madison?"

"I'm sure that . . . I saw Madison at the pool, and then—"

"Did you see Madison rip the amulet from your neck?" Claire forcefully interrupted.

I was silent as I struggled with the confusion.

"No," I finally answered truthfully.

"Because it wasn't her." Claire's voice sounded calmer now.

I looked back and forth between Ruth and Claire. Then to Jared. He was focused on both of them.

"Claire's telling the truth," he said. "At least, she believes she is."

I looked at Ruth. She was silent. I just couldn't believe it. It had *really* been her. *She* had ripped the amulet from my neck, then slammed my head as hard as she could against the tiled wall. Had injured me on purpose. In disbelief, I tried to read some reaction, some *emotion* on her face.

"I trusted you!" I shouted, outraged, at Ruth. I didn't know whether to reach for her throat or cry. "I trusted you," I repeated, more to myself than her.

"I'm sorry, Evelyn," Ruth mumbled.

"I'd feel that way if I'd been caught," Colin growled.

I put my hand on my forehead.

"All our talks, everything you said, only served to send me to Avalon? Jared and I almost died—do you understand that?"

"That was never my intention," Ruth objected. "I took the amulet and gave it to the girl, yes. And it was supposed to look as if she'd stolen it from you." Ruth looked at Claire. "She was supposed to lure Morgana out of the fog." She swallowed hard. "I'm terribly sorry about what happened to the girl. I . . . I thought I could take on Morgana myself." Again, she lowered her eyes.

Claire appeared close to fainting. Irvin had to support her while she held her hand over her mouth and attempted to suppress her loud, desperate sobbing—a devastated mother mourning her child. I felt incredibly sorry for her.

Tears ran down Ruth's face. "I hoped my mother's magic would pass to me as soon as I came close to Morgana. I had no idea how powerful she really was. After I saw what she'd done to the girl . . . Madison . . . I knew I couldn't . . ." She swallowed and breathed a deep sigh. "A fight would have been pointless. So I followed her to the clearing."

Images appeared in my mind: my flight from the headquarters, the damnati who had captured me and brought me to Morgana. Jared and Colin storming the clearing and killing scores of damnati. Jared's attempt to save me . . . the pact with Morgana.

"I saw it all," Ruth said. "I knew you were the only one who could do it. I knew you'd be strong enough in Avalon to challenge Morgana. So when these two"—she pointed at Gareth and Ian—"showed up at my home and said you needed help, I took my chance and encouraged you to go to Avalon." I looked at her but she lowered her eyes. "You were the key. Only you could open the portal."

"Bugger! We even drove you there," Colin snorted.

"Then you calmly hid in the forest and waited to see if Morgana would kill me?" Outrage and incomprehension resonated in my words.

"I knew you'd make it, Evelyn." She emphasized the words, as if it made a difference.

"That's interesting," I said sarcastically. Regret was evident in her face.

"It's your fault my daughter's dead!" Claire screamed, as if she feared Ruth might put me into a conciliatory mood. "You won't get away with it!" Claire tore herself from Irvin and charged Ruth with her arms extended as if she was going to strangle her. Ruth reflexively raised her hands in defense. A huge protective shield of orange-glowing light emerged from her palms in a semicircle and hurled Claire into a corner. The massive table tipped on its side, and the chairs, with us sitting on them, slid across the room. Ruth appeared to . . . dissolve into light. She was briefly gone, then rematerialized. I blinked.

Ruth stared at her hands in total shock.

Claire pulled herself up and rushed Ruth again.

Ruth again pushed her palms in Claire's direction—this time more deliberate, more targeted—swept her away, and disappeared into an orange glow.

Jared, back on his feet, charged at the being of light Ruth had become and attempted to grab her, but the light paled and disappeared.

"Jared, do something!" Claire shrieked.

"What the devil?" Colin mumbled.

"You must stop her!" Claire shouted.

Jared stood where Ruth had dissolved, then turned around. "She's gone," he said, and came over to me and helped me up. "Everything okay?"

I nodded and brushed the splinters from my clothes.

"No!" Claire protested. "After her! We must get her!"

"And how do you plan on doing that?" Enid asked.

"We . . . I don't know, but . . ." Claire completely lost control. "Madison's death was her fault!"

"Morgana killed Madison," I said. "Not Ruth. I saw it with my own eyes."

"But Ruth put her in that situation!" Claire yelled as if she were the only one who understood what had really happened.

"I'm sorry, Claire," Enid objected, as empathetically as possible, "but Madison made that decision herself. No one forced her to go into the fog."

"You can't be serious! Irvin!" She turned to him, looking for support.

"I'm sorry, Claire." Irvin took his stand. "Our top priority now is finding Morgana."

"What?" She turned to Jared with wide eyes. "Jared, I beg you!"

"Finding Morgana is our top priority," he affirmed. "That's my final word."

The council chamber door opened. I couldn't believe my eyes.

Karen!

"Oh, Jared, my boy!" She hurried to him and tried to hug him as Claire sobbed desperately in the background. Jared extended his arm to stop her.

"You're all right," Karen said, tears flowing down her cheeks. She attempted to duck under Jared's arm. Had I still been in possession of my magic, I would have killed Karen on the spot. Jared gave me a look that told me he'd take care of it.

"Get lost," he said in an ice-cold tone, then switched to a more formal tone. "I banish you for life."

"You . . . what? You're banishing *me*? That's impossible; you can't—"

"I can't?" Jared raised his eyebrows in a threat.

"Jared, don't be ridiculous," Karen objected, smiling, and attempted to stroke his arm. He stepped back. Karen froze. She finally seemed to understand how serious the matter was and that she was lucky to only get away with being banished.

She gulped, then put on a haughty tone. "It's not within your powers to pronounce a banishment against me."

"But it is within mine," Enid said, stepping forward. "I, high priestess of Legatum Merlini, banish you, Karen Mayflower, for life."

Karen stood there, slack-jawed.

"That's not all," Enid continued. "Gareth and I will now accompany you to the police."

Gareth stepped behind Karen and gave Aiden, who wanted to rush to his mother's aid, an authoritative look that tolerated no contradiction, let alone intervention.

"I'll testify against you, Karen," Enid said. "I'll tell them everything I know about the murders of Anna, Benjamin, and Zara Lakewood."

Karen's look turned to contempt. "Ha! You're just trying to exonerate yourself," she pronounced, as if Enid were bluffing. "You've known for years."

"I'm aware of that," Enid answered. "I've been silent far too long."

"Enid," Judith McHallern objected. It was the first time I'd heard her speak. Normally, the old lady only sat, bored, at the table, as if everyone and everything was an annoyance. For her, this objection was something like opening emotional floodgates. Karen gratefully turned to Judith and looked around the room as if seeking another ally. But even Aiden lowered his eyes and stared at the floor.

"Be gone," Jared said. "Be gone, and never show yourself here again."

Karen stared, uncomprehending, at Jared as Gareth ushered her toward the door.

"Let's go," Gareth ordered.

CHAPTER 16

"I don't know about you," Jared said, "but I really need a bath." He somehow managed to slip on his slanted smile.

"That almost sounds like an invitation," I replied, grinning back.

"It *is* an invitation, Miss Lakewood," he said. Then, lowering his voice in a dignified way, he added, "Lady of the Lake, Queen of the Water."

I smiled. "Right now, I'm just Evelyn."

"Okay, *just Evelyn*, how about it? Will you join me?" His grin broadened as he pulled me to him. I remembered being in the water in the grotto. Heat instantly flowed through me.

"Sure," I squeaked, swallowing the nervous tremor in my voice. Would it be different now that I'd lost my magic? Would I perhaps . . . feel *different* to him? Would it still be good enough for him?

As Jared let water into the bathtub, I looked at myself in the mirror. *Holy shit! Worn* came to mind. I didn't have injuries, not even a scratch—the water from the source had seen to that. Still, I looked pretty beat. There were deep shadows under my tired eyes—how long had it been since I'd had a good sleep? My clothes were dirty. Dried festival mud was all over my body. Clumps were in my hair.

Jared stepped behind me and put his hands on my hips. He didn't look any better. It was odd that I only noticed now. His arms were mud-encrusted, his face smeared with dirt. We were such an absurd sight that I laughed. How had the others managed to stay so serious the whole time? We looked like we'd completed the Tough Mudder in record time. Jared grinned in the mirror and kissed me on the side of my neck.

"It's about time we washed you," he said in a deep voice, and lifted me up. I swallowed. My whole body was tingling with anticipation. I clasped my arms around Jared's neck. He was shirtless.

"You're at least as dirty as I am," I countered. "Maybe we should shower."

"You want the whole package," he teased.

"Jared!" I shot back. He carried me to the shower, turned on the water, and set me down.

"Jared, no," I protested. "My clothes!" But he silenced me with a warm kiss. The water flowed along our entwined bodies, washing the mud, pain, exertion, and exhaustion away. Jared undressed himself, then helped me out of my soaking clothes, before gently lathering me in soap from top to bottom. When we were finally clean, he turned off the water, lifted me up, carried me to the bathtub, and gently set me down. The water overflowed as Jared bent over me. His lips trembled as he pressed them against mine. His hands started to glow as they wandered along my legs, brushed over my belly, and gently massaged my breasts.

His hands. His lips. His skin. I felt his magic. He was everywhere. He engulfed me and enclosed me completely. I pulled him to me and wouldn't let him go.

***

I awoke in bed twelve hours later. I stayed still and enjoyed the lingering warmth. We hadn't slept well for days, and were so tired we'd sunk into a deep sleep. I smiled. Last night had been incredible. We couldn't get enough of each other. If we hadn't been so tired, we wouldn't have stopped touching each other.

I tried to orient myself. My head lay on Jared's chest as it rose and fell. I supported myself on my elbows and stared into his sleeping face. As if he felt he was being watched, he opened his right eye.

"Good morning," I said.

"Good morning," he mumbled. "I hope I'm not dreaming."

"You're not," I answered, smiling.

He started up with a grin, grabbed me, and rolled us over. We started where we'd stopped the night before.

***

Breakfast consisted of scrambled eggs, toast, butter, and black tea. I was hungry as a wolf and loaded up my plate. Jared grinned.

"What?" I said with a full mouth. "I'm starving."

"Clearly." He laughed and loaded his plate more than I ever could have. "I'm starving," he joked.

"Good morning." Irvin sat down with us, opening a newspaper.

Enid was still at the police station. Colin had spent the night with Sally and had not returned.

"Where shall we start the search?" I asked, wiping my mouth with a napkin.

Jared thought for a moment. "We have to put ourselves in her shoes. What would you do if you were Morgana?"

"Hmmm," I said. "I don't think she'll let the matter rest."

"I don't think so, either. She'll try to regain Avalon."

"She's probably still very weak. So she'll lay low to recover her strength."

Jared nodded. "She's also lost her army."

"Yeah, she'll probably try to find some new followers. Only the worst people are good for that."

"So the question is, where are the evilest people?"

"According to police statistics, London has the most crime," Irvin said. "Maybe that's where we should start."

"Sounds plausible," I said, "but London's huge. How would we find her there? Providing she's even in London."

"Well, I know some people who might be able to help us."

"Members of the Order?" Jared asked.

Irvin nodded and rose. "I'll make some calls," he said, leaving the dining hall. At the door he almost bumped into Colin, who was grinning like the Cheshire cat.

"What's with him?" Colin asked, pointing at Irvin.

"Very busy," I said. "How's Sally?"

"I'm supposed to relay her greetings."

"Is she still upset with me?"

Colin sat down and locked his hands behind his head. "I saw to it that she was relaxed," he said and winked.

I rolled my eyes.

"Did you initiate her?" Jared asked.

Colin shook his head. "As long as Morgana's out there, Sally isn't safe."

"I guess you're right about that." I frowned. "Say, what day is it? I've completely lost track of time."

Colin glanced at his phone. "Um . . . Monday. Why?"

I shrugged. "Don't know. But, like, shouldn't we do something normal again?"

Jared laughed. "You're probably right. That or we could wander the country with a freak show."

Colin laughed. "You'd be the main attraction. Jared Calmburry: the Boy on Fire."

I snorted, and my tea went down my windpipe.

"Okay, serious now," Jared said. "As long as we don't know where Morgana is, there's really nothing we can do here."

"What time is it?" I asked.

"Nine-thirty. Do you really want to do something?" Jared asked. "We could have lunch in town."

"Why not? I haven't seen Sally for an eternity. I miss her."

***

Since Gareth hadn't returned, Ian accompanied us into Oxford. Irvin insisted. He didn't want to let us go unprotected, which was silly because Jared was far stronger than Morgana right now.

I bubbled with joy once the drive was finally over. I was about to see Sally again. We hadn't told her. I wanted to surprise her, and Colin had promised to play along. She was sitting alone at a table in the restaurant, poking at her food, when I came up behind her.

"Hi," I said, and a smile spread across my face.

Sally turned, eyes wide in surprise. "Evelyn!" she cried. She jumped up, bumped the table, and spilled soup on the man at the next one.

"Ow!" he screamed. Then he put on a sour face and slid his chair over. He calmed down when Jared put his hand on the guy's shoulder and apologized.

Sally threw her arms around me.

"I missed you so much," I whispered into her ear, and then pressed a big kiss on her cheek.

"Are you well?" she asked as we all sat down.

"Couldn't be better," I answered, grasping Jared's hand.

"You, too?" she asked Jared. "Those two said you were in trouble."

Jared nodded. "Yes, I'm well, too."

"I'm also well," Colin said. He sat beside Sally and ran his hand under her shirt.

"Stop it." She slapped his hand.

While we ate, Sally told us what we'd missed. We listened and laughed. Then talk turned to Felix.

"The police still haven't found him. That's the number one topic around here."

"I don't think they'll find him," I said, and tried to tell her with my eyes that we didn't need to worry about him anymore.

She frowned, gave me a probing look, then nodded. "I guess you'll let me know more later." This sounded more like a question than a statement. I only looked at her. One word could be a word too much. Any word could endanger Sally. The less she knew, the safer she was.

I couldn't help but look over the many people in the restaurant. All these people were clueless. They knew nothing of things happening right before their eyes, day after day. They drifted, untroubled, through their lives. Racked their brains about exams, parties, careers, not even sensing what creatures roamed this earth and what they were capable of.

Yet, looking at my fellow diners, I slowly decided that ignorance might be bliss. Surely not for me. I had searched for answers all my life. Only now did everything fit together and make sense. But for those who were able to grow up sheltered in the bosoms of their families, it would amount to the destruction of their worldview if they ever found out how much evil there was around them.

After all that had happened, it felt strange to sit in a plain, ordinary restaurant, yet it felt good to find some normalcy.

All in all, I felt fine. Especially with Jared next to me and Sally across the table.

"Man"—she shook her head—"you guys are full of secrets."

Jared took that as a cue to give us some time by ourselves. He clapped Colin on the shoulder and asked if he wanted to come along and run an errand.

"It's wonderful to have you back," Sally said and pressed my hand. Whenever I looked at her, she beamed at me. It was beautiful to have her close by.

I was so tempted to tell her what I'd experienced—because I wanted my friend to be part of my life and needed her feedback. But I remained steadfast. Maybe when all this was over and Morgana had been defeated and there was no more danger, but only maybe, we'd initiate her. In the end, that would be Colin's decision.

***

"And?" Sally asked, as we packed up our things. "Shall we go for a drink later? I'm buying."

"I don't know. Have you asked Colin?"

"Asked Colin? Do you think I need his permission?"

"No, I didn't mean it that way. It's just that—"

"Is *that* starting again?" Sally asked.

"It's not over yet. We still have to be careful, you know."

"Really? You disappear for half an eternity and don't even want to go for a drink with your bestie?"

"It's not that simple."

"Yes, it *is* that simple. Do you want to do something together or not?"

"Of course I do."

"Good, then let's meet around eight at Berry's," she said, and triumphantly charged off.

***

"We're going to Berry's at eight with Sally," I announced when I got into the car.

Colin turned to me. "You don't say. I didn't know about that."

"Now you do."

"Do you think that's a good idea?" Jared asked.

"I didn't have a choice. She totally ambushed me."

Jared reflected. Then he shrugged. "Colin, the ball's in your court."

Colin thought it over. "Why not?" he finally decided. "Morgana won't be stupid enough to come into the lion's den." He grinned. "If she knows what's good for her, she'll keep the hell away from us."

Ian started the engine and drove off.

***

"Enid, you're back again?" I asked when I saw her on the way to my room. "How did it go?"

"Well, I have to be off again right away. I'm only here to pick up a few documents for the police." It was clear she was very tense.

"Proof?"

She nodded.

"Is everything okay?" I asked.

"Yes," she said, nodding. "They just want to know everything in detail."

"What does that mean?"

She took a deep breath. "Karen was right when she said I'd incriminate myself," she finally admitted.

"If that's so, I'll come along and testify on your behalf. I—"

"No. I did it to myself. Now I must come clean. Don't worry about me, Evelyn."

"Are you sure?"

She nodded and stroked my cheek. "I regret that I kept silent for so long."

"There you are!" Colin called. "I've been looking for you everywhere."

"See you later," Enid said and walked away.

"Later, and good luck!"

Colin looked, astonished, at Enid. "She's back already?"

"No, she's just picking something up. Why were you looking for me?"

"Well, I thought a little training couldn't hurt. And I'm really hot for a good spanking from the Lady of the Lake."

"Is that so?" I crossed my arms over my chest. "I'd be delighted to assist."

"Training room, twenty minutes." He went off, chuckling.

***

After I'd changed, I wondered if Enid's nine-year-old daughter, Jessica, would want to watch Colin and me mix it up a bit. Of course, Colin was physically superior, but I'd gathered combat experience and learned a few tricks recently.

"Are you coming along?" I asked Jared, who'd taken a short nap.

"Wouldn't miss it for the world," he said with a grin.

"You should put on some pants," I said with a twinkle, pointing at his boxers. "I'll get Jessie—we'll meet in the training room."

***

The door to Enid and Jessica's room was open a gap. I put my hand on the doorknob but stopped when I heard Enid speaking quietly to someone. I looked in—and was a little surprised to see Irvin take Enid's face into his hands and kiss her gently.

"Don't worry," he said, brushing his fingers through her hair. "You have nothing to fear."

I cleared my throat. They turned around with a start.

"Evelyn," Enid said, her voice a touch too high.

"Please excuse me for bursting in like this. I'm looking for Jessie. Colin's giving me a training session, and I thought she might want to watch."

"Jessie . . . um," Enid said, embarrassed. "I think she's in the kitchen with Hilda."

"Okay, thanks." I turned, stopped, and turned back toward them.

"It's lovely seeing the two of you like this," I said, then walked off.

***

Jessie was overjoyed when I picked her up at the kitchen.

"Will Jared be there, too?" she asked excitedly.

I nodded. When we got to the training room, she joined Jared, and they eagerly looked on.

"Let's see what you learned," Colin challenged me.

"Okay. But this time, you attack me."

"As you wish." Colin was happy to oblige. "Ready?"

"Always."

Without a warning, he punched at me. I saw it coming, grabbed his wrist, and twisted his arm behind his back.

"Ah!" he cried, making Jared and Jessie laugh.

"Again," Colin demanded when I'd let go.

"As you wish." I focused on him. He'd be more careful this time.

He moved so fast I didn't stand a chance. I lay on my belly on the mat without an inkling of how he'd done it.

"Evelyn!" Jessica screamed with wide-open baby-doll blue eyes. Jared clenched his teeth hard.

"Everything's okay," I moaned to calm them down. But it wasn't. I couldn't move or feel my legs. My arm was stinging. I was struggling for air when suddenly an unpleasant tingling spread through my limbs, a sensation like going from cold to hot. Then feeling slowly returned. I tried to move my legs, then my toes. They worked. Man, had that ever given me a scare. I needed a few more seconds, but Colin helped me up.

"How did you do that?" I asked.

"That's Kyūsho Jitsu," he answered, almost proudly. "The art of vital points."

"How does it work?"

"Certain nerve pressure points are anatomically exposed on the body's surface. They can be stimulated with simple pressure. Acupuncture and other methods in Chinese medicine are based on this principle." He smiled. "It can also be used in combat. You focus on nerve pathways, especially nerve endings and crossings of nerve tracts, found close to the surface. They're distributed all over the body. Stimulation of these points by rubbing, pressing, or striking leads to a reflexive action resulting in pain, paralysis, or unconsciousness."

"Aha," I said, wiggling my toes again. "Where are these points?"

He took my arm and stroked its inside from the shoulder to the elbow.

"Here, for example." He pressed his thumb gently on a point near my elbow. The tingling immediately started again and spread over my entire arm. "The same goes for directed blows to the tip or side of the chin and the solar plexus."

I frowned. "That's it? I only need to hit that point to incapacitate my opponent or knock him unconscious? Why didn't you teach me this before?"

"It's not quite that simple. It takes a lot of practice."

"Then let's practice," I said, determined. We only stopped when my whole body had been afflicted with a numb, tingling sensation that felt like a thousand ants climbing all over me.

"Okay, that's enough," I decided. "What time is it?"

"Just after seven," Jared answered, coming over to me. He almost hadn't been able to bear watching as Colin repeatedly sent me to the mat. But that was the deal. He could watch as long as he didn't intervene.

"Already?" Colin asked. "I'll go pick up Sally. See you at Berry's."

***

Berry's was just as I remembered it. It hadn't been long since I was last there, but it had seemed infinitely far away.

"There they are," Jared said. He rolled his eyes and led me to the dark little wood table where Sally and Colin were making out.

"Why don't they just do it on the table?" I whispered to Jared. He gave a cheery, unrestrained laugh, the kind I hadn't heard from him in a while. It filled me with warmth, and I held his arm. "I love you!" I said. "It's so wonderful to see you laugh."

I gave him a long kiss, then pushed Sally's shoulder. "So, what's going on? Are you buying us a round or not?"

CHAPTER 17

"Jared." I heard Colin's voice and opened my eyes. It was the middle of the night, and we had been sleeping.

"Jared, wake up." Colin shook Jared.

"What's the matter?" Jared asked, sitting up.

"I think a damnatus followed us."

"What?"

"When I took Sally home."

"Are you sure?" Jared was suddenly wide awake. As was I.

"Not totally sure. But somebody followed us. I took Sally in and searched the area."

"Did you see anybody?" I asked.

"No. But I'm sure someone was there. I felt it."

Jared relaxed a little. "Colin, after what you saw in the fog, it's normal that you'd be worried about Sally."

"Don't you believe me?"

"Of course I believe you. If you want, we can look for him right now."

Colin reflected for a moment. "No," he finally said. "I looked all over. He's long gone by now."

Jared reached for his phone on the nightstand. "I'll call Ian," he said. "He'll watch Sally's house."

"No," Colin said. "I'll drive back to her and stay the night. I just . . . wanted to let you know."

"Don't worry," I said, stroking Colin's arm.

He nodded but still seemed a little rattled. "Time to find the witch," he muttered. Nothing more needed to be said.

***

The next day, we devoted our afternoon to research. Colin, Jared, and I retreated to the relic room. Colin took Excalibur from the glass case and practiced with it while Jared and I buried ourselves in books searching for evidence of Morgana. I was curled up on the big leather couch, snuggled against Jared, when Irvin rushed in.

"We have a clue. She's been seen."

"Where?" Jared asked.

"The City," Irvin said, out of breath. "Pack your things. We're leaving."

"Now?" Colin asked, lowering the mighty sword.

"Yes, now. How fast can you be ready?" Irvin's probing look was directed at me. As if it's a law of nature that women take longer to pack than men.

"Oh, twenty minutes, I'd guess," was my answer.

Irvin raised his eyebrows. "Really?"

"Yes, really," I said, somewhat sourly.

"But—" Colin protested. He only just had Sally back and was now supposed to leave her again.

"No buts," Irvin shut him down. "Move it. Enid and Gareth will follow as soon as they can."

***

I'd been ready for a while when Irvin showed up, exhausted, in the underground garage.

"Can we get started?" I joked.

He nodded, stored his travel bag in the boot, and slid into the passenger seat. Colin drove, and Jared and I cuddled in the back of the luxurious Mercedes E-Class.

The drive from Oxford to London took less than two hours. It led past open fields, rows of townhouses, and large factories. We needed another half hour to get to the city center.

Colin turned onto Wood Street and parked in front of the police station. Irvin announced us at the gate. A friendly blonde led us to an office with a silver sign on the door proclaiming "Detective Sergeant Adam Parker."

Irvin asked us to wait in the hall when the door opened and he entered. A good-looking man in his midthirties with unusually dense dark hair greeted him. The detective wore a gray suit with a loose tie. He nodded to the rest of us as Irvin made a sweeping gesture toward us.

"Evelyn Lakewood, Jared Calmburry, Colin Sullivan—this is Adam Parker," Irvin introduced us. "Detective sergeant with the City of London Police."

"Lovely to meet you, Detective," I said.

"My pleasure, Miss Lakewood."

I gave him my hand. "Ah, a firm handshake," he noticed with a smile. "I appreciate that in a woman."

Jared's face was impenetrable. When he shook Parker's hand, Parker went a little red in the face and wobbled slightly.

Jared got straight to the point. "Irvin said you had something we should look at." I couldn't suppress my grin.

"Yes," Detective Parker said in the same kind of tone my sister had used when she'd been on duty. "Follow me."

Jared took my hand. I glanced at him sideways and raised an eyebrow.

"You have no idea what oscillations this guy had in his energy field when he saw you," Jared whispered.

Parker led us into a small, windowless room where a presentation had been prepared. A still from a surveillance camera showed two men in a dark alley. The caption in the lower right noted that the scene had been recorded the previous night at 2:39 a.m.

"This should interest you," Parker promised, touching "Play." I stared intently at the monitor. A drug deal seemed to be going down. There was a bit of back and forth, but then something went wrong. The two started to argue. There was a tussle. A shining object suddenly gleamed on the black-and-white monitor. The image was strongly pixelated but still recognizable: a knife. It flashed up, then disappeared. The victim dropped to the ground. The knife's handle cast a shadow as it stuck in his chest.

The first man hastily searched the dying man's clothing. He pulled out two bags, then pocketed them before disappearing. He left the knife in the victim's chest. Nothing happened for a while.

"What?" Colin said.

"Just wait," Parker said, "and take a close look."

A few seconds later, another figure arrived—masked and wearing a black hood, but judging from the body outline, it was a woman. A well-built one, too. She went to the injured man, kneeled beside him, and brushed her fingers over his face. Her mouth moved; she was speaking to him. He nodded. Then his mouth moved, too. The woman began to smile, and then she rose. She spread her arms and pointed her fingertips at the prone figure. His body jerked. The knife pushed out of his chest and fell to the ground. Then the man's body stretched and bent at an impossible angle. It looked as if every bone in his body would break. He shook and twisted like a dying worm. Suddenly, he became rigid. The woman lowered her hands, then raised her right hand again, the palm facing upward. The man's stiff body rose, floated, turned in the air, and was shaken again by a quaking tremble. It took a long time but became more intense, faster. I blinked. Was I seeing right? A second figure detached from the man's body—was literally shaken from it. In size and stature, it was an exact copy of the man, with one difference. I wasn't sure about the quality of the image, but the second figure seemed strangely transparent, like a shadow. The man's body shook, wound, and bent, apparently suffering hellish pain, until the translucent shape completely detached.

Suddenly, it was over. There was complete calm in the scene on the monitor. The man floated, motionless, in the air, with the shadow copy beside him. The woman extended her fingertips, and the shadow moved toward her. Then she absorbed it—I was sure it was the man's soul—with her fingertips. She tilted her head back and slowly lowered her hand. The man got on his feet, looked at the woman for a long moment, then kneeled before her. She spoke to him again. Then he spoke. Always in the same interval, as if he was repeating her words. As if he . . . was taking an oath. Satisfied, the woman nodded and walked away. The man rose and followed her.

Detective Parker pressed "Stop" and gave us a look as if to say: *Well, I told you so.*

The door opened, and the hall lights briefly blinded me. Gareth entered, with Enid and Ian close behind.

"Adam." Gareth greeted the detective with a nod.

"Gareth." Parker nodded back.

We watched the surveillance recording again.

"Who knows about this?" Gareth asked.

"Just me and Constable Bailey."

"Do we have anything to worry about with him?"

Parker shook his head. "Bailey isn't the kind of guy who worries about much."

Colin and I exchanged a skeptical look.

"That means he's a drinker," Jared explained.

"Where did this happen?" Gareth stepped closer to the screen.

"Centre Point," Parker answered.

"That's a high rise at the center of the city, isn't it?" Jared asked.

Parker nodded.

"Earnshaw Street," Gareth determined after closely inspecting the still. "Right behind Centre Point." He turned around. "A hotspot for drug deals. Full of surveillance cameras. Can you see where she went?"

"To the southwest, toward Hyde Park, then her trail disappears."

"When was that?

"About four thirty this morning."

Gareth looked at his watch. "Well over fifteen hours ago," he said, then looked up. "Ian and I will look around Hyde Park."

Ian, always short on words, briefly nodded from his guard-like position by the door.

"Adam, can you spare a man?"

Parker nodded. "Preferably Bailey, he already knows the tape."

Gareth hesitated.

"He never drinks on duty," Parker assured him.

"What are we going to do?" Colin asked.

"You'll go to the safe house on Bishop's Park Road. They're already waiting for you there. I'll contact you as soon as I know more."

"Out of the question," Jared answered, with determination in his voice. "Morgana's nearby. I'm not going to sit around in some fat-cat mansion twiddling my thumbs."

"I'll check out the situation first," Gareth interjected. "You shouldn't expose yourself unnecessarily."

"Expose myself to what, danger?" Jared said, as if he hadn't understood right. "I'm the only one who can take her on! Your gun won't do you much good against her."

Enid intervened. "Jared, don't you think it'd be better if Gareth first—"

Jared cut her off. "No. Evelyn, go with Enid to the safe house. Pick a nice room. We may be here for a few days."

I opened my mouth to protest, but Jared leaned over and whispered, "You haven't got your powers anymore, remember that. I wouldn't be able to let you out of my sight for a second. You know what happened the last time you met her without magic. That can't happen again."

I opened my mouth again but closed it. He was right. Just then, I hated being a weak, useless human!

Jared kissed me.

"I'd like it if someone would accompany you. Colin?" Jared asked.

"Sorry, buddy. Not a chance. I'm not staying behind again and missing all the action."

"I'd be happy to drive the two ladies," Parker offered.

Jared's countenance darkened. He gave the detective a long, warning look.

"Jared, he's a member of Legatum Merlini," Enid said. "We can trust him."

"Very well," Jared acquiesced "You'll take Evelyn and Enid to the safe house. By the shortest route possible."

CHAPTER 18

"This is one of the richest districts in London," Detective Parker explained. He turned onto Fulham Palace Road and drove to Bishop's Park Road. Mansions with old trees and the most modern security systems lined the broad street. Some were in the splendid Victorian style of the late nineteenth century, others in the plain elegance of modern glass and concrete. The owners lived behind their wrought-iron gates, close to London's core, in the kind of seclusion only great wealth allows. Luxury rides lined both sides of the street. The parking spaces alone must have cost a fortune.

Parker turned into a driveway, stopped at a gate, and spoke to a security guard through an intercom. The gate swung open, and he drove up the driveway. Gray gravel crunched under the tires. The Victorian mansion was almost as large as the headquarters of Legatum Merlini, but in contrast to that medieval structure, this house appeared almost playful with all its stucco and countless ornaments. One side was completely overgrown with ivy, as if the house was a kind of sleeping beauty. As we got out of the car, we saw a familiar face. Judith

McHallern was coming out the door. Why hadn't anyone told me this was her house?

The widow appeared very fragile as she climbed down the stairs. She had tied her gray hair in an elegant bun, and her ankle-length dress somehow suited the house.

"Miss Lakewood," she coldly greeted me, pressing my hand. "Enid."

"Nice to see you, Judith."

"Where are Jared and Colin?"

"With Gareth. They're following a lead."

Judith turned and went back into the house. She didn't ask us in, but we nevertheless followed her into the large entrance hall. Dark wood lined the inside of the mansion. A dusty chandelier hung from the ceiling. Curved stairs with ornate rails led upward on both sides of the foyer.

"You'll find your bedrooms up the stairs to the right," Judith said, without looking at us. "You can pick a room there."

Enid gave me an apologetic look for Judith's rude behavior.

"You're still holding it against me that I went to the police because of Karen?" Enid asked so loudly that the old lady couldn't miss it.

Judith lifted her chin. "Loyalty was one of the finest virtues of Legatum Merlini in the good old days."

"Loyalty?" I asked, riled. "What about my family?"

"Sometimes you have to do what you have to do." Her answer was ice cold. She walked away without dignifying us with another glance.

"I beg your pardon?" I was about to go after her.

"Evelyn, let it be." Enid put her hand on my shoulder. "There's no point in arguing with her. She's a stubborn old woman who'll spend the rest of her days mourning the passing of the *good old days*."

She lifted my travel bag and held it out to me. "Come on." She nodded toward the staircase.

I hesitated, then followed Enid upstairs.

"Good-bye."

Detective Parker. I'd completely forgotten about him. He was standing at the entrance.

"Good-bye," I returned.

"Should you need something"—he took his wallet out, pulled a little white card from it, and gave it to me—"just ring me."

I took his business card. "Oh yes. Thank you."

Parker winked, then turned and left.

***

I took the first room I came across. It had dark wood paneling, like the rest of the house, but was somewhat brightened by lighter materials. There was easily enough room for Jared and me in the huge canopy bed. I hoped we wouldn't have to importune Judith's *hospitality* for too long, so I didn't unpack my bag. I was just placing my toiletry kit on the shelf of the adjoining bathroom when my phone rang.

"Evelyn," Sally said, her voice unusually serious. "Can we meet? I really need to tell you something. And I can't get hold of Colin. Do you know where he is?"

"Ah, yes," I answered. "London."

"What's he doing in London?"

"We're all in London, actually."

"And nobody told me? Are you trying to get rid of me?" Her indignation was palpable.

"We're not here for fun."

She groaned. "Is this one of those 'I'd love to talk about it but can't' things again? Grand!"

She was silent for a moment. I could visualize her sulking.

"When will you be back? It's *really* important."

"Soon." At least, that's what we hoped.

"And when is *soon*?"

"I'm not sure—maybe a few days."

"Swell!"

"Can't you tell me on the phone?"

"No!"

"I'll ring you as soon as we're back, okay?"

She didn't say anything.

"And then everything will be like before, I promise."

"Don't promise something unless you can keep it." Sally grumbled, then snorted. "Whatever. Call me when you're back."

"Will do."

"Evelyn."

"Yes?"

"Take care of yourself."

***

Some time later, a knock on the door woke me.

"Yes?"

Enid stuck her head into the room. "Dinner."

"They're not back yet?"

She shook her head.

"Okay. I'm coming."

I looked around the dining room and wondered if half the rain forest had been cut down to build this house. Polished mahogany was everywhere: floor, walls, tables, chairs—everywhere. Uniformed domestics—all of pension age—fussed back and forth between the kitchen and dining room. They poured wine into crystal glasses, arranged chairs, and finally served dinner under silver covers, which the domestics lifted in a kind of choreography. I lost my appetite when I saw liver with onions and something that looked already half-digested. I stared at the polished cutlery.

"Something wrong?" Judith asked, making it sound like a challenge.

Rage boiled inside me. I was walking a fine line between letting her talk and jumping across the table for her throat because of the quip she'd made about the murder of my parents and sister. She was not at fault for my family's death. Enid had assured me Karen was solely responsible. No, Judith was an old woman mourning the past. I decided it would be best if I didn't bother.

"No, everything's fine. Liver just isn't one of my favorites."

"I'd be delighted to make you an omelet, miss," a rotund maid offered. "I'll have it done in no time."

Judith gave the maid a devastating look.

"Please, don't trouble yourself on my behalf."

"Oh nonsense," the maid said. "You must eat. You're much too thin." She disappeared into the kitchen and returned in ten minutes with the best omelet I'd ever had. The trifle served as dessert was also rather good—quite in contrast to the conversation at the table, which was limited to "Please pass the salt," or, directed at the staff, "Thank you, you may clear the table now." Oh yes, and, of course, "Good night, ladies," when Judith left the room and declared the evening over. I rolled my eyes and looked at my phone.

"Anything new?" Enid asked.

I shook my head. "I'm starting to worry."

"I'm sure everything's fine." But even she sounded uncertain and gazed into space. "Jessie's about to go to bed. I want to Skype her and say good night. Will you manage?"

I nodded. "I'll read a little more in Ruth's Nimue book. Say hello to the tyke for me, okay?"

"Will do."

***

A gentle kiss brushed my lips. I started up.

"Keep sleeping," Jared said.

"Jared! Is everything okay? What time is it?"

"Two thirty. Sorry." He took off his jeans and got in bed.

"Did you find her?"

"No. Keep sleeping. We'll talk about it in the morning."

"Okay."

Jared was gone when I woke again. I sat up and rubbed my eyes. A note in Jared's handwriting lay on the nightstand.

There's a new lead.

A surveillance camera caught Morgana at the airport.

Don't wait for me.

I love you!

Great, I thought. Another day in the delightful company of *Miss Daisy*. Worse still, I found out at breakfast that Enid had left for Oxford to "handle a few matters." Whatever that meant.

I was bored stiff all day. I went through Ruth's book without discovering any new insights. There was no TV or DVD player. Not even a radio.

"Does the house have a library?" I asked one of the kitchen staff during lunch, which I ate alone in the kitchen. The icy silence at breakfast had not called for a sequel.

"Certainly," she answered. "However, it's attached to Mrs. McHallern's private quarters. Visitors aren't permitted access."

"Private quarters?" I repeated in disbelief. Had I traveled back to the nineteenth century?

The maid nodded, then went back to dusting.

"Oh. So I'm supposed to eat all day and loaf about?"

"I'm sorry, miss. Please discuss it with Mrs. McHallern."

I suppressed another comment. It wasn't the maid's fault, but I felt so frustrated. Jared was hunting for Morgana while I sat here killing time and hoping he'd return safe and sound. All that in the company of an old woman who harbored an undisguised dislike for me. To top it all off, it was the most beautiful early summer weather, but I was strictly forbidden from going outside. It was driving me mad!

Shortly before supper, I was so bored I dared to enter Judith's *private quarters* and sneak into the library. It wasn't what I'd hoped for, but all in all it was well stocked. All the classics were there, from Shakespeare, Tolstoy, and Jules Verne to Hemingway and Jane Austen. The whole canon. But that wasn't what I was looking for. I browsed a little, read bits from two or three books, then went back to my room in the hope that Jared would return.

CHAPTER 19

London by day and London by night are two completely different places. The contrast couldn't be starker. When the sun sets over the city and darkness takes hold of the streets, shadow-dwellers crawl out from their holes. Where crowds bustle during the day, dubious characters lurk in dark corners at night—making it easy for Morgana to find new recruits for her army of the damned. As far as we knew, this was her method: Every night she went out, waited for a rotten person to kill another, and then promised the wretch safety from damnation in exchange for his soul if he pledged servitude to her for the remainder of his miserable existence. She'd been caught twice on surveillance cameras while transforming a dying man into a damnatus. Twice. Two nights in a row. But we hadn't gotten any further.

Only a few minutes passed between the recording at Heathrow Airport and our arrival. We searched the entire area but found nothing. How did she manage to disappear so quickly? I didn't get it. From what we knew, only light magic gave a being the ability to appear and disappear at will. This magic was no longer available to Morgana; Ruth had gotten it back. Yet this was like catching a ghost.

Where are you hiding, witch?

The hunt drove me to the edge of madness. I couldn't think of anything else. Couldn't sleep, couldn't eat. Couldn't even think clearly. I had to find her at any cost. Only then would Evelyn be safe.

***

It was my fault she was in danger. A part of me wished we'd never met. She'd have been safe in Fleetwood. She had nothing to fear protected by Nimue's amulet. But the other part, my egotistical self, would have done it all over again. Colin said she had changed me, opened my heart. Made me a better person. I smiled. Well, that was true. I wanted to be a better person for her sake. I loved her more than I would have thought possible.

Dozens of girls had shared my bed. A few hours of warmth, a few hours of affection. But by morning I couldn't wait to be rid of them. The unavoidable "why didn't you call" looks I would have to deal with for weeks after only irritated me. Madison had been the worst of all. I wasn't able to simply avoid her as I had the others. She was a member of the Order. We crossed paths almost daily. Let alone Claire, who already imagined me as her *son-in-law*. Unbearable.

Pretty much sheltered from the real world by Karen, I drifted along. Went from one fling to another, trying to feel *something*—even if just for a moment. But I was never happy. Something was always missing. Something basic. For a long time, I thought it had something to do with the death of my family. Grieving did contribute its share. But I only knew what I was looking for when I saw Evelyn: It was *her*. I'd been searching for her my entire life without knowing it. And I finally found her. Or rather, she found me. Evelyn shot into my life like a comet and changed everything.

I didn't know what love was until I met her. She was the most beautiful girl I'd ever seen—no contest. Even if I had wanted to, I wouldn't have been able to get away from her. She cast her spell on me and wouldn't let go. When I closed my eyes, I saw her. In Avalon—how she'd opposed Morgana. Strong and beautiful like a queen, even a goddess. As long as I lived, I'd never forget that sight. She was unbelievable. How fast she'd learned to control her magic. She did in a few hours what took me years. It was her destiny. I'd see to it that she'd return. Back to the place of her destiny. Back to Avalon.

Morgana would die. There was no other way. I had to kill her. For my family. For me. For Evelyn. But time wasn't on our side. Morgana was becoming stronger every day.

***

"Jared, where to now?" Colin asked. He wore a ridiculously long black coat, making him look as if he'd just been sprung from the Matrix. But it was the only piece of clothing that allowed him to keep Excalibur on him without frightening people into calling the police because they thought the Highlander had descended from the Far North to pass judgment on them.

"Left, Neo."

Colin grinned, pulled dark sunglasses from his pocket, slipped them on, and cried out: "I am The One!"

"Will you two stop that nonsense?" Irvin scolded us as if we were twelve-year-olds.

"Calm down, old man," Colin said, patting him on the shoulder.

I laughed. "Have you been carrying those around all day just for this?"

"Worth it, wasn't it?" Colin put the glasses back in his pocket. "Well, you heard Harry Potter. To the left."

We turned onto a broader street. The booming bass from a club reverberated over the cobblestones. A queue, corralled by a velvet rope, had formed under the glowing neon letters "B4." The queue extended around the block. I stopped.

"Do you want to go in?" Colin asked.

"I sense damnatus energy," I answered. "You three stay here. They'll never let all five of us in."

Irvin, Gareth, and Ian stayed back, a little confused. Colin followed me. I walked past the queue despite loud protests and pressed two hundred quid into the hand of the broad-shouldered bouncer. He nodded, unhitched the rope, and waved us through.

The club was fairly full, but we could still move from one end to the other without much of a problem. I was gradually getting better at focusing on the energy of one or a few individuals in a crowd.

It didn't take long to find the damnati. There were two of them, freshly transformed. A few pale pink scars on their faces betrayed what they'd become. By tomorrow or the day after, they wouldn't be able to move freely in public. Their bodies would soon begin to rot. Like all damnati, they would putrefy alive. That was the price of their unholy existence. But no one seemed to have told these two, as they were in a festive mood, relaxing against the table on which a waitress was placing a bottle of twenty-year-old single malt along with two glasses. They laughed coarsely and toasted each other. One wore a tailored suit. He must have been a banker or a well-paid attorney in his former life. The other, more a creative type, wore torn jeans and a designer shirt. Both were lean and muscular. Studio muscles—no combat experience. I saw that at a glance. I had no idea what Morgana had caught them doing or who'd killed them, but both were the "I'll take what I want" type.

"Those two?" Colin asked when he noticed I was sizing them up.

I nodded.

Colin took a step toward them. I held him back.

"Too many people. We'll lure them out."

Damnati are stronger than humans, and freshly transformed ones yearn to try out their new powers. Preferably on someone they couldn't have beaten when they were still people. Colin and I would fill that role. We just had to draw their attention. Colin grinned. This was just his style.

"Ten quid says they'll follow me out the back entrance."

"Deal!"

Colin winked, turned, and staggered through the club as if he was totally drunk—straight at the damnati. When he'd nearly gotten there, he started to stumble, banged into their table, and knocked it over.

"Shoooorreey," Colin slurred. He leaned against the damnatus in the suit and wiped his wet hand on the guy's tailored shirt.

"That was a hundred-and-twenty-quid whiskey, asshole!" yelled the banker, who pushed Colin.

"Oh yeah?" Colin licked his fingers. "Itsh reeeally gooood."

"And this is an Armani shirt, ya tosser!"

That was my cue.

"Ish dere a probleeeem?" I asked, putting my arm over the shoulders of the creative-looking one.

"Fuck off!"

"No haaarm done," I said, and patted Colin on the shoulder. "Let's leave them to it, dude."

Colin followed me, staggering, across the dance floor. I took a furtive glance over my shoulder to be sure they were watching us, and then we left through the back entrance. Suit Guy looked at Creative Guy and nodded in our direction. Sure enough, they followed us.

There was only a single light high over the door out back. Otherwise, the alley was completely dark.

"Not so fast," Banker Guy said when he stepped outside, closely followed by his buddy. "You owe me a hundred and twenty for the whiskey and two hundred and thirty for the shirt."

"You won't need a shirt where you're going," I said in a calm voice.

They broke out in laughter.

"You have no idea the trouble you're in, kid," the banker bragged.

Colin opened his coat, pulled out the mighty sword, and jammed it into the ground; it split the concrete.

The damnati exchanged puzzled glances as they realized something was up.

"Where is she?" I asked without any show of emotion.

"Who?" the suit asked cluelessly. He didn't take his eyes off Colin, who, with his coat and sword, looked like he'd come to usher in doomsday.

"Morgana. She who made you what you are."

Their eyes widened with fright.

I raised an eyebrow and spoke slowly. "I'm only going to ask once. If I don't get an answer, my friend is going to cut you in half."

Colin pulled Excalibur from the concrete.

"Where is Morgana?"

"If you think you can frighten us with a *sword*, you're off your rocker, kid. Where did you get that? Pinch it from a medieval fair?" Creative Guy said, approaching us casually.

Colin lifted Excalibur, swung, and severed Creative Guy's head. It rolled across the pavement, eventually coming to a stop several yards away.

Colin breathed in deeply. "The only thing bothersome about killing damnati," he said, walking over to the headless corpse and wiping his blade on its shirt, "is having to get rid of their stinking cadavers. You'd imagine they'd turn to dust, burst into flames, or do something interesting, but no, someone has to clean up the mess."

Banker Guy froze with fear.

"Answer."

"I—I—I have no idea where she is! I swear!"

"When did she transform you?"

"Last night. I—"

"How is she going to contact you?"

"I—I don't know. Please!"

"Is there a meeting place?"

"No. She said she'd find us. We're supposed to be ready when the time comes."

He was telling the truth. I felt it in his energy.

Banker Guy crumpled and began to cry. "I don't know anything more. Please! I swear!"

At moments like this, when a damnatus was kneeling before me like a little pile of misery, pleading for his life or, rather, for what was left of it, I always asked one question. To remind both of us what a damnatus really is.

"How did you die?"

He looked at me, surprised. "What?"

I raised my eyebrows and stared at him.

"I . . . I was . . . poisoned."

"By whom?"

"A woman."

"Why?"

He said nothing, just lowered his head. I had my answer.

"You're a rapist, aren't you?"

He only whimpered. But I didn't sense a trace of regret in his energy. The only person he felt sorry for was himself. Hatred and contempt flared up inside me. That's why I'd asked the question—to extinguish even the slightest hint of pity. These creatures deserved no compassion. They were monsters.

"Kill him," I said, and Colin's sword swooped down.

I pulled out my phone and called Gareth. "Two dead damnati at the back of the club."

CHAPTER 20

The rattle of a belt buckle woke me up.

"Jared?"

"Hey, babe." He crawled under the covers and put his arm around me.

"Did you get her?"

Jared sighed. "No." He kissed me on the cheek. "I'll tell you about it in the morning."

"Okay," I mumbled, placing my hand on his chest. "Nice that you're finally here."

"Go back to sleep, honey." He kissed my forehead and soon fell asleep.

***

When I opened my eyes the next morning and found myself alone again, I was irritated. He'd disappeared two nights in a row. What was Jared thinking, leaving me alone all day with that old hag? I angrily threw the covers aside and leapt to my feet. This just couldn't go on. I decided to call him.

"Babe?" he answered on the second ring.

"Where are you?"

"Speakers' Corner." I heard a loud male voice in the background droning on about the doom of modern civilization.

"Jared, you've barely slept the past two nights. How long do you think you'll last?"

"I have to find her, Evelyn." His tone was appeasing but had a certain bite.

"I know, but I really can't sit around here any longer without doing something. Do you understand?"

"I can't take you with me, you know that. It's too dangerous."

"Jared!" That sounded like Gareth.

"I have to go. We'll talk later."

"Jared—" I said, but he'd already hung up. I clenched my teeth, wanting to hurl my phone against the wall. My anger had not yet dissipated by the time I got dressed. I tromped down the stairs.

"Good morning, Miss Lakewood."

Startled, I stopped on the landing. "Good morning, Mr. Parker," I said, wondering what business the detective had here.

"I thought you might want some company." He looked at me, then at his hands. He had a paper bag and a cardboard tray with two paper cups. The aroma of fresh coffee filled the air.

"Enid told me you were all alone here with Mrs. McHallern." I liked the way he pronounced her name. As if it were an imposition. I had to smile. Let's see how Jared would handle this.

"To be honest, I'm bored to death here."

Detective Parker grinned. "Do you feel like some fresh air?"

"Definitely."

It was so warm outside, I didn't need a jacket.

"Call me Adam, if you wish," he offered.

"Evelyn."

He gave me one of the cups.

"I wasn't sure what kind of coffee you'd like. Is a latte okay?"

"Yes. Thank you."

He smiled again and held open the bag. "You can't go wrong with croissants, right?"

I reached eagerly for one. "Good thinking."

I winked, wondering if I was really winking at him. Hopefully, he wouldn't take it the wrong way. I was simply happy for the diversion. I bit into the croissant, took a sip from my coffee, and enjoyed the sun on my skin. While we sauntered along Bishop's Park Road, I asked myself what Adam knew. Just because someone was a member of Legatum Merlini didn't mean he knew about Jared and Colin. I doubted Adam even knew who Jared was. He hadn't treated him differently from Irvin or Gareth. Then again, he hadn't seemed particularly baffled by what he saw in the surveillance video. This would be tricky, because I had to figure out what Adam knew without giving away too much. It was clear that he knew something.

"How long have you been a member of the Order?" A safe inquiry.

"About twelve years." He slurped from his cup. "I'd just begun service with the City of London Police. Gareth was my partner and trained me, in a manner of speaking." He smiled. "I helped him in a few extra-official matters, and at some point I was officially accepted into Legatum Merlini. With a ceremony and all the bells and whistles. But you know that."

"Not really." I frowned. "To be honest, I'm not even sure I'm a *member* of the Order at all. There certainly wasn't a ceremony for me."

"Oh, really?"

I nodded. I could almost hear Adam's mind working as he turned to me with an insightful look. I was pretty certain he'd come to the wrong conclusion. He had taken me for an ordinary member of the Order, but now he stared at me as if he saw in me what he'd overlooked in Jared. It made sense from his perspective, of course. Jared wanted to protect me at all costs and keep me away from danger. I, on the other hand, whiled away my days behind the closed doors of a safe house.

Adam looked at me almost in awe. Sure thing—he took me for Merlin's last descendant.

Adam swallowed. "Perhaps we should head back," he suggested, desperately trying to maintain a calm tone while probably visualizing what would happen to him if someone found out he was walking around outside with Merlin's supposed heir.

"I don't know who or what you think I am, Adam, but I'm sure you've got it wrong."

He gave me a quizzical look. The poor man looked completely lost. "If we return, I could—"

Suddenly, I was grabbed. Something clawed into my waist from behind and pulled me off my feet.

"Stop!" Adam shouted.

That smell. Damnatus stench. Anger and anticipation rose in me, and a hot shudder ran down my spine. I oriented myself. The beast had thrown me over its shoulder. I swung my legs around, clamped them on both sides of the stinking creature's neck, and squeezed. He gagged, gurgled, and then, trying to free himself, went down. I jumped off at the right moment, grabbed his arm, and twisted it until I heard a shoulder joint pop.

"Really? You're attacking me? In broad daylight?" I asked, twisting the arm even farther. The damnatus screamed and squirmed on the pavement like a run-over animal. "Where is she?" I demanded. I loosened my grip a little so he'd stop screaming. "Where's Morgana?"

"I don't know," he whimpered. "Please, don't!"

The hood of his sweatshirt slipped from his head, and I saw that the transformation hadn't advanced much. Probably some junkie she'd recently converted.

"You haven't been with her long, have you?"

"No. Please. She'll kill me."

I laughed. What did he think we'd do to him?

He didn't stop twisting, so I hit the nerve point in his elbow, just as Colin had taught me, and rendered the damnatus immobile.

Adam stood beside me, his weapon drawn, watching in disbelief at how I'd taken down a damnatus who was much taller and twice as heavy.

"Adam!"

He didn't react.

"Adam!" I said again, louder.

"Yes?"

"Call Gareth. Tell him we've got one. Tell them to come immediately!"

Adam blinked, confused, then pulled his phone from his pocket.

***

"He attacked you in broad daylight? In the middle of the street?" Irvin couldn't believe it.

"Yes."

"I asked you to stay home," Jared snapped at me, then whirled about. "And you, what the devil were you thinking, taking Evelyn outside?" Jared's face was close to Adam's. The air began to crackle.

"I didn't know," Adam stammered.

"Are you mad?" I admonished Jared. "Leave him alone. You should hear yourself! *Take me outside?*—as if I'm a dog?"

"Adam? So you're on a first-name basis now?"

"That's enough, Jared," I warned him.

"To get back to the damnatus." Irvin interrupted our squabble. "He attacked you, and you two overpowered him, then brought him here?"

"Not quite," Adam said. "To be honest, Evelyn took him down on her own." Astonishment and admiration resonated in his words. Colin grinned. Jared's look was reproachful. Mine, a warning.

“Did anyone see you?” Gareth asked.

“Yes,” I said, embarrassed. “He wouldn’t stop screaming. People were coming out of their houses to ask if everything was all right and why we were dragging that poor man across the street. Adam had to show his badge and explain that it was a police matter.”

Gareth clenched his teeth. We wanted to avoid attracting attention at all costs.

“Where is he now?”

“In the bathroom,” Adam answered. “I cuffed him to the radiator.”

Colin was the first to the bathroom. “Shit,” he swore, storming in.

Irvin, who was next, clasped his hand over his mouth.

Even before I could see what had happened, I sensed this damnatus wouldn’t be able to reveal anything. I stepped closer. The scarface sat motionless in a huge, stinking pool of blood, a razor blade still stuck in his arm.

CHAPTER 21

"If you ever speak to me like that again, you'll get to know another side of me!"

"I'm sorry, babe," Jared tried to appease me, then took my hand and kissed it. "I was just so worried about you."

"You're obsessed with this hunt for Morgana. You'd do well to sleep through the night for a change. You'd be less irritable."

"Yes, relax a little." Colin put his hand on Jared's shoulder.

"How can I?" Jared was still wired. "Morgana shows up someplace and is gone a second later. As if swallowed by the earth."

"I know," Colin said. "It's maddening."

"She's wearing Evelyn's amulet," Jared grumbled.

My hand wandered to the depression between my collarbones. You'd think I'd have become used to it, but I dearly missed my amulet and felt naked without it.

"It hides her from anyone wishing her harm," Irvin added, unnecessarily.

"I definitely want to harm her," Jared growled.

"Rest," I said, putting my arms around him. "Sleep tonight, and we'll think of something tomorrow."

Jared nodded. That night, he stayed with me.

***

"Lovely to still have you here," I said in the morning, without opening my eyes. I knew he was looking at me.

He laughed and kissed me.

"I had a strange dream," I said. I opened my eyes and ran my fingers through my hair.

Jared looked interested.

"I dreamed about a woman. She was dressed in black. She wore my amulet. It called out to me. I followed her. Suddenly the woman started to run faster than I ever could have. I pursued her even though I knew I didn't stand a chance. Then there was a door. She went through. I rushed after her, and we stood in a huge hall. Hundreds of people were there, but they weren't moving—men with briefcases, mothers pulling their stubborn children along, long-haired girls with headphones. Everyone frozen, mid-motion. As if someone had stopped time. The woman ran through the frozen crowd. Suddenly there was someone else. A man. He was wrapped in a red cape and wore a sparkling crown. He sat on a golden throne below a huge cross. He smiled and waved me over. Then I woke up."

"What do you think it means?" Jared asked, kissing my knuckles, one after the other.

I let the dream's images pass before my inner eye again. The woman in black running away with my amulet. The king under the cross. I frowned. King . . . cross. King . . . Cross. King's Cross. I suddenly put it all together.

"King's Cross!" I shouted, excited. "King's Cross train station!"

Jared stared at me.

"My amulet makes Morgana a Concealed," I explained. "There's no point trying to find her as long as she's wearing it, right?"

"Right." Jared listened attentively.

"But it's *my* amulet, do you understand?"

Judging from the expression on his face, he didn't.

"Maybe I can't find Morgana, but I can find my amulet!"

Jared gave me a startled look.

"I was able to do it once before. My mother discovered it in a flea market in London when she was pregnant with me, and the moment she wanted to put it back I began to kick like mad inside her. I could feel it—I could already feel it in the womb. So, if we stop looking for Morgana and I try to feel the amulet instead . . ."

***

"You dreamed of it?" Irvin asked when I told him and the others.

"Yes, of Morgana and my amulet and a huge hall and a king under a cross. King's Cross. She's at King's Cross!"

"And you know that just because you had a dream?" Colin inquired.

"If you've got a better suggestion, let's hear it." I was annoyed.

"It's worth a try." Irvin rubbed his chin.

The others didn't appear convinced.

That no one moved enraged me. "On with it! Let's go!"

"You want to come along?" Jared asked.

"Of course I'm coming along. Clearly you lot can't do it on your own."

Gareth frowned, then clenched his teeth. I'd insulted his honor.

"Whatever you want to say, spare me! I'm coming along."

"With all due respect, Mr. Calmburry," Adam intervened, "Evelyn can defend herself very well."

I could have kissed him. But the remark put Adam completely out of bounds as far as Jared was concerned.

***

Adam stopped his service vehicle right in front of the glass-arch facade of King's Cross. Colin parked the Mercedes behind him. We charged in, Jared, Colin, Gareth, Ian, Adam, and I. Irvin remained at the safe house to hold down the fort and organize help if necessary.

An incoming train hit its brakes with a seemingly endless hiss. The place was swarming with people. Except they didn't stand still, as in my dream, but dashed about everywhere in the huge train station, making our task considerably more difficult.

"Where shall we start?" Colin asked.

They stared at me. I had led them there, after all. I looked around. Dozens of tourists stood in a queue for their turn to take a picture at platform nine and three-quarters. A group groaned when a loudspeaker by their platform announced a twenty-minute delay of their train's arrival. Two child-care workers piloted their kindergarten-age group across the hall; the children walked in double rows, holding hands.

Damn, where was Morgana?

Had I been wrong? Had I just imagined it? Was my dream no more than a dream?

Uncertain, I turned to my companions, who were looking at me expectantly.

No—the amulet had called to me in my dream. I had felt it, I had. I exhaled and closed my eyes. Tried to focus fully on it and screen out the station noise.

"Excellent. Focus," Jared encouraged me.

Easier said than done. I tried to visualize the amulet. Every detail. The blue-green sheen, the delicately curved lines of its engraving, the warmth it radiated on bare skin.

Come on, you can do it!

I'd been able to fully focus on my magic in Avalon, too. I thought of it, remembered the feeling of letting it flow through my arteries. Even though my magic was gone, I knew how it felt. Suddenly, there was silence. Everything around me disappeared. Then I had it. The amulet was nearby. I could feel it very clearly.

I opened my eyes and began to move, slowly and deliberately. My confident stride parted the crowd. I walked around the upward-branching spider-web-like funnel-shaped central structure, beyond the crush of people. My amulet guided me. The others followed. I stopped in front of a fire door, looking into myself once more to be sure this was the right way. Beyond any doubt. My amulet was somewhere behind this door. I put my hand on the doorknob.

"Hey," someone called, running toward us. "No access for unauthorized persons." A railway employee blocked our path.

Adam pulled out his badge. "City of London Police," he said in a well-practiced tone. "You're interfering with an investigation."

The railway employee raised his hands and let us pass.

A short hallway was behind the door, with garbage pails on both sides, ending at another door.

"Keep on?" Jared asked.

I nodded.

Gareth pulled his gun out of its holster and went ahead of me through the second door, securing the area by first sticking in his gun, then his head. Jared followed.

Now, a broad metal staircase led down into a large room with bare walls. More garbage containers stood there. The air was stale, smelling of empty beer bottles and leftovers. The stench distracted me. I pulled my collar over my mouth and nose, closed my eyes for a few seconds, and let Nimue's amulet guide me again. I passed straight by the containers, Jared by my right side, Gareth with his weapon drawn to my left. I stopped before a concrete wall. Yet another container stood in front of it. There was no way forward, yet I clearly felt the amulet.

"Now what?" Colin asked.

I hesitated. "I don't know . . . but . . . I feel it very clearly. Behind this wall."

"We could try to push this thing away." Adam put his gun back into its holster, then leaned against the six-foot-high and twelve-foot-long metal colossus. It didn't move by a fraction, though Adam's face took on a worrisome shade of red from his exertion.

Jared chuckled. "This isn't going anywhere," he said, amused and even a little smug. "Please, step aside." He rarely had the opportunity to demonstrate his abilities before strangers.

Adam stepped back, crossing his arms over his chest. "Please," he said, sounding a bit smug himself.

Jared smiled, directed his palms at the container, and effortlessly sent it gliding to the other side of the room as if it were no more than a cardboard prop. Adam gasped, realizing that not I but Jared was the reason for Legatum Merlini's existence.

The container had covered a small opening. No more than a hole in the wall, it looked as if someone had recently taken a sledgehammer to it. Fresh concrete chips were still lying on the ground.

"After you, Detective," Jared said, pointing at the narrow, dark hole.

"Do you have to?" I whispered, walking beside Adam.

He shrugged and grinned. I crawled next into the opening, followed by Jared. It was pitch-black inside. Now the air smelled of old concrete, rusty nails, and rotting wood. Our flashlight beams lit up a large space. It was storage for the rusty parts of decommissioned freight cars. An engine graveyard. I probed my surroundings. Suddenly I noticed something. An old elevator grid stood out in the back right corner of the space. I went straight for it. Its green paint was flaking off. I looked through the grid. A black shaft led into the deep.

Adam shone his flashlight down. "I don't think there's anything here," he said. "It's a bunker. Must be a bomb shelter from the Cold War."

"Yes," Gareth confirmed. "Dozens of them were built back then."

"Can you still feel the amulet?" Jared asked.

"Yes, it's really close. I'm sure of it." My entire body was tingling.

He nodded. "Good. We'll go down."

I went around the elevator grid and found a narrow ladder.

"This way," I said, placing a foot on the steel structure to test it for stability.

"Not you, Evelyn." Jared stepped behind me, put his hand on my shoulder, and held me back. "You're going back to the safe house."

"Jared," I protested.

"No!" I saw in his eyes that he meant it. "You haven't got your magic anymore. I won't let you put yourself in harm's way. You will *not* endanger yourself."

I stared at him. He stared back.

"There's nothing more you can do now. I'll deal with Morgana, and then you'll finally be safe."

"Jared," I started again, but he wouldn't listen.

"I'll take her back," Adam offered.

Jared nodded. "Good," he said, but then he hesitated. Did he still not trust Adam? "Gareth will accompany you."

Gareth opened his mouth, then shut it again. He really wasn't excited about having to be my babysitter.

"I'll only feel comfortable if I know you're with Evelyn," Jared added. Great, an appeal to Gareth's honor.

"Nothing will happen to her. Only over my dead body," Gareth promised.

Jared took my face in his hands and kissed me.

I pushed away from him to put a little distance between us so I could look at him. "There'll only be three of you! That's way too dangerous."

"Morgana's weak. Trust me, there won't be any problems. Colin and Ian will easily deal with the few damnati she's gathered."

Colin grinned, and Ian didn't exactly seem to mind taking on a few monsters, either.

"What if you can't find her without my help?" I objected.

"It's a bunker. You go in at one end, out the other."

"But . . ." I was running out of arguments.

Jared couldn't help but grin when he saw he'd won. "See you later," he said, kissing me. "I love you."

I stomped off, offended.

"Wait," Jared called, running after me.

"Take this with you." With a serious look, he held out the blue dagger I'd taken with me to Avalon. The dagger Karen had thrust into Morgana's arm to make her bleed. "Just in case."

"Come." Gareth took my hand. I reluctantly let him pull me out. Adam followed us.

***

I sat in the back of the squad car, slammed the door, and sulked. I was fed up with Jared treating me like a child. Most of all, I was fed up with him being right. I was completely useless in the struggle against Morgana—worse still, a burden.

If only I had my magic!

Adam and Gareth were talking excitedly, but I wasn't listening. A burst of static from the police radio on the dashboard caught our attention.

"There's somebody on the subway tracks between Holborn and Covent Garden," a bored-sounding female voice droned.

"A suicide?" a male voice responded on the radio.

"Ah . . . nope," the woman said, as if looking for a note. "Some guy in a black cloak ran into the tunnel."

Adam jerked his head around and looked at Gareth. Then he grabbed the mic.

"Detective Sergeant Adam Parker here. Where exactly did this person enter the tunnel?"

"Um . . . Holborn," the woman answered after a long pause.

"That's less than five minutes from here," Gareth mumbled.

"I'm taking over," Adam radioed back. He turned on the light and siren and stepped on the gas.

Gareth turned to me. "Wait in the car, Evelyn."

"The devil I will!"

He frowned.

"Then we'll take you back to the safe house."

Adam looked at him, then took his foot off the pedal. There's nothing worse for policemen than having to give up in the middle of a chase. I knew that from Zara. I had their attention now.

"If you take me to Bishop's Park Road first, it'll be too late!"

"I will not put you in harm's way," Gareth repeated Jared's words.

"I can defend myself quite well, Gareth. Believe me."

"It's true," Adam confirmed.

"Yes, and it's only a single damnatus," I added. "If the three of us can't handle him, then I don't know who can."

Gareth stared intensely at me. Then he clenched his teeth. "All right," he finally consented. His expression had hardened.

I nodded to show him that he'd made the right decision. "Let's get him."

Adam grinned as he sped along Southampton Row.

***

When we arrived at Holborn station, we had to push our way through a crowd of several dozen people. The entire station had been blocked off. The mood was tense, with some passengers expressing their discontent. Adam went ahead, showing one of the transport policemen his badge. He nodded and let us through, which riled the crowd even more.

"Who's in charge?" Adam asked.

"The station head," the transport policeman answered.

"Me," a short, balding man squeaked behind us. "I notified you."

"Did anyone see the person?"

"Yes, a conductor said a man with a black hooded cape ran into the tunnel, and the alarm was triggered soon after."

"How long ago?" Gareth asked.

"About fifteen minutes. I don't know where he went. Another alarm hasn't been triggered."

"So he's still in the tunnel?"

"I'd assume so!"

"Thank you." Adam rushed off. Gareth and I followed. We ran along the platform to the southern end, where we dropped to the track level. Then we hurried along the gravely center between the tracks toward the tunnel. It was cooler right away. Gareth and Adam pulled out their flashlights. The tunnel curved, and the world disappeared behind us. It was totally dark in there, but the flashlights were sufficient. A damnatus had been here a quarter of an hour ago. How far could he have gone?

"Wait," Gareth said. Adam and I froze, straining to hear in the dark.

"I thought I heard something," Gareth said. "Onward!"

We started running again. Ten minutes later we had still heard nothing in the tunnel. No sign of a damnatus. How long would it take until we emerged at Covent Garden station?

"Wait," Gareth called, stopping us again.

"What?"

"Shh!"

Something stung my nose. I smelled sulfur. Biting, penetrating, all-pervasive.

"Do you smell that, too?" I quietly asked.

Both nodded. There was a dull thud, then a shuffling sound.

Gareth and Adam pulled their guns, cocked them with clicking sounds, and aimed—each with a flashlight in one hand, weapon in the other. The lights meandered about, searching in the dark tunnel.

Someone laughed. A satisfied, anticipating laugh. Like a spider that caught something in its web. An ice-cold sensation ran down my spine. I suddenly realized this was no damnatus. Whatever was lying in wait in the dark was much worse.

The creature laughed again, this time from the opposite direction. Adam quickly turned, casting his beam on a darkly dressed figure. It moved fast and was gone a second later.

"There!" Gareth called, firing three shots into the dark. It was dead silent for a moment. Did he get him?

Gareth moved ahead, shining the flashlight in the direction he presumed his bullets had gone. Suddenly a face appeared in the beam. It moved, so fast that the eye could barely catch it. A gurgling sound followed. Gareth tilted his head at an odd angle. He sank to his knees, and the flashlight fell from his hand and rolled across the concrete floor.

Oh my God!

Gareth slumped down on the ground. The light beam shone on his face. Blood streamed from his neck—the creature had slashed his throat.

I cried out in horror.

"Run, Evelyn, run!" Adam yelled, firing his gun. I turned and ran for my life. Shots rang throughout the tunnel. Then it was silent.

"Evelyn," I heard the creature sing. "What a beautiful name for such a beautiful woman." His voice was high and sinister. He was really close. I reached with a trembling hand for the dagger.

A crunching behind me, then a throaty laugh. I whirled around, turned in all directions.

"Evelyn," he sang my name again. Fear gnawed at me.

There! Eyes shone in the dark. Then they were gone again. My breathing was shallow and fast, betraying my fear.

"Evelyn." I heard the frightful voice from another direction. I turned.

"Evelyn."

He was everywhere.

"Where are you?" Fear made my voice tremble.

A snorting, snuffling noise—he was behind me. I turned, the dagger in my extended hand. Something suddenly struck me on the arm. The dagger fell to the ground with a clank.

"Where are you?" I screamed in naked terror.

The creature laughed, dark and rough.

"Catch me if you can," it whispered into my ear.

Oh God, he was really close.

I felt his breath, the sulfurous smell of a spirit, on my skin.

"Where are you?" I screamed. "Show yourself!"

Fear paralyzed me, making my voice sound childlike.

Suddenly it was silent. All I heard was my rapid, shallow breathing, the panicked pounding of my heart. I was in complete darkness. The tunnel was a forsaken place.

I heard fingers snapping. Saw a spark. A tiny flame, as if from a lighter, danced up and down before my eyes. I followed its movement. Suddenly—his face. Only a few inches away.

"Boo!"

I stumbled back, forgot to breathe, tripped, fell, and remained motionless on the ground. The creature laughed.

"E-ve-lyn," the cruel voice sang again. He held his face into the glow of the light and bent down over me. I gasped for air. His skin was pale, almost green; his face furrowed; his teeth sharp and pointy. The creature grinned, letting a forked tongue flick out. His eyes were white with tiny pupils. A worn top hat sat on his greasy hair; a ragged tux cloaked his body. I crawled backward. I felt steel under my fingers. Smooth and hard. A . . . blade. *The dagger!* My hand closed around the handle. I thrust it forward. Thanked God when I felt resistance. I'd struck him.

The creature produced a sharp cry and shrank back, holding his bleeding arm. Then he turned again, distorted his face into a frightful grimace, and pounced. The flame died. I scrambled to my feet as fast as I could and ran off into the dark. Deeper and deeper into the black tunnel. Something gripped my ankle. I fell, hit my chin on the ground, tasted blood. I coughed, spat, and gasped for air. My mouth suddenly felt full. I ran my finger over my teeth. They were all there, but I had bit my tongue—therefore all the blood. My tongue swelled to double its normal size. The hand that had brought me down now grasped my calf, with his other hand at my knee, working its way up my leg. I clutched the dagger with a trembling hand and swung it. I felt that I'd hit him again before I heard his scream. He let go.

Suddenly, the tunnel lit up. Tiny dancing light balls whirled about me. It looked like the cave in Avalon. Was Nimue's magic returning to me?

The creature clasped both hands over its face. A deep wound gaped in its cheek. The light became brighter, then bundled. Formed into a . . . human shape. Into . . . a woman.

"Ruth?"

"Quick, come here!"

Ruth pulled me up, put her arms around me. The monster charged at me, but then the tunnel was gone.

I was pulled off my feet, and everything around me blurred. There was nothing but light. Blinding, glowing light. I felt soft ground under my feet. I blinked, then opened my eyes. Ruth's brown curls tickled my nose. She slowly let go. I took a step back and looked around.

"Where are we?"

"Primrose Hill."

CHAPTER 22

Seen from above, even a pulsating, all-devouring city like London appears strangely peaceful.

Primrose Hill is a two-hundred-foot-high hill, at the north end of Regent's Park in the Camden Borough, from which one can enjoy an undisturbed view of the city to the southeast and of Belsize Park and Hampstead Heath in the north. A broad expanse, crossed by romantic footpaths and dotted with splendid trees, it seems to watch over the city and its inhabitants. A wonderful place. But right then I was incapable of noticing the beauty surrounding me. I ran about, disturbed, aimless. Grabbed my forehead and tried to control my breathing rhythm and conceive a clear thought.

I almost died down there!

Ruth stood there motionless, watching me.

"How did you find me?" I asked.

She smiled, sad and honest. "I was always near you."

I was still in too much turmoil to stand still. "What was that thing down in the tunnel?"

"He's called Old Nick. He's been living for centuries in the London Underground."

Gareth! Adam! I broke out in uncontrolled sobbing, sank to my knees, and buried my face in my hands.

Ruth approached me. She squatted beside me and put her arms around my shaking body. "I'm so sorry, Evelyn."

"Jared," was my next thought. Crying fits repeatedly shook me.

"He . . . he's in a bomb shelter under K-King's Cross. Can you bring him here?" I asked. "P-please, Ruth, look for him. Please!"

"I can't leave you alone here."

"Please, Ruth!" I pleaded, then added in a firmer voice: "You owe me that."

She was silent, seemed touched. "All right," she finally agreed, "but first I'm taking you to safety."

Again she put her arms around me, there was light, and I lost the ground under my feet and was pulled into a whirl of brightness. When the light paled, I was back at Bishop's Park Road in front of Judith's house.

"Hurry," I said, as Ruth dissolved into light.

I went into the house, sat on the bed, and waited. Seconds felt like hours.

Finally, I heard steps. I shot from the room to the stairs. The front door burst open and Jared stormed in, climbed the stairs in a few bounds, and took me into his arms. Relief flowed through me. He was all right. Thank God, he was all right.

"Gareth and Adam are dead," I sobbed.

Jared nodded. Pain also distorted his face. Ruth had told him. I looked over his shoulder to the door. Was she still there?

"She's gone." Jared answered my unspoken question, pressing me tightly to him while I desperately tried to stop my tears.

A short while later a car raced up the gravel driveway. There was a tumultuous noise outside the door. A few seconds later, Irvin came in, followed by Colin and Ian. Between them they held a wildly flailing damnatus, whom they furiously attempted to subdue. Colin turned red. I saw him lose control, then ram his fist into the damnatus's face, knocking him out. The scarface hung limp in Ian's relentless grip.

"Take him away," Jared said to Ian, "and keep him alive. I'm not done with him by a long shot."

Colin hurried up the stairs. "Are you all right?"

I nodded. I couldn't speak.

Jared pulled me tighter into his arms, gave me time.

Then, a long while later, he asked: "What happened down there?"

***

We sat in the living room. Jared to my right, Colin to the left. Irvin and Ian sat across from us. Judith stood in the doorway, struggling with all her might to keep her composure. I met her chilling hate-filled glare.

I sobbed as I told them what had happened. I had to stop a few times.

"You're sure it wasn't a damnatus?" Irvin asked.

"Yes. It was something else. Something far more powerful. For sure."

"You injured it?"

I nodded. "I got it twice. With this." I pulled out the blue dagger with dried black blood on it.

Irvin took the weapon from my hand to inspect it. Suddenly, his face showed concern. "What did the creature look like?"

"Hard to say. It was pitch-black down there. I only caught glimpses of him."

"Try," Irvin pressed.

I strained to remember. "He was pale, had deep furrows in his face, wore a tuxedo and top hat . . . Ruth had a name for him—Old Nick."

"Jesus, Mary, and Joseph!" Judith burst out. "You woke the devil." She clasped her hands over her mouth.

"Judith!" Jared admonished her harshly.

Irvin slumped back into his chair.

I swallowed. "The devil?"

"He has many names," Irvin said, then paused for a while. "Old Nick is an ancient demon. It was more than lucky that you had the dagger with you. I bet there aren't many weapons that can injure him." Again he examined the dagger, looked at it from all sides. "Then it's true," he mumbled.

"What's true?" Colin asked.

Irvin gazed into the distance. "Enid and I were never entirely sure, but it's said that this blade was forged in dragon fire."

"Which means?" Colin asked when Irvin failed to continue.

"It means there are very few creatures it can't hurt. We know only one other weapon that has this power." Irvin looked at Colin. "Excalibur."

"Excalibur was forged in dragon fire?"

Irvin nodded. "That's why it's so mighty. An ancient magic is attached to dragon fire. A magic that worked its way long before the age of humans on Earth."

Jared nodded. *"Primordial magic."*

"Primordial magic?" I repeated.

"A raw, pure, unadulterated form of magic. Mightier than anything one can imagine." Irvin rubbed his finger over his mouth. "Old Nick is from that age. He, too, masters this primordial magic."

"You woke the devil," Judith quietly repeated, again glowering at me. Then she raised her voice and pointed her finger at me. "She has brought nothing but misfortune on us all." She took a few steps toward me. "Get out. Get out of my house!"

Jared rose and stood in front of me. "It's not her fault!"

"Oh yes, it is! It has been from the start. Gareth should have killed you when he had the chance. Now he's dead—because of you!"

"Shut your mouth!" Jared commanded abruptly, but there was no stopping Judith now.

"She has brought nothing but misery upon us, can't you see?"

Jared's magic flared up and engulfed him in a gentle golden light. The air around him began to crackle. He stared at Judith. His look was inscrutable.

"I'm removing the protection from this house," he said. The building shook to its foundations for a moment, and then it was over.

"You can't do that!" Judith screamed.

"I just did." Jared turned around to us. "Pack your things. We're driving back to Oxford."

"What about the stinker?" Ian asked. "I locked him in the basement."

"Maybe we should leave him there?" Jared gave Judith a challenging look. Exasperated, she dropped into a chair.

"Stuff him in the boot," Jared snapped.

CHAPTER 23

As long as I wore Nimue's amulet, I was safe. But they'd come dangerously close, so close I could clearly feel his magic. Then he'd disappeared, as if swallowed by the Earth. My mood darkened. I didn't know many creatures who had the power to appear and disappear at will. *Light guardians,* I thought. Were they allied with the Calmburry boy?

Oh, how I longed to get the light magic back. Without its ability, I was forced to hide here in the darkness until I recovered my strength. Forced to move like a *human.* To climb up through the dirty hatch every night to find new recruits for my army, only to climb down into the same dirty hole to hide underground at the first light of day.

But time was on my side; I gained strength every day. Every soul I absorbed, no matter how rotten, contributed its share to healing my wounds. I would soon have my old strength again. Then I would strike back—and kill them all. My sister's brood would be wiped from the face of the Earth once and for all.

Eowyn. I had always hated her. She killed our mother, who bled to death during the birth of the second twin. What was left were two motherless children competing for their father's affection. I saw through her hypocritical attempts to manipulate me with her feigned love. But her act worked on our father. He always preferred *her*, though there wasn't the slightest difference in our appearance. I was the only one who recognized what she was really like: driven by envy and ill will toward her own sister. Eowyn knew I was the stronger, *better* one of us. She couldn't bear that.

I discovered my abilities early, and even though Mother was no longer there to teach me their use, I learned fast. I was a natural. Always better than my sister. She was careful handling her magic. Shied away from exploring its limits. Finding out what she was really capable of. But timid and weak as she was, she had our father's full attention. I, on the other hand, was punished harshly for even the slightest misstep.

One day, when I was ten years old, the stable boy caught me testing my abilities on the beastly dog that always nipped at my heels. The stable boy grabbed me by the arm, pulled me aside, yelled at me, and threatened to tell Father what I had done. He called me a *changeling*.

What happened next was his fault. He wronged me. If he hadn't angered me so much . . . I was still a child. A child that didn't know what she was capable of and how destructive her powers could be. I didn't want to kill the stable boy—it was an accident.

But Father beat me black and blue. Eowyn rushed in, pulled his arm, pleaded tearfully for him to spare me. It spared me more of a beating, but I had seen through her deceitful intervention. It served one purpose alone—to deepen Father's disfavor of me. She wanted his love for herself. And she got it. Eowyn was his darling. Father could hardly wait to drive me from the house.

When we came of marriageable age, he selected a husband for me while she got to remain for another year with him. At first I resisted and begged Father not to marry me off to a complete stranger. But one look at him, and I was struck in the heart. Kenneth Calmburry was a dream of a man: strong, gorgeous, powerful, and from a good family. My sister was green with envy. She wanted to have him, just like she wanted everything else that was mine. But I was the older one. Father had selected Kenneth for me. Those were the plans for me. A life at his side.

I loved him. Loved him so much. Not a love as humans are capable of experiencing it, no. I loved Kenneth the way gods love one another. But he wanted her. Eowyn. My twin sister.

The humiliation ripped a hole inside me that hasn't yet closed, a wound that has never stopped bleeding. *Her* happiness was my torture. She had taken everything from me—Mother, Father's love, and my beloved. Eowyn was living my life, and no spell could relieve my torment.

She bore him eleven children. Three I cursed on the day they were born. They died before their first birthdays. Eowyn, who suspected I was behind the deaths, laid a mighty protective spell on her family. I couldn't break the spell, so I cursed the fields. The harvest failed. A famine visited the country, and I succeeded in killing two more of her brats. The four remaining sons—Mael, Byron, Kelby, and Merlin—as well as the two girls, Imogen and Moyra, were protected all the more. I couldn't break the magic, so I decided to take Eowyn's powers for myself. I used her weapons against her. I lured her into a trap with feigned love and a dishonest wish for reconciliation. But she betrayed me and tried to kill me with her magic, though she knew it would cost her own life. I survived, although it took years for me to regain my strength.

When I'd recovered, I dared trying to win Kenneth's love. I went to him. Still grieving, he took fright, calling me by my sister's name, thinking she had returned. I didn't contradict him and finally led the life that was my destiny. A life at his side. Until the day Merlin returned home from his travels and recognized me for who I was.

Kenneth believed the boy, so I revealed myself. Told Kenneth that he could start a new life with me since Eowyn was dead. But he spurned me a second time. Pushed me away and told me to get out of his sight.

His rejection filled me with rage. I wanted to see him suffer. He needed to suffer the way I had suffered. So I confessed that it was I who had killed his beloved wife and five of his children.

He put his hands around my neck, his eyes burning with immense hatred. *Die, witch! Die!*

He meant to kill me and left me no choice. I conjured up the darkest forces, pleaded with them to save me, and consigned my soul to them in return. They heard me. Gave me power. More power than I had ever known before.

I killed Kenneth. My love was dead. One thing remained: Revenge! Revenge on the brood of that woman responsible for my misery. None of her offspring must live.

But I couldn't kill them, for my sister's protective spell was stronger than ever before. I had to take a different approach.

First, I cast a spell of discord on the remaining family members to drive a wedge among the siblings. It did not fail me. An intense quarrel broke out over Kenneth's inheritance. The strife I had sown in the family lifted the protective magical veil.

One day, three of the six heirs gathered with their families in the parental home to divide Kenneth's possessions amongst themselves. That night I cursed one of the children. In his sleep, the boy wandered through the castle to the stables, where he lit the animals' fodder with an oil lamp. Mael, Byron, and Imogen died in the fire with their families. I let them burn the way I did. Burn with the pain raging inside me.

But three still lived. Kelby, Merlin, and Moyra had stayed out of the dispute, so Eowyn's spell still protected them. No matter what I tried, I couldn't get to them.

If it wasn't in my power to kill them, I could at least see to it that Eowyn's line died out. First I sent Irish monks who converted Moyra to Christianity and persuaded her to lead an austere life as a nun. She never had any children.

Kelby loved a woman on whom I cast a spell of infertility. So he, too, was without heirs. Only Merlin resisted. He never loved anyone enough for me to subjugate him. I was never able to grasp him. None of my curses were powerful enough to hit him. But I did not give up. Waiting paid off. One day, an unexpected opportunity opened: *Nimue.* He loved her with his whole heart. She left her home for him. Left her magic on Avalon to be with Merlin as a *human*. It was almost too easy. I kidnapped her, threatened to kill her, and succeeded in getting Merlin to enter a pact. I had learned from my errors, had realized that magic cannot be taken. Magic must be given. I was prepared for a trick, but Merlin was still able to betray me, just as his mother had. Yet again, I barely escaped with my life, and, as before, it took years to regain my old strength. I decided to find a helper. More yet, I needed an army. Merlin was dead, but he had set a horde of descendants loose in the world. I swore I would find them. Every last one. And wipe Eowyn's heirs from the face of the Earth. So I did. I killed all of them—except one. Jared Calmburry is the last of them. The final heir of Merlin, the final heir of Eowyn.

***

"Someone's here." Mad Willie reached for his sword. Of all the damnati who had survived the battle of Avalon, he had been in my service the longest. Once, he was a mighty pirate lord, stabbed to death in his sleep by his mutinous first officer. He had become my faithful servant, had carried me from the island when that girl cheated me out of my magic.

"I know." I had felt the demon when he was still miles away.

"It's been a long time," I said, without turning around.

Old Nick stepped from the shadows, slowly approaching me.

"Mistress?" Mad Willie asked. I lifted my hand to halt him. Old Nick and I had long been acquaintances. Our paths had crossed several times over the centuries. He'd never attacked me. The demon had a soft spot for me.

Old Nick took off his worn top hot, gallantly bowed, and kissed the back of my hand without taking his eyes off me.

"It's always a pleasure to see you again, dearest. You're as beautiful as ever."

"Flattery won't do you any good. I thought we'd gotten beyond that."

"That wasn't flattery, dearest, only the plain truth." He straightened up again, then put on his hat.

I put on my superior smile. "What do you want, Nick?"

"I want to help you," he answered, pacing in my confined quarters.

"Help me?" I raised my eyebrows. "Stop the games, and get to the point."

"What has earned me your reproach, dearest?" he asked, ever the hypocrite.

I snorted. "I've known you long enough to know you haven't come to me out of kindness. So, what do you want?"

"Why do you question my integrity? It's inauspicious. I really want to help you. We serve the same power. That makes us allies, doesn't it? I'm merely concerned for your well-being, dearest. A creature of such exquisite beauty should not be forced to spend her days in such"—he made a sweeping motion with his cane, went over to the bunk beds, took the corner of one of the wool blankets between his thumb and index finger, and rubbed it before turning away with a look of disgust—"*accommodations*. It's unworthy of you, dearest."

"Stop calling me 'dearest.'"

"What have I done to anger you?"

I curled my lips. "So you want to help me, right?" *If he wants to play, then let's play.*

"Certainly, dear— . . . Morgana."

"Then, as you surely know, I've been cheated out of my magic."

"It's my understanding that it wasn't *your* magic that you were cheated out of but the magic of others you've incorporated over time."

I answered him with an icy look.

"But that's just splitting hairs," he deflected. "To answer your question, yes, I did hear about it." A twitch at the corner of his mouth revealed his glee.

"As you've correctly noted, this forces me to spend my days in this"—I spread my arms—"*accommodation.*"

He nodded. "Correct," he said with a stretch. There was a touch of distrust in his look.

"So if you want to help me, give your magic over to me."

He chuckled. "My apologies, love, but I can't do without my shadow magic."

My look darkened, and my voice sounded deep. "Then why don't you tell me why you're really here."

His mood turned serious. The game was over. "I want the girl."

"The girl?"

"That girl, Evelyn."

I raised my eyebrows. "That's it?"

"That's it."

I looked at him, weighing his words. Was he trying to trick me? "What do you want with her?"

"That's no concern of yours."

I gave him a long look, tried to unravel the lie. He was telling the truth. If all he wanted was the girl, why not? Evelyn must exercise a strong attraction for someone like him. I had felt it myself when I absorbed her soul. She was so pure, so unspoiled, and so vulnerable because of all the pain and grief she had suffered. Truly perfect. I had to admit that it had been difficult for me to separate from her. What were his plans for her? In the end, it didn't matter to me what happened to her. Still, I hesitated. I had always dealt with the basest sort of human being. Murderers, thieves, rapists. It was always the worst who grasped after any straw in the face of death. They were the ones who were willing to serve me to evade their just punishment. I had gathered entire legions of the damned over the centuries. For that is what they were—damned. Damnati. They had always proven useful, yet I despised the hideous creatures.

"You want the boy, don't you?" Old Nick asked, seeming impatient.

"Yes, I want the boy."

"Then the rest need not trouble you."

"You can deliver him, just like that?" I asked skeptically.

"Not quite, but I have something else for you that will bring you much closer to your goal. You're still very weak. Worrisome to imagine what the boy would do to you in your current state." Old Nick grinned. "To be honest, you've seemed a bit out of shape for some time. Wagging tongues claim that this *schoolgirl* nearly finished you off."

I whirled around angered. "She's Nimue's heiress. She bears her magic!"

He raised his hands defensively. "All right, all right. It's just that I thought after the fiascos with Eowyn and Merlin you wouldn't almost croak a third time trying to transfer someone's magic to yourself."

How did he know that? "What are you trying to say?" I took on a threatening posture.

"I thought you'd be better prepared."

"I was." I had become loud without wanting to.

Old Nick made a swiping hand motion. "Never mind," he said. "I want the girl, and in return I can give you something that will let you recover your strength much faster."

I crossed my arms over my chest. "And that would be?"

"Light magic," he answered, waiting to see if I'd take the bait. And I did. The idea alone almost made me euphoric. During the years I had possessed this magic, I had become familiar with its capabilities. To disappear and reappear wherever one wished, as impossible to catch as light itself.

"You know a light guardian?" I asked, trying to appear casual.

"A woman who's a light guardian," the demon specified, grinning. "But not just any; it's the one whose magic was once . . . yours."

I looked up. "Mary Hayman's daughter?"

"That's the one."

"How do you plan to get her? Not to mention get her to give up her magic?"

Old Nick took a deep breath. "I've been roaming this world for a very long time," he said slowly. "There's much I've learned about humans. They're selfish, greedy, cowardly, and vicious." He grinned, showing his pointy teeth. "But to save those they love, people are willing to give just about anything."

CHAPTER 24

The drive from Oxford to London was one long torment, with the acrid stench of our *guest* spreading inside the car. We had to keep the windows open all the way. As soon as we arrived in the garage of the headquarters, we rushed out of the car.

"My God." Colin coughed. "Does that shit ever smell!"

Even Ian, who had the self-control of a palace guard, turned his nose up in disgust.

"Ian, would you be so kind as to get him to the dungeon," Irvin said.

I looked at Jared, surprised. "There's a dungeon here?"

He shrugged. "It's a really old house."

Enid, closely followed by Jessica, came down the stairs and put her arms around Jared, then Colin and me at the same time. Her face was covered in tears. The news of Gareth's death had hit her as hard as the rest of us. Maybe even harder. "Come," she said, trying to sound encouraging. "Hilda has made you something to eat."

"Evelyn," Enid's daughter shyly squeaked as she tugged on my jacket.

"Hi, Jessie." I bent down to pick her up. She put her slender arms around my neck with a firm grip and buried her face in my shoulder.

***

Enid kept crying during the meal. Irvin did his best to comfort her. Gareth must have meant so much to her. I also found it difficult to hold back my tears. Jared didn't say a word. He looked into the distance, stone-faced. I barely managed to eat a bite. No one seemed to have much of an appetite. Not even Colin.

"Where did you find the damnatus?" I asked. The silence was unbearable.

"Down in the bunker," Colin answered with lowered eyes. "There were four of them. Blocked our way—we killed three right away."

"And Morgana?"

Colin shook his head. "Ruth came before we were able to penetrate further into the bunker. She told us two of our people were dead and she was only able to save you at the last minute."

Tears again rolled down Enid's beautiful face.

"Of course, Jared immediately went with her." Colin paused, then added: "But I'm sure we were very close."

"I'm so sorry." I lowered my eyes. If I hadn't insisted on going into the tunnel, they would have probably caught Morgana. And Gareth and Adam would still be alive.

"It's not your fault," Jared said. It sounded as if he wasn't sure of that. He pushed his untouched plate aside, placed his hand on Colin's shoulder, and got up. "Let's go."

***

When I entered the underground room aptly described as the "dungeon," it was like being projected back into the Middle Ages. It had stone walls, chains, iron manacles. There were even torches on the walls.

"This room was never changed," Jared explained when he noticed my disturbed look. "It's just as it was when this house was built."

"You don't say."

The damnatus was cowering in chains on the floor. Broad metal cuffs were fastened to his wrists and ankles.

Jared stepped in front of him, flanked by Colin and Ian. Irvin and Enid stayed in the background with me. Jared looked at the creature for a very long moment. He just stood there and stared. Then he shifted his weight from one foot to the other.

"Your name?" Jared's voice was hard and cold.

The prisoner was silent, averting his eyes.

"Your name?" Jared repeated. You didn't have to know him particularly well to know that he wouldn't ask a third time.

The damnatus didn't answer again.

Jared clenched his teeth, extended his right arm, and produced a pulsating energy ball in his hand—it almost looked as if his arm was burning—and thrust it into the damnatus's chest. His scream echoed throughout the room.

"H-Heinrich," he gasped.

"How long have you been with Morgana?"

The damnatus hesitated. Jared raised an eyebrow in warning.

"Since 1942."

"Were you with her in Avalon?"

I looked at the damnatus, trying to remember if I had seen him there. I wasn't sure; these monsters all looked the same to me. Especially when the transformation had advanced so far that nothing human remained.

Suddenly, the damnatus raised his gaze and looked at me. "Yes."

"Did you help Morgana flee?"

"Yes." A satisfied twitch in the scarred corner of his mouth betrayed his pride in having won this small victory over Jared and me.

Colin stepped forward and brutally struck him in the face.

Dark blood dripped from a wound above the right eye. But he was conscious. This damnatus was able to take more than I had expected. Colin's blow would have surely knocked my lights out.

"How many of your kind has she created since you escaped?"

The damnatus was silent, tilted his head, and grinned.

Jared clenched his fist and let his curse pass, lightning fast, over the belly of the damnatus. The prisoner's whole body shook, and his rotting teeth chattered.

"Sixteen," he yelped. "Sixteen."

"Is she still in the bunker?"

"How would I know? I'm here." He raised his arm to rattle his chains.

"Let me rephrase the question. Is the bunker Morgana's only retreat?"

"The bunker? You're going to have to be a bit more specific."

Colin punched the damnatus again, knocking him backward.

"Yes," the damnatus answered, spitting blood.

"Yes, what?"

"Yes, it's her only retreat."

"What are her plans?"

"To reconquer Avalon."

"How will she go about that?"

"With an army."

"What do you know about the deaths of our two men?"

"Your men? Nothing."

Jared gave him a penetrating look.

"Is he telling the truth?" Colin asked.

Jared frowned, then nodded.

The damnatus repeatedly looked at me. Something dark and unpredictable shone in his eyes.

Jared abruptly blocked his view. "If you look at her one more time, you'll die," he said in an ice-cold tone.

"I'm already dead," the prisoner answered, and continued to stare at me. A rotten grin spread across his face. "You can't stop her," he said, and laughed—the crazed, desperate laugh of someone who knew the end was near. Colin punched him so hard that blood spurted all over.

Jared turned to me. "Is everything okay? You're very pale."

"It's all right," I answered bravely.

He came to me. Took a look at me. "Perhaps it's better if you left. You don't have to watch this."

I swallowed with difficulty and nodded. Yes, perhaps it'd be best if I left. I felt nauseated. Ready to puke, to be honest. I had to get some air. I turned and left.

I heard Jared ask, "How did you die?" Then the heavy door shut with a clang.

***

It was already dark and a little chilly outside. I sat on the stone stairs at the headquarters' entrance, let cool air flow through my lungs, and exhaled. I just sat there for a while, breathing, running my fingertips over the rough stones. This was the exact spot where I had my first chat with Gareth. Tears came to my eyes at the thought. I couldn't stand sitting there any longer. So I took a few steps across the lawn before realizing I wasn't alone.

"How are you?" a familiar voice asked.

I looked up. Ruth stood in front of me. The light of her appearance hadn't entirely faded.

"Ruth! What are you doing here? If the others see you . . . Claire's in there."

"I wanted to see how you were." As she came closer, I saw that her hands were trembling, and, looking at her more closely, I was certain she'd been crying.

"Could I have a hug?" Her voice quaked, sounded brittle.

"Is everything okay?" I asked, keeping my distance.

"Yes. I'm just a little shaken by the events of the last few days." Again she took a step toward me. Suddenly she looked up. Her eyes widened. She stared past me. I turned to see Jared coming outside.

"Get away from her!" He stretched his arm out and shot an energy ball at Ruth. Then everything happened so fast I couldn't react. Ruth pulled me to her and clamped both arms tightly around my body, and everything became bright.

"Sorry," she whispered, and then I lost the ground under my feet. Light spun around us. When I thought we'd be lost in the whirl, my feet hit the ground again. I pushed her away.

"Where have you taken me?" I shouted, half blind. I blinked several times, then opened my eyes wide, trying to recover my vision and adjust to the darkness.

I recognized this place. We were on Primrose Hill. I frantically looked around. It became clear what Ruth had done. She had taken me to *her*. Not ten yards away from Ruth and me, Morgana stood under the cover of a tree. Several dozen scarfaces had set themselves up like a protective wall behind her. I couldn't believe how many there were. The damnatus had lied to us. There weren't just sixteen; there were at least a hundred. Morgana had been busy.

A satisfied smile spread across her immaculate face. Even though she wore torn jeans and a hoodie, Morgana looked exalted, almost regal. As if she wore the finest dress of silk and velvet. She held something in her hand. A strangely shining rope or chain—I couldn't quite see from the distance. I looked along it. The other end was around the neck of a woman cowering on the ground. She whimpered, then looked up.

Morgana's prisoner was about thirty years old and had auburn curls. She was crying, her beautiful face distorted by mortal fear. I suddenly understood. I had seen this woman before. In a photo in Ruth's flat. No doubt about it: this was Hanna Hayman, Ruth's daughter.

Ruth pushed me in the back. The shove was so unexpected, I almost lost my balance.

"Here she is!" Ruth cried in desperation. "I've done what you two asked! Now give me back my child!"

Done what *you two* asked? I looked up and noticed someone else. A figure stepped out from behind the tree. He wore a tux and a top hat, swung a cane, and whistled a children's tune. He looked at me, doffed his hat, bowed, and said, "Good evening, love."

Then he put his hat on over his straggly hair and grinned with his shark teeth, a long gash in his pale cheek.

I took a deep breath. That was him! *Old Nick*—the demon from the tunnel. I suppressed a scream.

He sauntered up to me. "I'm delighted to see you again so soon."

I turned and ran.

"You're going nowhere," the demon calmly said. High flames shot up in front of me. I turned in the other direction, where more flames shot up. I was caught in a ring of fire.

"You were down in the tunnel, weren't you? You killed Gareth and Adam." Hatred seared inside me.

"Quite possible," the demon said and approached.

I took a defensive posture and faced him. I held up my hands, hoping for warm waves of magic, but my hands remained cold. I pushed them forward, again called for my magic, attempted to conjure Nimue's power—but nothing happened.

"Interesting," Morgana mumbled as she approached. She pulled Hanna after her like a dog. "So you left Nimue's magic in Avalon," she concluded from my futile attempts to defend myself. She grinned at me scornfully. "That'll be the first thing I'll check on when I return to the island."

The demon casually walked around me and observed me from all angles, like a customer inspecting goods. He stepped behind me and sniffed my hair. The hairs at the back of my neck bristled.

Ruth spoke again. "Well, let her go!" she demanded hysterically.

"Not so fast," Morgana answered casually. "That was only the first part of our agreement."

"The first part?" Ruth asked, thunderstruck. "You didn't say anything about a second part. Give me my child back now!"

"It must have slipped my mind."

Ruth's eyes widened, first uncomprehending, then determined. She dissolved into light, then reemerged next to her daughter. Ruth put her arms around Hanna and tried to make her disappear along with her, but only Ruth vanished. She materialized again nearby.

Morgana laughed. "Did you really think it would be that easy?" She yanked the chain again to further tighten it around Hanna's neck.

"What do you want?" Ruth asked.

"Oh, I imagine you know the answer," Morgana said and laughed again.

Ruth swallowed, stared Morgana in the eyes, then looked down. "My magic." That wasn't a question—it was a statement.

"Bingo!"

Ruth hesitated. Morgana looked her over, alert and impatient. Then she put on her fake smile, aimed her hand at Hanna, and hurled a curse at her neck. The young woman cried out in pain. Ruth cried out, too.

"No!" she yelled, her voice almost breaking. "No!"

Morgana smiled, an expression of anticipated triumph. She knew she had won. Ruth would give Morgana *anything* to protect her daughter. That was certain.

"You know what that means," I said, and looked Ruth in the eyes. "It will kill you. You will die just as your mother did."

"But Hanna will live," Ruth answered determinedly.

I gave her a tired smile. "Do you honestly think she'll just let her go?"

I could tell from the expression on Ruth's face that she hadn't considered this. But I had her attention and needed to convince her. It was my only chance of getting out of here alive.

"She'll throw your daughter to her damnati." I nodded at the scarfaces, then paused to let it sink in. "Trust me, that's worse than death."

"Mother," Hanna whimpered.

Old Nick grabbed me by the neck, pulled out a knife, and held the blade to my throat. "Careful," he warned. "No one likes uppity girls."

Now or never. "You have to get Jared here," I shouted. "Now!"

"Shut up!" Morgana ordered. The blade at my neck twitched. I feared Old Nick would cut my throat if I said another word.

Ruth looked torn. She frantically looked back and forth between Hanna and me. Everything would be lost if I didn't convince her now.

"Get Jared! At once!" I yelled. I fully expected the blade to dig into my throat, but nothing happened. I realized that whatever Old Nick had in store for me, he didn't want to kill me. At least not yet.

"Jared will kill me," Ruth objected, trembling.

"*She* will kill you! Don't you get it? Jared's your only hope!"

"Make her shut up!" Morgana snapped. "If the light guardian disappears, our agreement is void."

"Better shut your trap," Old Nick hissed in my ear as his grip on the back of my neck tightened. "I don't want to have to kill you, my beauty."

I pulled together all my courage. If Ruth didn't disappear now, I'd die anyway—or spend the remainder of my days in the deepest darkness of the London Underground.

"Ruth! Go!" I yelled so loudly my neck hurt.

Nick yanked my head back. "Big mistake," he said. "Very dumb."

I saw light glow from the corner of my eye and knew that Ruth had listened to me. Relief flowed through me. He would come. Jared would come.

Then I felt the pain—a sharp burning pain like I'd never felt before. Warm blood flowed from the wound and ran down my neck. A scream raged inside me. I tried to swallow but couldn't. Blood bubbled out of my mouth. The demon let me go, and I fell face-first into the dirt. Coughed, spat, tried to breathe.

"What a shame," Old Nick complained. "Are you happy now?"

"Happy?" Morgana shrieked. "Do you know *who* will show up here any moment?"

I rolled on my side and grabbed my throat. Tried to stop the bleeding. In vain. It flowed in streams from my neck.

That's it, I thought. After everything I'd gone through, *survived,* I'd die here in a pool of my own blood. Even if Ruth brought Jared immediately, it would be too late for me. He could only watch me bleed to death.

The scent of the meadow mixed with the sweet, metallic smell of my blood. I felt the cold, hard earth under my cheek.

It'll be over in a moment.

Then I started to count. *One, two, three, four* . . . I continued. *Five, six, seven* . . . counted toward the advent of my own death.

Eight, nine. In a moment it'd be over; the pain would stop. I'd be dead. *Ten* . . . I waited for the inescapable . . . *ten.* I was stumped. I'd been sure I'd be dead once I'd counted to ten. But—I was still alive. I was alive! I tried to swallow—and could. Carefully I felt the cut. It was no longer bleeding. More yet: the wound was almost closed, had nearly healed. What on earth? I could think of only two possible explanations. First: Old Nick hadn't injured me as badly as he had pretended. Second: I was still covered by the protection of the source, and the water I'd drunk caused my wound to heal so quickly that I'd ducked death once more.

Whatever had happened, this wasn't the right moment to figure it out. It was time to act. The advantage was mine now. Everyone, or at least Morgana and the damnati, thought I was dead. I remained lying there, trying not to move, so I wouldn't give myself away. I carefully looked through the dense curtain of my hair. Hanna was lying on the ground, crying. Morgana yanked the chain around her neck. Dawn was coming.

Old Nick grinned, pulled off his top hat, and bowed. Then he clicked the heels of his pointed boots and dissolved into smoke.

"Stay here, you coward!" Morgana shouted, but the demon was already gone. She looked around. Nervous, searching, panicking.

The light became dense, then gradually paled. Speed was of the essence. I had no time to see whether Ruth had found Jared or returned alone. My window of time was only those few seconds while Morgana was distracted. I pounced on her, tore Nimue's amulet from her neck, then knocked the chain out of her hand. I pushed Hanna aside with all my strength; she tumbled over the meadow, briefly looked up, reached for her neck, and took off the chain.

I looked around to see if Jared had come. Ruth had found him. At the same moment, something grabbed my hair and pulled me to my feet. Ruth rushed to Hanna. I saw the light, and then they were gone. Thank God—they were safe.

A damnatus yanked my head around. "You're tough, huh?" he said, almost respectfully. He laughed, but his face froze when he saw Jared. I used the element of surprise, rammed my elbow into his stomach, and tore away from him. Then Jared unleashed a force of nature. The hill trembled, lightning struck trees and the ground, the air crackled. Jared's body shone from the inside out.

He had waited so long for this moment. Had hunted and pursued Morgana. Now she would feel the full force of his revenge. He bundled his power, then unleashed it.

Jared was mightier than I would have thought possible. His anger struck the damnati first. He swept them away like rag dolls. Then his pitiless gaze turned on Morgana.

"We meet again," he said.

I ran to him and stood by his side. "Finish it," I said, narrowing my eyes.

Two damnati came out from behind a tree and positioned themselves as protection before their mistress. Jared, with a small motion of his fingers, snipped them away. Morgana's eyes widened. There was naked fear in them. Then she ran—rushed away, zigzagging like a rabbit. Jared thrust his hands forward, sending a curse after her. It struck only an inch away from her. First I thought he'd missed, but then I realized he was only toying with her.

"Turn around and fight!" he demanded.

She jumped and ran in another direction. She wasn't able to hide anywhere in the open plain. Again, Jared's spell only missed her by a hair's breadth.

"Coward!" he called, at the same moment that Morgana turned and hurled her magic at him.

Jared lifted his hand and effortlessly deflected it. I had felt her power on my own body. Though I didn't feel it now, I knew this was only a fraction of what Morgana used to be capable of.

"No, you won't get away this time."

Morgana was so far away, I could only guess at her shape in the dark, but I knew Jared felt exactly where she was.

"Duck," he suddenly cried. I ducked and evaded a curse the witch had hurled in our direction. It collided with Jared's magic. I was thrown back, stumbled, then looked up. Morgana was nowhere in sight.

"Stay put," Jared said. He tilted his head back, spread his arms, closed his eyes, and let his magic flow through him. Time stood still. He would finish it now. There was no escape for Morgana. Jared would crush her. The plasma pulsed when it left his body and bundled into a buzzing sphere.

Suddenly, a woman screamed. Jared looked up, stopped the destroying curse. His incomprehension was evident.

"Not so fast, not so fast," a deep voice calmly said. From nowhere, Old Nick appeared in a black fog before us. He was not alone. He had his arm around a delicate female figure. His knife was at her throat. She was dressed in a nightgown, her feet bare. She looked at me with shocked eyes.

Oh God, no! I tried to swallow my horror.

"Evelyn," Sally's voice trembled. "What's happening?"

Morgana rushed to Old Nick and hid behind him, seeking protection.

"You see, dearest," he said to her. "It's always good to have an ace up your sleeve." He laughed hoarsely.

Without thinking, I rushed forward.

"Easy, easy," Nick warbled, pulling Sally's head back. The blade of his knife flashed in the moonlight.

I stopped, Jared with me.

"Sally, are you all right?" I asked.

She sobbed. What a dumb question. Of course she wasn't all right.

"Are you injured? Has he harmed you?"

"No," she finally answered. Then quieter: "Please, help me."

"Let her go," Jared yelled, "or I swear I'll burn you alive."

Old Nick laughed alongside Morgana. She suddenly seemed brave.

"And how are you going to do that?" she asked smugly. She dared to come out of Nick's shadow, stepped forward, and stroked her long fingers over Sally's cheek. "If we burn, she'll burn with us."

"What do you want?" I shouted. "Ruth's gone—your plan didn't work. You know we can't get you the light magic, don't you?"

"Yes, unfortunately." She feigned disappointment.

Sally whimpered when the witch pulled her to herself and placed her long fingers around Sally's neck. Nick skillfully flung his knife into the air, then put it in the inside pocket of his tuxedo.

Helpless rage took hold of me, and I shouted, almost screeched, "What do you want? Jared's magic? You'll never get it!"

She had to know that he'd rather die than leave her his magic. He would thrust it with full force into the witch as Merlin once had done. But he would destroy her.

"Nooo," she replied, drawn out. "Not *his* magic . . ." Her eyes focused on me with a covetous gleam. *"Yours."*

"What?"

"You will accompany me to Avalon and show me where you hid Nimue's magic. Then we'll let the girl go." She gave a sinister laugh.

"Evelyn's going nowhere," Jared said, and I knew he'd never allow me to go with Morgana. Even if it meant Sally's death.

"As you wish," Morgana said. She closed her fingers around Sally's throat and effortlessly lifted her into the air. Sally's bare feet kicked and she clawed her fingers into Morgana's hand, trying to free herself from the relentless grip. Her face turned red, then blue. Her eyes protruded.

"No!" I screamed in a panic. "Let her go! Let her go!"

Jared let his magic pulse. "If you don't let her go, I'll kill you right now." Only an idiot would have doubted him.

I thought I saw light from the corner of my eye. I looked as the heads of the others turned that way as well.

Ruth? Had she returned? I looked around but couldn't see her.

Then the light bundled directly before Morgana. It blinded me so much that I had to shield my eyes. When I looked again, I could barely believe it.

Ruth had returned—with Colin.

He didn't hesitate. He immediately raised the mighty sword and charged wildly at Morgana. Jared ran after him. In a fright, Morgana loosened her grip on Sally's neck, and she managed to break free. Sally plopped to the ground, wrestling for air. Colin was unstoppable. He swung Excalibur, and it descended on Morgana in a semicircle. At the last moment, she yanked her head away and lifted her arms to protect herself. She avoided decapitation, but Colin didn't miss. The mighty blade severed Morgana's right arm at the shoulder. The limb hit the ground with a thud. Her shrill scream echoed over the hill.

Jared had almost reached Sally when Old Nick also charged toward her. Jared thrust his hands forward, sending a curse down on him with the unbridled force of lightning. The demon whirled through the air, spun around, and slid across the meadow. But he quickly regained control, rose, and was back on his feet in midmotion.

Old Nick looked firmly at Jared. His eyes flared. "Not bad for a little guy," he acknowledged generously, swinging his black cane in a circle. The demon grinned with his pointy teeth. "We'll meet again," he promised. He bowed gallantly, clicked his heels together, and was gone in a puff of smoke.

Jared's curse had made a tree burst into flames. I ran to Sally and pressed her against me at the same moment that Colin raised Excalibur for the final blow. He roared like a bull. Then everything went so fast that I could barely follow.

The sword was near Morgana's neck when dark shadows flashed across her glowing eyes.

"No!" Jared shouted, but she raised her remaining arm and directed her magic at Colin with brute force.

Running, Jared threw both hands forward and released his unbridled power, brightening the night as if it were day—and struck the witch with full force.

Morgana was dead.

CHAPTER 25

Silence. Indescribable silence. It enshrouded everything.

Then Sally began to scream. The soul-piercing cry of a heart torn from a breast.

Colin lay on the ground. Morgana's curse had struck him in the middle of his chest. Sally threw herself on his lifeless body.

"Colin! Colin!" Her cry tugged at my heart.

The three of us kneeled beside him. Blinding tears streamed down my face. I felt Colin's chest and pressed down on it. Pounded on him, tried to get his heart to beat again, tried to *force* it to beat. Why weren't they helping me?

"Do something, Jared!" I cried. "Do something!"

Jared took my wrists, firmly gripped them, and forced me to stop.

"I can't," he said in a voice that sounded strange. "He's dead."

My thoughts drifted, incapable of understanding what had just happened. It was impossible. Colin could *not* be dead.

Sally's cheeks were covered in tears, and she desperately stroked Colin's face, kissed him. Kissed him again and again, as if her lips could bring him back to life.

Jared's expression was frozen—the grief for his friend, his brother, so overwhelming that he was incapable of letting it out. He kneeled beside Colin and just looked at him. Stared into his brother's empty eyes. Silent. Motionless.

Hours must have passed while we kneeled beside Colin's body. Dawn came, announcing the day. Somehow I found the strength to call Enid so someone would pick us up. It wouldn't be long before dog walkers and joggers swarmed Primrose Hill. When I told her what had happened, she sobbed so loudly and intensely, I was almost unable to understand her.

I hung up and sat down beside Sally.

I only said, "They're coming."

Soon we heard footsteps in the grass. It wasn't who we'd expected.

"Get lost," Jared said, without looking up. His voice was so cold. Ruth stood next to us, looking sadly at our dead friend.

I whirled around, enraged. "Why did you bring him here?"

"I—I just wanted to help," she said, her voice muffled.

"Get lost." I repeated Jared's command, sounding just as cold. "I don't ever want to see you again. Go!"

A tear ran over Ruth's cheek, and then she dissolved into light.

***

When Ian finally came, he and Jared carried Colin's body to the car. There were dozens of onlookers. Joggers, barking dogs. Some began to scream at the sight of the dead witch and hundred-plus damnati corpses scattered over the hill.

Jared lifted his arm and made a gentle sweeping motion in the air. A delicate gold rain came down on those standing around. They halted as if they'd just forgotten what they were doing, then went about their business.

We were already at the car when the convoy arrived, a seemingly endless motorcade of Jeeps and hearses. They'd clean up thoroughly, removing every trace of last night's tragedy. No one would know what had happened. No one would know how Colin had really died. As a hero.

None of us said a word. Sally, who sat in the backseat with me, had Colin's head in her lap and endlessly stroked his cold face. Jared sat in the front, rubbing his hand over his eyes. Tears even ran over Ian's normally ever-so-composed face.

***

Grief pervaded the headquarters. Oppressive, almost palpable. Adam, Gareth, and Colin: three lives, one purpose. Casualties in the war against darkness in this world. My brain still refused to believe I would never see them again.

Sally was completely distraught. She held on to Colin and cried like a banshee when he was taken from her. Thrashed so wildly that Jared had to hold her. When no one managed to calm her, Jared gently engulfed her in his magic and carried her trembling, whimpering body to Colin's room and put her in his bed. I lay down with her and put my arms around her. Held her tightly and shared the pain.

"Try sleeping a little," I whispered in her ear. She began to cry again. So I asked Jared to let her sleep as he'd once done with me.

He gently placed his hand on her forehead to let calming waves of his magic flow through her.

"Evelyn," Sally whispered. "R-remember that I wanted to tell you s-something important when you were in L-London?"

"Yes, of course. What was it? Please, tell me."

Completely exhausted, she opened her eyes a tiny gap and looked at me. A last tear ran from the corner of her eye.

"I'm pregnant," she whispered. Then she finally fell asleep.

CHAPTER 26

I had to get out. I had to get some air.

I'm pregnant. The words ran through my thoughts. I walked about aimlessly. Tried to run away from desperation, escape the pain.

"Why?" I cried. "Why Colin? Haven't you taken enough from me?"

The grief brought me to my knees. I collapsed. Pounded the earth with my fists, screamed, and cried.

I felt Enid watching me from the window. I looked up. Even from this distance I could see her pain-filled, teary face. She gave me a short nod, then walked away.

Strong hands pushed under my arms. Jared pulled me into his arms and held me. We both cried. Grieved for our lost friends.

"The funeral is tomorrow," Jared finally said in a calm voice. "He'll be interred with Gareth. Irvin's preparing everything."

"They've found Gareth?"

He nodded. "The sent a special task force into the tunnel and recovered his body."

"And Adam?"

"No. Only Gareth."

I shuddered at the thought of what Old Nick might have done to Adam. I swallowed against the tightness in my throat. We spent several minutes in silence.

"*He* must have been the one who followed Colin and Sally from Berry's to her house," I said. "Not a damnatus. Nick knew exactly where to find her."

"Yes," Jared said. We were still tightly wrapped around each other. Jared's closeness was the only thing giving me comfort. He kissed me, mingling our tears. Then we went into the house.

***

In the afternoon I went to Sally's home to tell her mother, Pamela, that Colin had died in a traffic accident and Sally would stay with me for a few days to recover. But Pamela insisted on seeing her immediately. So we packed a few clothes, and I took her to the headquarters. I couldn't have cared less about the reproachful looks of some members of the Order when, after Ruth, I brought another stranger there. Sally needed her mother, and I was willing to do anything to ease her pain. Jared agreed.

When I entered Colin's room with Pamela, Jared was sitting by Sally's bedside, holding her while she cried. The shoulder of Jared's shirt was soaked with her tears. Pamela sat down, took her daughter in her arms, and brushed over her disheveled hair while incessantly whispering comforting words into her ear. Sally couldn't stop crying, but she seemed to do better with her mother there.

***

Colin and Gareth were buried the next day in Rose Hill Cemetery in Oxford. Sally barely managed to stand during the funeral. Jared and Irvin had to support her to keep her from collapsing. The sorrow overwhelmed her. It was difficult for me to imagine how much she suffered from the loss. Sorrow was a feeling I knew too well, but Sally hadn't lost just her friend and lover, she'd also lost the father of her unborn child—unaware that this child was king Arthur's last heir.

***

A few days passed. Pamela moved in with Sally in Colin's room. Once Sally had recovered enough, she started to ask questions. She wanted to know what that creature was who had kidnapped her in the middle of the night and taken her to the hill. She wanted to know who had killed Colin, how it had all happened. Jared decided to accept both women into Legatum Merlini. There was a ceremony, an oath, and then he initiated them. He told them everything possible about all of us.

Flabbergasted, Sally repeatedly stroked her tummy when she realized what a special child slumbered under her heart. She smiled for the first time in days. I believe this child, this extraordinary child, brought Sally back to life.

Four weeks later Pamela went back to work. Sally was stable enough to manage on her own for a few hours. Normality returned to our lives. Jared, Sally, and I attended classes again. Life continued, and we tried to look forward.

***

"Isn't it amazing?" Sally asked one afternoon as we were taking a short walk outside the headquarters. "The world just keeps turning without noticing in the least that someone so important is missing."

She caressed her belly. A small ball was outlined under her shirt.

"Yes," I said. "But Colin will always be here with us. In our hearts."

Tears ran over Sally's cheeks. She still cried almost every day. Sometimes she retreated for a few minutes, said she had to go to the restroom, but when she returned, her eyes were red and swollen.

"Are you okay?" I asked, squeezing her hand.

"It's getting easier," she said. "It lessens each day."

We went a few more steps as clouds drew up and darkened the sky. Sally rubbed her arms, shivering.

"Dinner's ready," Jessie called, sticking her head out the front door.

"We're coming," Sally said. Sally had immediately taken Enid's daughter into her heart. They often sat together on the couch in the evening, and she let Jessie listen to her belly. She swore she felt a kick once, but according to Enid it was too early for that.

"Come on," Sally said. "It's going to rain any minute."

"I'll be there soon," I said. "Give me a few minutes."

"Okay."

I wanted to be alone for a bit and walked over the lawn, then sat down on a garden bench. Suddenly swirling light dots appeared from the storm cloud above me and moved in. They bundled into a shape in front of me.

"What do you want?" I said without looking up.

"I've got something for you," Ruth said, and pulled a worn notebook from her coat pocket.

"What is it?"

"My mother's last notes. I've just found them. She hid them well."

I looked at her skeptically.

"I always asked myself why she was so obsessed with Nimue. She never stopped looking for the truth, as long as she lived."

I hesitantly accepted it. "Why didn't she ever stop?"

Ruth smiled. "You'll find the answer in there." The light dots began to dance around her while she spoke. When Jared came racing over, she disappeared.

"Where is she? Where's Ruth? I felt her energy." He turned around, searching.

"Gone," I said, looking at the book in my hands. "She gave me this."

"What is it?"

"A notebook of her mother's."

I sat down again and brushed over the smooth surface. "She said I'd find the answer here about why Mary never stopped searching for the truth about Nimue."

He gave me a concerned look, sat next to me, and looked at the brown binding.

I opened it. It was a diary of sorts. A place and date were noted above each of the brief entries.

> *Oxford, March 15, 2000*
> *Mayflower has published another academic paper. It's entitled "Excalibur: Symbols of Power." She shines at conferences with her insider knowledge of the "Merlin myth," but she's endangering the entire Calmburry family with her boundless arrogance.*
>
> *Oxford, May 2, 2000*
> *A damnatus in Oxford. I killed him. Morgana has picked up Mayflower's scent. I must do something.*
>
> *Glastonbury, June 5, 2000*
> *The fog is impenetrable. All my attempts to open the portal have failed. I'm not able to make it through.*
>
> *Oxford, December 20, 2000*
> *I must not give up! Morgana's bringing so much darkness into this world. I must stop her. The Calmburrys are in grave danger.*
>
> *Glastonbury, February 25, 2001*
> *It's futile. The portal won't open. I can't make it in. I must lure her out.*

Fleetwood, August 19, 2001
It's hard to find them. There are three of them. Direct descendants. Anna, Zara, and Evelyn Lakewood. They have no idea.

Fleetwood, August 20, 2001
The youngest one wears Nimue's amulet. Can she open the portal? Dana will keep an eye on the Lakewoods for me. Better not involve them, so they'll be out of danger. But if I find no other way, I'll try to lure Morgana out of the fog with the amulet.

Oxford, September 25, 2001
My time on Earth is limited. The time has come to initiate Ruth.

Oxford, January 21, 2002
More damnati in Oxford. I was able to do in two, but the third got away. What does he know? God help us all! The Calmburrys are in grave danger.

Fleetwood, February 1, 2002
I've decided against involving the Lakewoods. Nimue's amulet will hide the girl from anyone wishing to harm her. I don't want to endanger her. Still looking for the source.

Oxford, February 3, 2002
I can't do it alone. I don't have a choice. I must warn the Order. Mayflower is far too careless. She must become aware of the danger.

Oxford, February 6, 2002
Mayflower's arrogance knows no bounds. She is not aware of any failing.

Oxford, April 2, 2002
They are dead. Morgana has found them. They are dead. Burned in a plane crash.

Oxford, April 2, 2002
The boy has survived! Thank God! The boy has survived! Merlin's legacy has not yet been lost.

Oxford, April 7, 2002
A man was here. He said he has orders to kill me. But he won't do it. He says his duty is to the Order, not Mayflower. He advises me to disappear. Others will come. They will never stop looking for me.

London, April 18, 2002
I have found her! She's alive.

That was the last entry. There were only two lines underneath it:

8 Roffey Street
London E14 3NH

CHAPTER 27

It rained. Again.

Shivering, I pulled my hood over my head and walked faster. The brown paper shopping bag was dangerously soaked, and I didn't feel like collecting my shopping out of a puddle.

I longed for the warmth of summer. The feeling of sun on my skin. I sighed. I'd been living in London for more than sixty years, but I was fed up with this rain. Not because of the water, no. Water never bothered me. Quite the contrary. But the cold, the cold got to me. Not that I was ever ill. That probably wasn't even possible. I'd never had a cold for as long as my soul had lived in this body, not in—how many years had it been? I'd stopped counting.

I put the bag down in the tiny kitchen. My flat on the Isle of Dogs in London's East End felt barely larger than a dollhouse. It was a decayed townhouse, quite typical for the Docklands before the start of mansion building by the riverside. I never had company. Which was somewhat due to my never getting along that well with people. Also, my flat would have looked very strange to any mortal. Starting with the freestanding bathtub that took up almost all the space in my living room where one would expect a couch instead; it would surely make an odd impression. But what would first have caught the eye of any visitor to my house would have been my swimming flatmates. My place had more aquariums than any pet store from here to Liverpool.

I brushed off my boots.

"Well, did you miss me?"

I loved my fish—they were the only things that meant anything to me. They were all I still had. Everything else had either been taken from me or fallen to dust. *Morgana.* A bitter taste came to my mouth at the thought of the dark witch. My home, the love of my life—she had taken everything. I scattered fish food into the aquariums and watched how the thin flakes that were not gobbled up first floated to the surface, eventually became soggy, then slowly sank to the bottom. *To be a fish,* I thought. *No worries, no fears, no grief, no pain.*

I wondered how much suffering a soul could bear and whether an immortal's soul could bear more than a mortal's. I had no answer. All I knew was that I'd reached my limit. I'd seen everyone die: my daughter, my grandchildren, my great-grandchildren. I breathed against these painful memories. Losing only one more beloved person would have been too much. So I'd gone away. Lived my life alone. Lost sight of my descendants. To be honest, I wasn't sure if anyone was left. Living day by day without feeling seemed the better option. At least better than having to forever relive the pain of loss. Thus, I continued to live. Day by day, year by year, century by century.

***

The doorbell rang. I looked at the door in shock. The doorbell almost never rang. At most, it was the postman when he wanted to leave a parcel for a neighbor. It was probably him, so I decided to ignore it. There was another ring. Again I waited. Then there was a third ring. I got up, sighing, and went to the door.

"Yes?" I said, peering through the narrow door gap without looking up.

I heard a nervous clearing of a throat.

"Nimue," said a young woman with a trembling voice.

It hit me like an electric jolt. I'd not been called by my proper name for centuries. I looked up at eyes the color of the Lake. Her eyes, my eyes—were the same. Then I recognized her.

I undid the safety chain and opened my door.

***

Nimue stood behind the open door. "My dear," she said. I heard the deep feeling in her voice.

I nodded, feeling unsure, even timid, and hesitantly moved toward her. Nimue came the final step forward and took me into her arms. I broke out in tears. We only let go of each other after several minutes.

Her gaze wandered over my shoulder. "Amazing," she said, taking a step toward Jared to have a closer look. "You're the spitting image of Merlin."

He smiled.

"Come," she said, asking us in. We followed her through the living room into the kitchen.

Jared and I exchanged surprised looks at seeing the multitude of aquariums scattered about the flat and the bathtub under the living room window.

"Tea?" asked Nimue.

"That'd be lovely," said Jared, without betraying his amazement.

She turned on the faucet to fill the teakettle, then spun around and looked at me. How beautiful she was . . . She looked just like my mother.

"What's your name?" she asked me.

Damn! Hadn't I introduced myself yet?

"Evelyn. Lakewood," I answered, somewhat embarrassed. "This is Jared Calmburry."

Nimue placed the teakettle on the stove. "Calmburry. You're the last one, right? The last of Merlin's bloodline."

"Yes. My family . . . they're all dead."

"I heard about it. I'm sorry."

Jared nodded and looked at the floor.

"And you?" she asked me. "Are there more of us?"

I shook my head. Slowly and sadly.

"I had a sister. Zara. She and my parents—they're all dead."

"My poor child," she said, appearing to hold back tears. For a moment, I thought she'd cry, but then she composed herself.

The teakettle whistled. Nimue swallowed, took it from the stove, and poured hot water into the teapot.

"So . . . how long have you been living in London?" I asked awkwardly. She smiled. Given the circumstances, this banal routine question almost seemed absurd. I would have preferred to retract it.

"About sixty years." She poured tea into cups and placed them before us. "Every ten to fifteen years I make a break and start over again. New name, new home, new job. People get suspicious if you don't age even a day in twenty years."

"I'd imagine," I said.

Nimue placed sugar and milk on the table. "First, I worked at the London Aquarium."

Jared grinned. "Lots of water there," he remarked while pouring sugar into his tea and stirring.

"Yes." she grinned back.

We were silent for a while. The clinking of the stirring spoons was almost unbearable.

Suddenly, she raised her eyes. "How did you find me? Please don't misunderstand, I'm delighted you're here, but I've always taken care to wipe my trail clean. So how did you find me?"

I frowned. "*We* didn't find you, to be precise. I didn't even know you were still alive. A woman by the name of Mary Hayman found you. Her daughter gave me Mary's notebook. It had your address."

"Who's Mary Hayman?"

"A light guardian. She died about thirteen years ago. Morgana killed her."

Nimue flinched at Morgana's name.

I looked at her closely. I couldn't even fathom how much she'd suffered because of the old witch. "May I ask you a question?"

She cleared her throat. "But of course."

"Why did you never return to Avalon?" I looked intently at her face. Pain distorted her youthful look.

"Because I *couldn't*." Nimue lowered her eyes. Looked at her hands. I could see the memories flooding her. She took a deep breath. "The first time I tried, Morgana killed a nymph right before me." She paused a second. "When I tried the second time, she killed ten nymphs. When I tried the third time, she burned down half the island." She closed her eyes. "The cries in the fire are etched into my memory forever."

"I'm so sorry," I said, tears threatening to spill over.

Nimue took a moment before opening her eyes again. "Merlin was dead, Avalon was unreachable for me—I had nothing worth fighting for, so I hid from Morgana by disappearing into ordinary life," she told me with a heavy voice. "I married and had a daughter. I named her Viviane." It seemed she had to make a great effort to pronounce her daughter's name. "You . . . you look like her," she added ruefully.

I swallowed.

"What happened?" I asked.

"She died. Anno Domini 632."

Although I had never known her, I felt a deep sadness over Viviane's death.

"How did she die?" I didn't want to intrude, but I just had to know.

She shrugged and tried to hold back her tears. "She was simply . . . old."

Jared frowned. "Then she wasn't like you?"

"You mean immortal?"

He nodded.

Nimue shook her head. "No. Only water from the source in Avalon can bestow immortality. Once you drink from it, you partake in immortality."

My mind went blank, and then I turned to Jared—who returned my stare. Taken aback, uncomprehending. It took a while before I even had an approximate idea what this might mean. Could it be?

"The fog . . . you made it through Morgana's fog?" Nimue mumbled, her voice barely audible. Judging from the expression on her face, she was just as surprised as Jared and I. "You were there, weren't you?" she finally said.

I couldn't speak, not a single sound. I just stared at Jared. He stared back.

"You—" Nimue started, then stopped, struggling for the right words.

Nothing happened for a long time. Then I cleared my throat, which suddenly felt dry. "Are you trying to say that even if you drink only once from the source, you're . . . *immortal*?" I asked in disbelief.

She nodded. Slowly. She did not look away from us. Then she suddenly sucked in air. "I'm more than one thousand, six hundred years old, Evelyn."

I jumped up, clasped my forehead, and started pacing the small flat. Jared remained seated and stared into space. We were both completely overwhelmed. Suddenly, Jared got up and took me in his arms. Then he let his golden magic light up and enveloped me in it.

Calm and confidence returned.

I looked at Nimue, who watched Jared with wide eyes. Her lips were slightly open. A tear flowed from the corner of her eye. She blinked, stood up, and went into the kitchen.

Jared kept holding me. "You and I—forever," he whispered into my ear.

My eyes widened. How did he know this line? Did I ever tell him that these words had become my and Zara's mantra after the death of our parents? Was it pure chance that he chose the exact same words? Or maybe it was destiny?

"You and I—forever," I repeated. That's the way it was going to be. Jared and I. Forever.

Then we kissed.

When I joined Nimue a little later in the kitchen, she was rinsing the cups. Soon, she turned to me. Pure love shone from her eyes. "Why did you come here, dear?" she asked. It didn't sound as though she was upset. Rather, it sounded like genuine interest.

I smiled. "I want to return something that once belonged to you." I looked at her for a moment, then reached for the back of my neck and undid the lock of the fine silver chain I wore around it. She curiously followed my movements. When she saw the amulet, her eyes widened, and she clasped her hands over her mouth.

"Is that . . . ?" she asked with a trembling voice.

I nodded. "Your amulet."

"M-Merlin made this for me."

I placed the blue-green gem into Nimue's shaking hands.

"I once gave it to my daughter," she said quietly. My eyes rested on her beautiful face. "She passed it on to her daughter."

"It must have gotten lost at some point," I said. "My mother discovered it at a flea market in London."

She looked at the amulet for a moment.

"Keep it." She returned the amulet to my hand and closed my fingers around it. "It has been passed from daughter to daughter. One day it will belong to your daughter."

I hesitated and stared at the jewel in my hands.

"Please. Keep it."

I nodded. "Thank you."

I stared at the shimmering stone for a long time, then suddenly had to laugh. "It helped us find Morgana, you know?"

Nimue frowned and again drew her eyebrows together. "*Find* Morgana?" she repeated in disbelief. "Are you mad? Keep away from her. You don't know what she—"

"Morgana's dead," I said in a calm voice. "Jared killed her."

She looked at me, incapable of putting her astonishment into words.

"Dead?"

I nodded slowly and clearly as Jared stepped behind me.

"That's not the real reason we're here." I looked her straight in the eyes.

"I didn't just come to return the amulet to you. I've come to take you home."

EPILOGUE

She went ahead through the fog. She hadn't been here for more than a millennium, but she knew the route well. Nimue turned to me with a smile. Her blond, almost platinum hair shone in the mist. I felt a sting in my chest, seeing her. She looked like my mother. Wonderfully beautiful, forever frozen at the age of twenty. She took my hand and led me through the silver fog, which respectfully whispered "Mistress" as we passed through it. Then we arrived.

Nymphs, barghests, goblins, pixies . . . they'd all come to greet their mistress. They accompanied us to the source. Then Nimue went into the cave. Alone. I waited.

I must have fallen asleep at some point. When I awoke, she was kneeling beside me. She gently brushed my hair. Then she helped me up and looked at me.

"I want to give you something, dear," she said. Pure love shone from her sea-green eyes. "Close your eyes."

I did. The next moment, I felt her fingertips on my forehead—gentle and without pressure, but I clearly felt her touch. On the skin, but also inside. A golden-green glow penetrated my closed lids. I felt the warmth from Nimue's fingertips, and it spread over my face and streamed along my backbone, through my legs to my toes.

"Open your eyes," Nimue said. Then she kissed my forehead and let part of the golden-green light pass over to me.

ACKNOWLEDGMENTS

I wish to thank my dear colleague Mila Summers and all the members of the Facebook group *Schreibmotivation am Abend* [Writing Motivation in the Evening]. Without you, I'd probably still not be done.

I thank Michael Osmann, Audrey Deyman, and my editors for all the work they have put into this book.

I thank Claudia Ummenhofer, who handles matters for me of which I understand nothing.

I thank Petra Förster—you were the first to believe in me; Nina Vosschulte, who built me a bridge across the sea; and Elizabeth DeNoma, who finally made my dream come true. Thank you, you wonderful women, for accompanying me on this journey.

I thank Anna-Maria, the most beautiful girl in the world, for teaching me to recognize what life is all about. Thank you, my treasure, for bringing me back to the light.

And of course, I thank you, my readers. Without you, all this would mean nothing.

ABOUT THE AUTHOR

Photo © 2014 Fokus Fotographie

Sarah Kleck studied education, psychology, and sociology at the University of Augsburg in Bavaria. Currently, she works as a human resources officer and lives with her husband and two little girls in Germany near Lake Constance. *The Revealed* is her second novel.

ABOUT THE TRANSLATORS

Left photo © 2012 Audrey Deyman, Right photo © 2013 Michael Osmann

Michael Osmann and Audrey Deyman are trained medievalists, linguists, former orchardists, and mythology enthusiasts. They live in Ontario's Beaver Valley near Georgian Bay, where they enjoy the company of their children, dogs, cats, poultry flock, and the local wildlife.